MYST

FIC
HO

P9-CFS-889

Norfolk Library

DNR	DATE DUE		
7/3/18			
JUL 14 2018			
JUL 30 2018			
AUG 12 2018			
SEP 25 2018 ✓			
OCT 29 2018			

Norfolk Library
9 Greenwoods Road East
Box 605
Norfolk, CT 06058

LIKE TO DIE

ALSO BY DAVID HOUSEWRIGHT

Featuring Holland Taylor

Penance

Practice to Deceive

Dearly Departed

Darkness, Sing Me a Song

Featuring Rushmore McKenzie

A Hard Ticket Home

Tin City

Pretty Girl Gone

Dead Boyfriends

Madman on a Drum

Jelly's Gold

The Taking of Libby, SD

Highway 61

Curse of the Jade Lily

The Last Kind Word

The Devil May Care

Unidentified Woman #15

Stealing the Countess

What the Dead Leave Behind

Other Novels

The Devil and the Diva

(with Renée Valois)

Finders Keepers

LIKE TO DIE

David Housewright

MINOTAUR BOOKS

NEW YORK

This is a work of fiction. All of the characters, organizations, and events portrayed in this novel are either products of the author's imagination or are used fictitiously.

LIKE TO DIE. Copyright © 2018 by David Housewright. All rights reserved. Printed in the United States of America. For information, address St. Martin's Press, 175 Fifth Avenue, New York, N.Y. 10010.

www.minotaurbooks.com

Library of Congress Cataloging-in-Publication Data

Names: Housewright, David, 1955– author.
Title: Like to die / David Housewright.
Description: First edition. I New York : Minotaur Books, 2018. I
    Series: Twin Cities P.I. Mac McKenzie ; 16
Identifiers: LCCN 2017060155 I ISBN 9781250094537 (hardcover) I
    ISBN 9781250094544 (ebook)
Subjects: LCSH: McKenzie, Mac (Fictitious character)—Fiction. I
    Private investigators—Minnesota—Fiction. I GSAFD: Mystery fiction.
Classification: LCC PS3558.O8668 L55 2018 I DDC 813/.54—dc23
LC record available at https://lccn.loc.gov/2017060155

Our books may be purchased in bulk for promotional, educational, or business use. Please contact your local bookseller or the Macmillan Corporate and Premium Sales Department at 1-800-221-7945, extension 5442, or by email at MacmillanSpecialMarkets@macmillan.com.

First Edition: June 2018

10 9 8 7 6 5 4 3 2 1

FOR RENÉE

ACKNOWLEDGMENTS

Special thanks to India Cooper, Tammi Fredrickson, Keith Kahla, Alice Pfeifer, Alison J. Picard, and Renée Valois for all their assistance in writing this novel.

I am especially grateful to Lisa Nicholson, the creator, founder, manager, and chief bottle-washer of Calavo Salsa Lisa, for her kindness and generosity, for telling me her remarkable story, for allowing me to tour her facilities, and for introducing me to the tastiest salsa I've ever had. I promise you that Lisa bears little resemblance to the character in the book, although she could pass for a femme fatale anytime she wants.

The State of man does change and vary,
Now sound, now sick, now blithe, now sorry,
Now dancing merry,
Now like to die.

—WILLIAM DUNBAR
"Lament for the Makers"

ONE

My inner voice screamed at me. *Don't do it. Do. Not. Do It.*

I studied the face across the table from me; the smirk. How I wanted to wipe that smirk off that face.

It's a trap. You know that, right?

No, I don't know that, I told myself.

Yes. You do.

Dave Deese leaned forward and smirked some more. "I'm supposed to sit here all night?" he asked. "Show me something, McKenzie."

He's trying to goad you into making a mistake.

I tossed three red chips into the center of the table. "Call," I said.

Deese's smirk became a smile. He threw his cards down. Three jacks.

Dammit.

I laid down my own cards—a pair of tens. Deese rubbed his hands together in delight and dragged the pot toward him.

"You are the worst poker player I've ever seen," said Bobby Dunston.

"That is so untrue." I pointed at the man sitting next to Deese. "Ian hasn't won a game since college."

"Actually, I was the big winner last month," Ian Gotz said. "I didn't make a fuss about it because, unlike you guys, I don't have self-esteem issues."

"You're an accountant," Harry said. "Of course you have self-esteem issues."

"Says the man who carries a gun wherever he goes."

"I'm a special agent of the Federal Bureau of Investigation. It's required. Whose deal is it?"

Ian pointed at Bobby Dunston. "How 'bout you?"

"The St. Paul Police Department makes the same demands," he said.

"And you?"

Gotz was pointing at me.

"I never carry when I play poker for fear of shooting Dave."

"Hah," Deese said. He gathered the cards together and started shuffling.

"What's your point?" Harry asked.

"Penis envy," Ian said.

"Excuse me, what?"

"Have you guys ever shown each other your guns to see which is bigger?"

Bobby and Harry stared at each other for a beat.

"Mine is," Harry said. "U.S. government issue."

Bobby thought that was awfully funny.

"It's not how big your gun is," I said. "It's how well you use it."

"Is that what Nina tells you?" Deese asked.

"Let's not go there."

"Talk about self-esteem issues," said Harry, whose real name was Brian Wilson, same as the Beach Boy, but who everybody called Harry because of his uncanny resemblance to the character actor Harry Dean Stanton.

"Five-card draw," Deese said. "Aces wild, jacks to open, trips to win."

"Is it even possible for you to play a straight game of poker?" Bobby said.

"Dealer's choice. Are you the dealer? Ante up boys, ante."

We played three more hands. I lost them all.

"You know, it's okay to throw in your cards every once in a while," Bobby said. "You don't have to play every hand."

"I only play when I have decent cards," I said.

"The trouble is, you think all of your cards are decent."

"McKenzie's an eternal optimist," Deese said.

"Do I call you names?" I asked.

"Last hand?" Harry suggested.

"Why last hand?" Deese wanted to know.

"Because it's late and I'm still ahead."

"I knew there had to be a good reason."

"Hey," Ian said. His eyes flew from Bobby to me. "Before you guys leave, can I talk to you?"

"That sounds ominous," Harry said.

"Sure," I said.

"What about?" Bobby asked. "You have a problem?"

"Not me," Ian said. "Erin Peterson."

"Salsa Girl?" Deese said.

"What about her?" Bobby asked.

"Someone's messing with her," Ian said.

"You mean someone besides you?" Deese said.

"Cut it out. This is serious."

"How serious?" I asked.

"Yesterday someone filled all of the locks in her building with super glue. She had to call a locksmith to have them drilled out and replaced before her employees could get inside to work. It was a big deal because Friday is when she loads the reefers that deliver her product throughout the Midwest. It put her way behind schedule. She had to pay overtime to get her salsa out."

"What's a reefer?" Deese asked.

"Refrigerated semitrailer," I said.

"Look at you knowing how things work," Harry said.

"Her business is located off University near Raymond, right?" Bobby said. "That's the Western District. Who'd she talk to?"

"No one," Ian said. "Erin never called it in."

"Why not?"

"She said she was afraid of bad publicity."

"What'd her insurance company have to say?" I asked.

"I doubt she called them either."

I glanced Bobby's way.

"Revenge prank?" I said.

"Has Erin fired anyone lately?" Bobby asked. "Layoffs?"

"No layoffs," Ian said. "Her business has been doing very well. She's in fifteen states now. If she fired someone for cause— that I couldn't say."

"It was probably a dissatisfied customer," Deese said. "The new batch of salsa she's selling, the one with the green chilies, I don't care for that at all."

"Industrial espionage," Harry said. "A business rival is attempting to sabotage her product. Maybe I should interview her."

"Really, Harry?" I said. "You want to make a federal case out of it?"

"Any excuse to spend time with Salsa Girl is a good excuse."

"She is a fetching lass."

"Her name is Erin," Ian said. "I wish you would stop calling her Salsa Girl. She doesn't like it."

"Not even in bed?" Deese said.

"Stop it."

"How long have you kids been dating now?"

"We haven't been dating. We're just friends."

"Friends with benefits?"

"Stop it."

"No kidding, Gotz," Harry said. "You've been brooding over this woman for how long now? Six years? Seven?"

"So what? McKenzie has been pining after Shelby for twenty years."

"Closer to twenty-five," I said.

Bobby raised an eyebrow. "Is that right?" he said.

"Don't you know?" Ian asked. "You must know."

Of course he knows, my inner voice reminded me.

"This is the first I've heard of it," Bobby said. "I thought they were just good friends dating back to college."

Ian stared back as if he had accidentally opened a deep emotional wound and didn't know what to do about it. Bobby gave him a slight smile and a head shake to let him off the hook.

"Besides," Deese said, "unlike you, McKenzie has moved on. You've met Nina, right?"

"She's not as pretty as Shelby," Ian said.

"That's for sure," Bobby said.

"Hey," I said.

"On the other hand," Bobby added, "you guys are going to mention my wife once too often, and the next time will be once too often."

"Are we playing cards or what?" Harry asked.

"You're dealing," I reminded him.

"What we're saying, Ian," Deese said.

"We?" Bobby said.

"It's time to move on."

"What I'm saying is that Erin and I are friends," Ian said. "Like McKenzie and"—he paused when he saw the look in Bobby's eye—"the woman whose name will never again be mentioned. Besides, I'm her accountant."

"This is where I would make a joke about going over her figures," Harry said. "But I know none of you would laugh."

"I wouldn't," Ian said.

"That's because you have no sense of humor," Deese said. "Deal the cards, Harry."

"Ian," Bobby said, "if Erin doesn't want to call in an act of vandalism, there's not much I can do about it."

"Actually, I was thinking McKenzie," Ian said.

"Why me?"

"Why not?" Harry said. "You're like that amateur sleuth on the Hallmark TV channel who finds dead bodies every time she goes to a garage sale."

"You watch the Hallmark Channel?" Bobby said. "That's the saddest thing I've ever heard."

"The wife likes it."

"And you claim Ian is whipped."

"McKenzie, what about it?" Ian asked.

"After my last disaster, I've retired from the amateur sleuthing business."

"Who are you kidding?" Harry said.

Only yourself, my inner voice told me.

Bobby put an elbow in my ribs. "C'mon," he said. "Flirt with someone else's girl for a change."

"She's not my girl," Ian said.

"In seventeenth-century Europe flirting was referred to as coquetry," I said.

"Only you would know that," Bobby said.

"Okay, Ian," I said. "Tell Salsa Girl that I'll call her Monday morning."

"Umm."

"What?"

"She made me promise not to tell anyone what happened."

"Oh, for God's sake."

"Couldn't you drop by Erin's office unexpectedly just to say hello and see how she's doing?"

"Since I've never once dropped by Erin's office unexpectedly just to say hello and see how she's doing, I think she's going to be suspicious."

"Tell her you've come to complain about her new salsa," Deese said.

Harry finally got around to dealing the cards. He gave me an ace, but nothing else. Still, you have to bet the ace, don't you?

It was rare when Nina arrived home before I did, especially on a Saturday night. She not only owned Rickie's, a high-class jazz joint and restaurant on Cathedral Hill in St. Paul, she insisted on managing it every minute it was open. Even more uncommon was to find her watching our HDTV in the living room area of the condominium we shared.

I said, "Hi."

Nina said, "How'd you do?"

"I lost fifty-four bucks."

"You are the worst poker player in America."

"So I've been told. What are you watching?"

"This is the damnedest thing I've ever seen. The tall blonde with the fake boobs is screaming at the tall brunette with the fake boobs for flirting with her man ..."

"Wouldn't you?"

"Meanwhile, the tall redhead with the fake boobs and store-bought hair claims they're ruining her party and wants them both to leave except they can't leave because the party is being held on a yacht in the middle of the ocean. I didn't know being a housewife was so dramatic."

"Clearly you don't get out enough. Speaking of which— you're back early."

"I work too hard."

"Yes, you do."

"Jenness told me to go home."

"I'm sure she said it in the nicest way."

"She said she's either the weekend manager or she isn't the weekend manager, so what's it going to be? So I said, 'Fine. Manage.' It's not like I've poured twenty years of my life into the place."

"Too bad there weren't any cameras. You could have your own reality TV program."

"Do you think I'm a workaholic?"

"I think your business is running smoothly, your daughter is off to college, and you have a bundle of cash in the bank. You should take more time for yourself."

"Doing what? Watching TV?"

I gestured at the $60,000 Steinway I bought her a year ago.

"I thought you wanted to get back into music," I said.

"Who'd hire me?"

"I have a friend who owns a jazz joint. I could put in a good word for you."

"Would I have to audition?"

"She does have pretty high standards."

Nina turned off the TV and tossed the remote on the sofa.

"I'm taking tomorrow off to clean the place and do the laundry," she said. "You're going to help."

"Okay."

"I'm also thinking of taking Monday off. We could go antiquing in Stillwater if you're up for it. I'll even buy lunch."

"Works for me, but I need to meet with Erin Peterson first."

"Salsa Girl? Why?"

"Favor for Ian Gotz."

"What's wrong?"

"Probably nothing. Ian is worried about her, is all."

I told her why.

"Could be a vengeful lover," Nina said.

"What makes you say that?"

"Some men, if a woman breaks up with them, they feel the need to punish the woman. You've met my ex-husband."

"If it's an ex-boyfriend that's troubling her, do you think she'd confide in me?"

"I doubt it. You need to remember who's asking for the help. It's not Erin. It's Ian. Do you honestly think she's going to look Ian's friend in the eye and tell him that she's being vandalized by someone she was cheating with?"

"I don't think cheating's the right word. Ian and Erin are—"

"Just good friends? Is that what you were going to say?"

"That's what he says."

"I don't care what he says. I see the look in his eye when she's near. Ian might be Salsa Girl's port in the storm, but she's the love of his life. She knows it, too."

"You think?"

"I think. Besides, the only times I've spoken to her were at gatherings with you and your friends, and she was very private. Very secretive. Erin loves talking about her business, but not herself. I know very little about her except what she does for a living. We always say that we should get together since we seem to have so much in common, single women who've built successful businesses from scratch, only nothing ever comes of it. Each time I've tried to arrange something, Erin says she's too busy. I'm not sure she has much of a life outside of her work."

"Sound like anyone we know?"

"I've got a life. I have Erica."

"Who's at Tulane University."

"I have friends. Like the Dunstons."

"Mostly they're my friends, but okay."

"I have my music."

"Which you hardly ever play."

Nina stood, feet apart, her fists pressed against her hips. "I have you," she said.

"I agree that should be enough for any woman."

"You're right. I need to get out more."

TWO

Winter had been uncharacteristically courteous to the Twin Cities, if not the rest of Minnesota. There had been no staggering body blows, no flurry of uppercuts or hooks or brutal kidney punches. Instead, we were treated to a few light jabs that barely landed, mixed with a couple of gentle combinations as if, instead of pounding us into the canvas, instead of knocking us out, it was content to win on points. Yet there was no trusting winter. Less than forty-eight hours after posting a high of seventy-two degrees, it sucker-punched us with three inches of snow and temperatures well below freezing. Hell, we've had measurable snow as late as June. That's why even now in mid-April, we viewed each gray cloud as a threat and feared that every stiff wind carried danger.

I saw the clouds and felt the wind while I stood in the parking lot in front of a sign that read PETERSON/SAX ENTERPRISES, INC. HOME OF SALSA GIRL SALSA. I was wearing a brown leather jacket that was too warm for the weather, yet zipped it tightly closed anyway while I conducted a cursory reconnaissance.

The building was located in a sprawling industrial park on the west side of St. Paul near Highway 280. On the north were the heavily traveled University Avenue and the Green Line high-speed train. On the south was the always-congested I-94 freeway. You could hear traffic noises from both like surf in the distance. Yet the park itself was surprisingly quiet. Pelham Boulevard ran along the edge of the park, but it wasn't particularly well traveled. I saw only a few vehicles on the street and even fewer moving in and out of the park's service roads. There were no sidewalks and no foot traffic whatsoever.

Inside the building, I was met by a young thoroughbred of a woman with long legs, wide brown eyes, and a flowing mane. She smiled at me and said, "May I help you?"

"I'd like to see Ms. Peterson."

"Do you have an appointment?"

"No."

"I'm sorry, but Ms. Peterson is very busy, and—"

"Tell her it's McKenzie."

She smiled some more. I smiled back. Apparently it was unusual for strangers to come in off the street and ask for the boss, and she was curious to see how the scene would play out.

"Just a moment," she said and disappeared down a corridor. It was only a moment before she reappeared.

"This way," she said.

I followed her. She led me to an office. Inside the office, leaning her backside against the edge of her desk, was Salsa Girl. She must not have believed spring had sprung either, because she was wearing a long-sleeve sweaterdress with a hem that ended below her knees and knee-high boots. Her arms were folded across her chest. She looked like she was actually glad to see me.

Every time I saw Erin Peterson reminded me of the first time I saw her. It was at the arena where we played hockey. She was sitting alone in the stands. I was sitting on the bench with my teammates. You wouldn't have missed her even in a crowd, which there wasn't.

"Who is that?" I asked.

None of us knew, yet we were all convinced that she was a guest of one of the hockey players. It was kind of a tradition among us—as soon as a guy became seriously involved with a woman, he took her to a game and introduced her to his friends. It was also a tradition—or a consequence of just how boring we were—that the woman almost never returned to watch us play again.

Finally Dave Deese said, "I think that's Gotz's new girlfriend. Erin something."

We were all impressed by Ian's good fortune, yet Deese blew it off.

"Just another dumb blonde," he said.

"You're basing this assessment on what, exactly?" Bobby asked.

"Well, look at her. She's blond. She's dating Gotz. How smart can she be?"

Personally, I hadn't met that many dumb blondes. Certainly blondes didn't seem to be dumb in any greater proportion than the brunettes or redheads I've known. Meeting Erin in the bar after the game, however, discovering who she was and what she did, pretty much shattered my confidence in the stereotype once and for all. Forget her dress, which was made of some magic material that seemed to both hang loose and cling to her generous curves. Ignore the winter-blue eyes—if you could—and her warm smile. There was a quiet center to her that you rarely see in people, and almost never in someone younger than forty, that impressed me even more. She didn't greet us as much as absorb us into her life. The way she spoke went beyond mere communication. It was a reflection of a belief system that valued intelligence, grace, and self-control. You've heard the term 'woman of substance'? That was Erin Peterson.

"Rushmore McKenzie," she said. "You honor me."

"Hardly."

She came off her desk, unfolded her arms, and hugged me. I hugged her back. The thoroughbred watched. Erin broke the embrace before it became uncomfortable or evolved into something else.

"Alice Pfeifer," she said. "This is my friend, McKenzie."

I offered my hand. "Alice," I said.

She shook my hand. "Mr. McKenzie."

"Just McKenzie," I said.

"Alice is the most important person in the building," Erin said. "Without her, Salsa Girl Salsa would shudder to a halt."

"That's not true," Alice said.

"It is; it is." As if to prove it, Erin draped an arm around the young woman's shoulders and gave her a squeeze. For a moment they reminded me of Nina and Erica, the proud mother showing off her daughter.

"McKenzie," Erin said, "to what do I owe the pleasure?"

"I was in the neighborhood. Thought I'd drop in and see how you've been doing."

"I'm doing quite well, thank you."

"No problems?"

"None beyond the usual trials and tribulations of managing—wait." A troubled look clouded Erin's eyes, and she removed her arm from Alice's shoulders. "Ian. He sent you, didn't he?" She turned her attention toward the young woman. Her voice was quiet, almost tranquil, as always. "What is it with men that they have such a difficult time keeping a secret?"

Alice shrugged her reply.

"I should explain," Erin said. "McKenzie is—what should I call you?"

I didn't have a ready answer, although I was asked the question all the time. Unlicensed private investigator? Semiprofessional busybody? Unabashed kibitzer?

Bored rich jerk? my inner voice said.

"How 'bout concerned friend?" I said aloud.

"I should go," Alice said.

"No, don't," Erin said. "McKenzie isn't that kind of friend. Unless something's happened I haven't heard about. You and Nina?"

"Nina sends her love," I said. "She wants to know when you two are going to get together."

"See, Alice, not that kind of friend. McKenzie, the thing with my door locks—it was just a prank. Kids."

"Not a chance."

"Oh? That's your considered opinion?"

"You're isolated here. There isn't any residential housing within a half mile in any direction. No parks. No malls. No stores. Do you honestly think a bunch of kids went out of their way to pull a practical joke on someone they didn't know in a place they never hang out?"

"It could happen."

"Did it happen to anyone else in the park?"

"Not that I'm aware of."

"Well, then."

"That doesn't mean I require your services."

"Yet they're at your disposal."

"What kind of services?" Alice asked.

"McKenzie is an ex-cop," Erin said. "He now works as a kind of roving troubleshooter."

Roving troubleshooter—I like the sound of that, my inner voice said.

"Maybe ..." Alice said.

"No maybes."

"But ..."

"No buts."

"Erin?"

Erin's usually calm voice rang with authority. "Alice," she said.

"Yes, ma'am." Alice gazed down at her shoes. She might have

been the most important person in the room, but she wasn't the boss. Erin sighed dramatically as if she regretted pulling rank on her assistant.

"Alice always calls me 'ma'am' when she's disappointed in me," she said. "McKenzie, you've never been here before, have you?"

"No."

"Would you like a tour?"

"Sure."

"I need—" Erin stared at her watch for a few beats. "I was promised a telephone call from California in three minutes. 'Course, they're never on time. Alice, do me a favor. Give McKenzie a tour of our production plant, and I'll join you in approximately eighteen minutes."

"If it isn't an imposition," I said.

"Alice?"

"No imposition at all."

"Good. I'll meet you out on the floor. I'll explain more thoroughly, McKenzie, why you have no reason to be concerned about me. Scoot. Scoot."

We left the office. Erin closed the door behind us.

"California?" I said.

"It's a long story," Alice said. The sound of her voice gave me the impression that she'd love to tell it but didn't think she should.

"You seem more concerned about what happened the other day than Erin," I said.

Her eyes found mine and quickly darted away. Again I felt she wanted to explain but chose not to. I didn't press the matter, deciding it would be better to ask Salsa Girl myself. Why risk getting the kid in trouble with her boss?

We scooted down the corridor back to the reception area. Alice deposited my jacket in a closet and pulled out a long white linen lab coat that fell to my knees.

"Put this on," she said.

I did. She slid into one as well.

"I don't like to leave the office uncovered," she said. "We have a couple of other girls who work here, but they're both part-time. One of them should be here, but she called in sick. If you're wearing jewelry, take it off."

I didn't wear jewelry, but I asked anyway. "Why?"

"So it won't fall off into the product."

"That's a thing that happens?"

"You'd be surprised. Our people can't wear nail polish or makeup, either."

Before we went any farther, Alice also gave me a board with a nondisclosure agreement clipped to it. By signing it, she said, I was basically agreeing that anything I saw or heard in the Salsa Girl production plant would remain in the Salsa Girl production plant. I took her word for it and signed without reading the document even as my inner voice told me, *Don't ever tell your lawyer what you just did.*

Afterward, I was led into a "staging area," where I was required to don a white hairnet, wash my hands, and submerge the bottoms of my shoes into a foot bath. From there, I was ushered into the production plant itself. It was brightly lit and had a wall of windows. It was also cool. Most of the employees—I counted over a dozen—wore sweatshirts and sweaters under their white jackets and hairnets. I asked Alice about it.

"The temperature is kept at a constant sixty-five degrees," she told me. "The salsa itself is kept at thirty-four to thirty-six degrees. The threshold temperature is forty. That's when spoiling agents start to work. It's why the cold chain is so very important to us—keeping the product at the correct temperature from the moment it's packaged until it arrives in the stores. We guarantee freshness for sixty days after purchase, but it's actually closer to eighty. We estimate five days maximum to move the product to various distribution centers, although it rarely takes longer than three, if that; add another day for warehousing and one more to rotate the stock into the store coolers. That gives us plenty of leeway.

"What you need to remember, McKenzie, is that we don't sell Salsa Girl off the shelf like Tostitos, Pace, Wild Harvest, Green Mountain, Old Dutch, Newman's Own, or any of those other jar salsas guaranteed to last twenty years after the apocalypse. Our salsa is refrigerated. That's why it tastes so good. 'Course, the trade-off is that we often miss out on impulse sales; people don't usually think to go to the produce or deli section of a store to buy salsa. But for those who do, for those who demand a quality salsa, freshness is paramount."

The plant was painted white with a concrete floor and a lot of stainless steel equipment. Alice led me across it to a large room in the back. There were huge stainless steel tubs and cabinets in the room, a conveyer belt that led to a washing machine, and a lot of equipment that looked as it would chop off your fingers, if not your entire hand, unless you were careful. There were also cardboard boxes and plastic bins filled with tomatoes, onions, jalapeños, and other fruits and vegetables. An older man, who wore a uniform similar to ours plus rubber gloves and a surgical mask, was examining the boxes and their contents. He looked as if he had done it for a hundred years and expected to continue doing it for a hundred more. He seemed miffed that we interrupted his work.

"This is our prep room," Alice said. "And this is Hector Lozano, who really is the most important person at Salsa Girl."

Lozano removed his mask and nodded at Alice as if he believed her.

"This is where we inspect and store all of our ingredients, make sure they're up to our standards," she added.

Lozano spoke with a thick Hispanic accent, and I wondered how long he had been in the States. "*La Señorita,* she will tolerate only the best," he said.

"This is also where we wash everything, peel the onions, de-stem the jalapeños," Alice said. "Most of our tomatoes and onions are sourced locally; we have a distributor across the river. Some of the other ingredients, the jalapeños, for example, come from Mexico. We bring them up in our own trucks."

There was an open box filled with large, ripe tomatoes near the door. I reached for one. Lozano slapped my hand. I pulled it back, looked at the swelling on my knuckles and then at Lozano. He adjusted his hairnet as if nothing had happened. Alice laughed, took my elbow, and spun me toward the door.

"That hurt," I said.

"Hector takes his job very seriously."

"Still ..."

Alice slowed so I could get a good look through an open door into another room, this one filled with carefully sealed ten-gallon buckets and bags with labels that I couldn't read from a distance.

"This is where we mix our spices, our recipes," she said.

I noticed that she didn't allow me to go inside.

We stopped next to a large stainless steel tank mounted on a metal stand three feet above the floor. A man was standing on a ladder and stirring the ingredients inside the tank with a paddle. Alice said that it was one of two mixing tanks. She explained that all of the ingredients were blended together in the tanks before being siphoned to a "filling hopper." From there the salsa was pulled through flexible tubing called "filler cylinders" and poured into plastic pods. I watched three women working the assembly line, filling the containers, sealing them, and placing labels on the lids. The lids indicated the flavor of the salsa—the company offered half a dozen varieties—and featured an illustration of a smiling Salsa Girl that bore no resemblance at all to Erin Peterson.

"As you can see," Alice said, "most of the work is done by hand."

I watched as the containers moved along rollers into still another room, where the batch numbers and expiration dates were sprayed onto the labels with an ink-jet printer. The next stop was a packing area, where the containers were loaded into boxes that were sealed, labeled, and stacked on wooden pallets. One of the men doing the packing eyed me furtively. I was sure I had seen him before but couldn't place him. 'Course, I'd met and spoken with so many people over the years, first as a cop with the St. Paul Police Department and now as an unlicensed private investigator, that nearly everyone seemed vaguely familiar to me.

Music was being pumped into the plant, most of it in Spanish. Two-thirds of the employees were Hispanic. The rest were African American, Asian, and white, and I wondered if they ever switched it up—one day Latin tunes, the next hip-hop, the next something else. I was going to ask Alice if they ever listened to jazz, but her attention was drawn away by a half-dozen containers that had somehow slipped through without labels. Alice scooped up the containers and carried them back to the woman who was doing the honors. While she was gone, I noticed again that the man packing the salsa was watching me while pretending not to. That's when I put a name to his face. Tony Cremer, a good-looking kid who once made his living stealing cars that he sold to chop shops, boosting them out of the parking lots of shopping malls and apartment complexes—Hondas, Toyotas, and Nissans mostly, sometimes Ford and Dodge pickups, whatever could be stripped for parts—until I caught him.

"You behaving yourself, Tony?" I asked.

He didn't like the question.

"You want somethin' from me, Officer?" Cremer asked.

"Me? Nah? Tell me, though—does Ms. Peterson know about your checkered past?"

"Yes." The word came out like a hiss. Cremer added that unlike some people he could name, Ms. Peterson believed in giving a guy a second chance.

"Good for her," I said.

As far as Cremer was concerned, I was just another cop trying to screw up his life. He proved it by stepping close enough to make me feel uncomfortable. "You gonna ruin it for me?" he asked.

I don't know why I told him, but I did. "I'm not a cop anymore."

"Don't mean you're not still an asshole."

"How many cars did you boost before I stopped you? And you call *me* an asshole?"

"What I did—everyone thieves, man. You know that. Some thieve big like the Wall Street guys, some small like me. The only difference is that I got caught."

"I'm glad to see that you've turned it around, Tony," I said. "But that kind of reasoning can only lead you back into trouble."

"Like you said, you ain't a cop no more."

"What do you know about the super glue in the door locks the other day?"

"I don't know nothin' about that. Why would I? This has been a good place for me. Why would I fuck it up?"

"Just asking."

"You tryin' to hang that on me, Officer? You gotta know, a man don't shit where he eats."

"I'll keep it in mind."

By then Alice had returned. She must have felt the tension between Cremer and me.

"Everything all right?" she asked.

"He was interrupting my work, is all," Cremer said.

"Sorry," I said.

Cremer returned to his task. Alice led me away. She whispered, "He makes me nervous."

"How so?"

"The way he watches me."

"You are a pretty girl."

"Not like that. He watches like he's waiting for me to do something wrong."

Something that he can use against her? my inner voice asked.

"It's probably just my imagination," Alice added.

"Or not," I said. "Always trust your instincts. We have them for a reason."

Alice led me to the room where the pallets loaded with packed boxes of salsa were stored. Most of them were wrapped in plastic. Another worker was arranging them near the large back door. It was cold inside; near freezing, I guessed.

"This is the finished-goods cooler," Alice said. "From here the salsa is loaded onto the trucks. On Mondays we have a truck that takes the product to Texas and New Mexico and another for local deliveries, those within half a day's drive. For all of our other customers, we have a distributor that picks up the product on Fridays and delivers it to distribution centers across the Upper Midwest and Great Lakes Region. We're in fifteen states now. McKenzie, I don't think what happened with our locks was a prank. I think someone wanted to send us a message. Someone who knew how important Fridays are to us."

I was surprised by the sudden shift of topic and wondered if Cremer had something to do with it.

"What message?" I asked. "Why?"

"McKenzie," Erin said. I turned and found her standing there. "What do you think?"

"I'm impressed," I said. "You've done very well building all of this."

"Thank you."

"I was just asking Alice—how much salsa do you sell?"

"Approximately seventeen thousand units."

"A week?"

"A day."

"That's—"

"Twenty-two hundred and fifty gallons, give or take."

"Wow."

"Yes, we think so, too."

"Exactly how much do you guys make a year?"

"Gross? I'd say between four and six million dollars."

"In other words, you're not going to tell me."

"Why do you need to know? Do you want to invest in the company?"

"Yes. Yes, I do."

"If I had known you back in the day, I would have taken you up on your offer. You wouldn't know it to look at his always casual attire, Alice, but McKenzie is loaded. How much money are you worth these days?"

"Between four and six million," I said.

"Let's move out of here."

Erin opened a door, and I soon found myself standing in a corridor that separated the production plant from the outside loading dock; there was a huge folding door that led to the dock. The difference in temperature between the corridor and the finished-goods cooler room came almost as a shock.

"This is where we ship from," Alice said. "In case you haven't guessed."

"What's that?" I pointed at a large metal cage. There were several boxes and buckets neatly arranged behind the white bars.

"Chemicals," Erin said. "Mostly cleaning supplies, sanitizers for our mixing tanks. When I was starting out, the Department of Agriculture came for a visit. The first question they asked—

'Do you keep your chemicals away from your process?' They were afraid we might poison our customers."

"Sounds like just another unnecessary regulation hampering the small business person."

"Who are you calling small?"

"Ma'am?" We turned to see a man approaching. He was dressed for outside, not in a white coat. He didn't seem to know if he should be walking fast or running and settled for something in between. "Ma'am?"

"Is there a problem, Jerry?" Erin spoke as if problems were something that happened to other people, never to her.

"The door locks last week, you know, with the super glue?"

"What about them?"

"Someone did the same thing to the trucks."

Erin closed her eyes and became very still. If she was silently counting to ten, she was counting fast, because a beat later her eyes snapped open.

"Show me," she said.

Jerry half walked, half ran toward a door. He slowed when he realized that Erin was not running after him but walking casually. Alice and I walked with her.

"McKenzie," she said. "Have you tried my new recipe?"

"Is that the one with green chilies?"

"No, no. Fire-roasted tomatoes. I originally made it for my customers in Texas and New Mexico. It's done so well down there, I thought I'd try it in the Twin Cities. Possibly it has too much heat for this market. We'll see."

I didn't say it, but I admired how calm she appeared.

Once outside, we walked to the truck parked with its back end flush against the loading dock. It was painted with the company's name and colors and the smiling face consumers knew as Salsa Girl. I noticed the refrigeration unit resting above the cab. Normally I wouldn't have paid any attention to it.

"I left it here last night like always," Jerry said. He poked his key at the door lock. "See? It won't go in."

"I see," Erin said.

"I checked the other truck. Same thing."

"I see."

"I told you something like this would happen," Alice said.

"Alice, please."

"I told you that our enemies wouldn't stop."

"Alice."

"Ma'am."

Enemies? my inner voice asked.

"May I?" I asked aloud. I stepped past Erin and ran my finger over the opening of the lock cylinder. It was smooth.

"I need to make a few phone calls," Erin said.

"I know where we can get other trucks," Jerry said.

"We can't use just any trucks," Alice told him. "We need reliable refrigerated vehicles. Otherwise we'll break the cold chain."

"I am aware of the situation," Erin said.

"Did you try the passenger doors?" I asked.

Jerry was staring at Erin like a child who was afraid he would be blamed for something he didn't do.

"Jerry," I said, "did you try the passenger doors?"

"Huh? Yeah. I ain't stupid."

"Let's take a look."

It wasn't that I didn't believe him; I just wanted to see if the face of the lock cylinder was as smooth as on the driver's side. It was. I cupped my hands and pressed them against the window so I could get a good look inside the cab. Manual locks.

Erin watched quietly.

"Talk to me, McKenzie," she said.

"Ideally, if you want to sabotage a lock, you fill it with glue, shove a toothpick in there, and break it off. That way the entire mechanism will need to be replaced. That's what they did with your door locks, right? But I don't think your vandals did that here. There are no jagged edges protruding; the glue is smooth. I think they might have just covered the opening, thinking that was enough. It's possible the lock assembly itself is fine."

"Meaning what, exactly?"

"Give me five minutes."

I circled the building to my car parked in front, examining the building and the light poles that surrounded it as I went. I opened my trunk and withdrew a rag and a flat piece of stainless steel, twenty-four inches long and one inch wide, with a notch cut in one end and a rubber handle on the other—a Slim Jim, $9.98 at Walmart. I returned to the truck and inserted the Slim Jim between the weatherstripping and the window, using the rag to protect the glass from scratches. I worked on the passenger side because the driver's side had wires and other components I didn't want to damage. I moved the tool back and forth gently until the notch grabbed the lock rod. I pulled up and the door unlocked. I had hoped to accomplish the task quickly to impress the women. It actually took me close to five minutes. They seemed to be impressed anyway. At least Alice smiled, and Erin said, "my hero."

Jerry pushed past me, climbed into the truck, and crossed over to the driver's side. He opened the door.

"Hey," he said.

"You'll need to be careful not to lock the door again until we can get the lock fixed," I told him.

"What about the other truck?" he asked. "That goes out later today."

"I'm on it," I told him.

I opened the door, but this time it took me over ten minutes. I knew that Tony Cremer would have done it much more quickly. 'Course, he probably would have just smashed the window and climbed in. He didn't care about the condition of the vehicles he stole; he was selling them for parts, after all.

When I finished, Erin said, "I'm grateful."

"You're welcome."

"Let's talk."

Salsa Girl and I returned to her office; Alice remained on the loading dock to supervise. Erin told me to take a seat in front of her desk. I did. Meanwhile, she opened a drawer of the credenza behind her desk and pulled out a bottle of Woodford Reserve Distiller's Select Kentucky Straight Bourbon Whiskey. There was enough gone from the bottle to suggest that this was not an uncommon occurrence, and my inner voice asked, *When was the last time you saw a woman drink straight bourbon?* I didn't have an answer.

"Drink?" Erin said.

"No, I'm good."

"When have you ever turned down good bourbon?"

"I have a long day of antiquing in front of me."

Erin filled a glass with two inches of liquid.

"Have you ever actually bought anything while antiquing?" she asked.

"Me personally? No. I'm not really interested in antiques. I find it all kind of boring, to be honest."

"You're telling me that you go just because Nina wants you to go?"

"That's right."

"Sounds like true love to me."

Erin drained half the bourbon from the glass, closed her eyes, sighed dramatically, opened her eyes, and refilled the glass. She returned the bottle to her credenza and sat in the chair behind her desk.

"Apparently, I'm being—what's a good word?" Erin gazed out her window across the parking lot to the bridge that allowed

Pelham Boulevard to cross I-94 while she searched for one. I offered my own.

"Harassed," I said.

"I was thinking something stronger."

"Tell me the worst thing that could happen to you and work backward from there."

"The worst thing would be a recall. If my salsa became contaminated with something, listeria monocytogenes, for example, and I had to pull my products from the stores. That's not counting the additional fallout from potential lawsuits. Listeria causes food poisoning. Adults and healthy children might become ill, but it's rarely serious. In pregnant women, though, the infection can result in miscarriage, premature delivery, serious infection of the newborn, even stillbirth.

"What's next?" Erin went on. "I suppose an employee could deliberately damage my equipment to the point where it takes me a few days or weeks or months to fix or replace it and I would be unable to meet my obligations ... A vendor might miss delivery of my boxes, my containers ... My suppliers might not ship quality fruits and vegetables in a timely fashion ... If I develop a reputation for unreliability, for a lack of quality control ..." Erin sipped some more bourbon. "Things can go bad in a hurry, McKenzie. You could lose your business in a minute."

"On the plus side," I said.

"There's a plus side?"

"The damage done to you so far has been external, not internal. Your doors, your trucks, but not your equipment, not your product. Also, it's been superficial. He could have burned your trucks to the ground. He could have blown up your building."

"He?"

"It could just as easily be a she. Alice said you have enemies."

"She was speaking generally. Whoever is doing this is my enemy."

"Whoever is doing this knows how important Mondays and Fridays are to you; he knows when you ship your product. Have you fired anyone recently?"

"Not for three years."

"Reprimand any employees? Threaten their jobs unless they shaped up?"

"I haven't. Alice or my production manager—if they've had words with any of my people, they haven't mentioned it to me."

"Would they have?"

"Not necessarily, but McKenzie—I have only twenty employees including part-time. I pretty much know what's going on with them all the time."

"Have you passed over anyone for promotion lately? Failed to pay a bonus or give a raise to employees who thought they deserved it?"

"No."

"Changed vendors?"

"I went with a more reliable packaging company for my containers, but that was eighteen months ago. My other vendors—you're always trying to bargain for a better price, better quality, better service, of course, and negotiations can sometimes become contentious. However, I've used these people for a long time. Bernal Mexicana in Delicias, Mexico, has been with me for over five years."

"Have you pulled your products from a store?"

"If you knew how difficult it is to get my products into stores you wouldn't ask that."

"Have you broken up with a boyfriend recently?"

Instead of giving a quick response, Erin looked at everything in her office except me. She was going to lie, as Nina predicted, and I waited for it. While I waited I noticed that there was nothing in her office that could be labeled personal. No photos of

Mom and Dad, no pics of Erin and her friends. Just a couple of Scovie Awards—whatever they were—and a few framed newspaper and magazine clippings extolling her company, all of them with photos of Salsa Girl but not of her.

Finally Erin fixed her blue eyes on me. "Like I have time for a boyfriend," she said.

"Refused someone who wanted to be your boyfriend?"

Erin shook her head slowly.

"A hookup that went badly?"

"McKenzie, please."

"Well, you pissed off somebody."

"I don't know who. I don't know how."

Alice knocked on the opened door and stepped inside Erin's office.

"We're good," Alice said.

"Are we?" Erin asked.

"The truck is on its way to Texas. We didn't lose much time; Jerry said it'll be easy to make up. I spoke to Doug." Alice pivoted toward where I was sitting. "Doug is our maintenance man. While they were loading the truck, he used acetone to remove the super glue from the locks. If it had actually been injected into the locks like it was with our building doors, he said it probably wouldn't have worked; that we would have had to replace the locks like you said." She turned again to face Erin. "I was thinking: if this happened on the road, if the locks were sabotaged while the driver was at a rest stop or in a diner having a bite to eat ..."

"You have a vivid imagination," Erin said.

"She does," I said. "Alice is also right. If your truck was forced to sit for as long as it took to repair it; if your cold chain was broken ..."

"I'm aware of the ramifications, McKenzie."

"Erin, your security's a joke. I took a look around your building, the parking lot. There are no closed-circuit TV cameras anywhere. No gates. Your neighbors are at a distance. Do you have a security company keeping watch on your facility? Vehicle or foot patrols?"

"The landlord inspects the grounds a couple times a week, but that's more to check on the tenants."

"Swell."

"Up until now, security wasn't an issue."

"Times change."

"So I've been led to believe."

"Police," I said.

"No."

"Bobby Dunston."

"No."

"You're a tax-paying citizen, Salsa Girl. If you ask for help, he'll quietly arrange to expand some officer's beat to include the industrial park. There'll be a police presence."

"I said no, and I wish you wouldn't call me Salsa Girl."

"What are you going to do, then?"

"What are *you* going to do, McKenzie?"

"Me?"

"Doing favors for friends is what you're all about, isn't it? Isn't that what leads you on all those grand adventures I sometimes read about, that Ian Gotz tells me about?"

"Yes, but ..."

"The question is—are we friends, McKenzie? You only know me through Ian because he's escorted me to parties and gatherings with you and Bobby and the others, the hockey players, your buddy with the FBI."

"We've known each other for a long time, Erin."

"Yes, but does that make us friends?"

"Sure."

Erin took a deep pull of her bourbon while she thought about it. She was gazing at Alice when she said, "I'd like to take advantage of your friendship."

"Okay."

Erin's eyes found me again.

"One thing," she said. "If at all possible, I don't want the world at large to know what you're doing or why. The reason I keep saying no to the police, if word gets out, the story won't be about a small business person being victimized by vandals. That's not how it'll be played. Instead, the headlines will read 'Salsa Girl Assaulted' or some such thing. That's unacceptable. I can't have that."

"I'll do the best I can."

"Where do we start?"

"We start with installing a decent surveillance system. I know some people."

"This is going to cost me a lot of money, isn't it?"

"Yes, but my services are free."

"What else besides cameras?"

"I'll make some discreet inquiries."

"*Discreet* inquiries—I like the sound of that." Erin finished her drink and gazed up at Alice. "Happy now?"

"Yes, ma'am."

"One last time, McKenzie—are you sure I can't offer you a drink?"

"A short one, for the road."

THREE

"I still think there could be an ex-lover involved," Nina said.

"Erin said she didn't have time for a boyfriend," I said.

"Which might be the motive, the reason the person or persons unknown are doing this to her."

"Motive? Person or persons unknown?"

"I'm starting to sound like you, I know."

By then we were inside the Midtown Antique Mall in downtown Stillwater with its sixty-five dealers, three floors, and enough nooks and crannies to keep even the most ardent treasure hunter content. We explored them all. Or rather I should say Nina explored them all while I followed along and worked my smartphone. These days if you want to learn about someone, you start with the internet, because that's where most people store their lives when they aren't using them.

As it turned out, Erin Peterson's success story wasn't all that unique. It was one she shared with luminaries like Debbi Fields, Marie Callender, and Chef Ettore Boiardi: She made something so good that friends told her, "You should sell this." Instead of cookies, pies, and spaghetti sauce, though, in her case it was salsa.

According to the origin story on her website, Erin's journey began with "Potluck Fridays" at the University of Wisconsin in Madison, where she majored in business. Apparently her friends had decided it was a good idea to eat heartily before beginning a weekend of heavy drinking at what many people consider to be one of the most infamous party schools in America. Her most frequent contribution to the meal was salsa that she made from her mother's recipe. Her classmates loved it and began referring to her as "the salsa girl."

Erin discovered it wasn't all that much harder to make a lot of salsa than a little. At the urging of her classmates, she began producing large batches that she sold in jars out of the apartment she shared with two roommates and at Memorial Union and other spots around campus. On a whim, she brought her salsa to the Dane County Farmers Market in the square surrounding the Wisconsin State Capitol.

I mentioned it to Nina, who was examining a hand-carved cribbage board made to resemble a battleship, complete with gun turrets and conning tower.

"Remember that huge farmers market that we went to in Madison a few years ago?" I asked. "About two hundred vendors? That's where Salsa Girl started her business."

"That's nice," Nina said.

What happened, Erin showed up with about a hundred jars of her salsa and a card table. She didn't know the rules, the biggest of which was that you had to be a member to sell your wares at the market and that there was a five-year waiting list. By the time she was discovered and ejected forcibly from the premises, however, she had nearly sold out. What encouraged her most, though, was that she heard that some of her customers had returned to the market the following week hoping to buy another jar from the salsa girl.

Fortunately, there were other markets where Erin could sell her salsa, and she began doing so, to the detriment of her studies.

One day she was taking a quiz dealing with business statistics when she asked herself "What am I doing here? If I want to learn how to run a business, why not start with this business?"

She finished the quiz and handed in her paper, but never returned to class to learn how well she had done. Instead, she left school and went back to her home in Minnesota. She told her mother her plans. "She was furious," Erin said both on her website and in an article published in the *Minneapolis/St. Paul Business Journal.* "That changed, though, when I hired her because I was unable to keep up with the demand by myself."

It was at the farmers market on the Nicollet Mall in downtown Minneapolis that Erin met Randy Bignell-Sax. Randy was a member of the Bignell family, who owned and operated both Bignell Bakeries and Minnesota Foods. He was so impressed by the quality of Erin's hand-crafted product, which was now being sold in two flavors under the label Salsa Girl Salsa, that he invested enough working capital for Erin to be able to move to her first manufacturing plant—well, second if you counted her mother's kitchen. From there Salsa Girl expanded to a third location, and finally the one where I found her that morning. She expanded to six flavors and quickly paid off her business loan from Randy, although he retained a 10 percent stake in the company.

"That must be where Peterson/Sax Enterprises came from," I said.

Nina was inspecting a stereoview photograph through a stereoscopic card viewer. It allowed her to observe the two side-by-side photographs on the card as a single 3D image.

"Wow," she said. "You need to see this."

"What is it?"

"The ice palace from the 1887 St. Paul Winter Carnival."

I took a look. The palace was actually a castle made entirely of thirty-five thousand blocks of ice taken from the Mississippi

River. At 217 feet long, 194 feet wide, and 140 feet high, it was, in a word, breathtaking.

"They built this by hand, can you believe it?" Nina said. "Why can't we build something like this? The ice palace they built for the Super Bowl was a tar paper shack compared to this. I'm going to buy these."

Nina took a box full of stereoview photograph cards to the register in the front of the store. In the meantime, I continued my internet search. There was little left to learn. I discovered a few more articles that appeared in local media outlets like *City Pages* and *CBS Minnesota*, yet they all told nearly an identical story. There was no mention of Erin's mother's name or where they lived in Minnesota, and no photographs of either her or Erin except for a shot of Erin and her production manager dressed in white lab coats and hairnets and standing in front of a mixing tank. Erin was barely recognizable.

She didn't have a LinkedIn page, and her Facebook page, listed under the name Salsa Girl, was used strictly to promote her business. Instead of a pic of her, it displayed the same likeness of Salsa Girl that appeared on the product labels and other company literature.

"That surprises me," I said.

"What surprises you?" Nina asked.

We were on the sidewalk and headed north. I told her about my findings.

"Why would she post her photograph?" Nina asked. "Or her mom's?"

"Why wouldn't she?"

"I have a website. I have a Facebook page. Weekly email marketing, too. Have you ever seen my photograph? Or Erica's? Have you read any personal information?"

I hadn't, except under the ABOUT US tab on her website where Nina mentioned that Rickie's had been named after her daughter.

"What we look like and where we're from has nothing to do with what we're selling," Nina said.

Still, it occurred to me that I knew nothing about Salsa Girl except for what I could find on her website. It made me wonder about my relationship with other friends as well, guys I've played hockey with for years. I was thinking to myself but spoke out loud: "What's Andy Adams's wife's name? Does he have kids? Where does he work again?"

"Who's Andy Adams?" Nina asked.

"Guy I play hockey with, always wears an old Minnesota Fighting Saints sweater."

"I don't remember him."

"I barely remember him myself, and we had beers after we played the last game of the season just two weeks ago."

"You're not having an existential crisis, are you, McKenzie?"

"I might be working myself up to one."

"Wait until we get down the street first."

"Why? Where are we going?"

"Isaac Staples Sawmill. Can you think of a better place to question if your life has any meaning or purpose than in an antiques store located in a hundred-and-seventy-year-old building?"

A few hours later, I was sitting on a sofa in Bobby Dunston's man cave that I had helped him build in the basement of his house and drinking a Leinenkugel. Bobby had major league baseball on his HDTV. At least Kansas City was playing major league baseball; I had no idea what the hell the Twins were doing.

Bobby and I had known each other since before kindergarten, and it was easy for us to sit together for long stretches without speaking. But as I watched the Royals hit a lazy pop fly to yet another one of Minnesota's ever-expanding cadre of inadequate shortstops I had to say, "Do we really know anybody? I mean, do we even know who our friends are?"

"What are you talking about?" he said.

"Take Andy Adams, for example."

"What about him?"

"What do we know about him? Really know?"

"You mean besides the fact that he never passes the damn puck?"

"I've been contemplating the nature of friendship."

Bobby stared at me for a long count, an expression of alarm on his face. Finally he stood and walked to the bottom of the staircase leading to his kitchen.

"Nina," he shouted. "Nina Truhler."

Nina appeared at the top of the stairs; Shelby Dunston was standing behind her.

"What is it?" she asked.

"What did you do to McKenzie? The last time I saw him he was perfectly fine; now he's talking gibberish."

"He's having a moment of personal reflection and self-doubt."

"That's what I mean. I've known him for over forty years and he's never had a moment of personal reflection and self-doubt. You broke him."

"It wasn't me. It was Salsa Girl."

"Salsa Girl?" Shelby said. "I want to hear this."

Shelby hustled down the stairs, crossed the room, and sat next to me, her long legs tucked beneath her. She rested an elbow on the back of the sofa and rested her chin in her hand. Her wheat-colored hair fell across one eye, and for a moment she reminded me of Veronica Lake in all those 1940s gangster movies.

"Well?" she said.

"Well what?"

"Salsa Girl."

"Oh, for—she asked me to do a favor."

"And?"

"And I said yes."

"And?"

"What do you mean 'And'?"

"You do favors for friends all the time. What's the problem?"

Nina answered for me. "The problem is, before she asked for the favor, Erin asked McKenzie if they were friends and he said yes."

"And?" Shelby said.

"I've known her for about seven years," I said. "We all have, but only because of Ian. Now that I've had time to think about it, I realize that I know nothing more about her than what's on her website. I'm wondering if it's true. If we are friends. Not only her, but it's occurred to me that half the people I know, the guys I play hockey with, the cops I worked with, the people I've done favors for—they're strangers to me."

"That's true of everybody," Shelby said. "I have one hundred and seventy-seven friends on Facebook, and I think I've actually met about thirty of them in person."

"I have regular customers," Nina said. "One of them put me down as a reference on her résumé. Some of the others, they behave as if we're cousins or something. I don't even know their names."

"That's the point," I said. "I have friends"—I quoted the air with both hands—"with whom I've never had a meaningful relationship."

"Like who?" Shelby asked.

"Erin Peterson."

"I've never been able to warm up to her," Nina said. "She's always friendly enough, yet at the same time—I don't know. She doesn't seem to care about anything except her business."

"I wouldn't say that. She gives a lot of money to charity, mostly women's groups—Women's Foundation of Minnesota, Tubman, the Sojourner Project."

"How do you know?"

"She told me. McKenzie," Shelby said, "if you want to know something about the woman, why don't you just ask her?"

"Hey?" Bobby's voice changed. If you didn't know him you might not have heard it; the calm authority. "Exactly what does she want you to do?"

I answered his question. He asked several more. Bobby was the best cop I knew, even better than I was. We started together at the St. Paul Police Department twenty years ago. I retired to accept a reward on a rather ambitious embezzler—$3,128,584.50 before taxes—that a financial wizard named H. B. Sutton had nearly doubled for me. The plan was to give my father, who raised me alone after my mother died, a comfy retirement. Unfortunately, he died six months later, leaving me both rich and bored. Meanwhile, Bobby stayed with the SPPD, eventually moving up to commander in the Major Crimes Division.

"Who are you going to get to supply the surveillance equipment?" he asked.

"I was thinking Marshall Lantry."

"Isn't he a criminal himself?" Shelby asked.

"He's never been convicted," I said.

"Half the people McKenzie knows are criminals," Nina said.

"Yes, but are they his friends?"

"In the meantime," I said.

Bobby knew what I was asking. "I *don't* do favors for friends," he said. "Not even for you. Especially not for you."

"Police officers are regularly assigned to patrol those areas where criminal activities are known to occur, and if the patrol commander of the Western District was made aware that—"

"How would she be made aware of crimes that the victim has refused to report?"

"Someone would need to reach out to her."

"Uh-huh. That's what I thought. McKenzie, in case you haven't been paying attention, there's a heroin epidemic sweeping the Twin Cities. I don't have the time or the resources to waste safeguarding another one of your girlfriends. Explain it to him, Shel."

"Honey," Shelby said, "what Bobby's trying to say is that there's a heroin epidemic sweeping the Twin Cities and he doesn't have the time or the resources to waste safeguarding another one of your girlfriends."

"Exactly how many girlfriends does he have, anyway?" Nina asked.

"There's you, me, Heavenly Petryk ..."

"C'mon," I said.

"McKenzie," Bobby said. "You know that Salsa Girl is lying about all of this, don't you?"

Both Nina and Shelby seemed outraged by the suggestion.

"How can you say that?" Shelby wanted to know.

"The sabotage of her building and trucks is obviously acts of retribution; it's payback," Bobby said. "It's highly unlikely that she doesn't know who's behind it."

"Yet entirely possible," I said.

Bobby spread his hands wide and shook his head. He looked exactly like he did the other night when I bet my ace against his full house.

Nina seemed distracted after we left Bobby and Shelby's house in the Merriam Park neighborhood of St. Paul and drove to the condominium we shared in Minneapolis. I knew why, too. The woman was suffering withdrawal symptoms. She had not set foot in her club since Saturday night, hadn't even made a phone call to check up, and now she was wondering if the place might've been burned to the ground and her employees were too frightened to tell her.

"When we get home, instead of going up, maybe I'll drive

over to Rickie's just to make sure everything's all right," Nina said.

"Everything is fine and you know it."

"Jennifer Grimm is singing in the big room tonight. It's the first time we've had her. I'd like to make her feel welcomed."

I glanced at the illuminated digital clock on the dashboard of my Mustang.

"The woman must be in the middle of her second set by now," I said.

"It wouldn't hurt to drop in for a minute to say hello."

I would have argued with her, except Nina running off to the club left me free to wander over to the industrial park that housed Salsa Girl Salsa—just to make sure everything was all right.

I parked my Mustang in the far corner of the back parking lot. At my rear was a cyclone fence that separated Salsa Girl from a yard filled with dozens of semitrailers. On my left was a nearly identical fence that kept pedestrians from climbing down into the valley that was Interstate 94. There were trees along the fence and no lights. I picked the spot because it rendered my car virtually invisible to anyone who wasn't looking for it; there were a few lights mounted on poles near the building and Pelham Boulevard, but they didn't reach where I sat. It also gave me an unobstructed view of the Salsa Girl loading dock. True, I couldn't see the front of the building, yet I could see the driveway that led to it. If anyone pulled in, I'd know it.

Even though it was cold, I rolled down the Mustang's windows so the glass wouldn't cloud over. You'd think forty-five degrees would seem warm after a long winter, but it didn't. I sat behind the steering wheel in my brown leather jacket, gloves, and stocking hat with the logo for the University of Minnesota, my alma mater thank you very much, and stared at the back of the building with a pair of binoculars that I kept in the glove compartment for just such occasions. The binoculars trembled in my hand because of the cold. I thought briefly of starting the car and turning the heater to high but ignored the suggestion. I was supposed to be hiding, remember?

The thing about conducting fixed surveillance, it's stressful. There's the physical stress—shivering behind a steering wheel is not fun. Worse is the mental stress. You can't listen to the radio or iPod, read articles or watch videos on your phone, or text your friends. Nor can you risk nodding off. If you did, you could very well miss the one thing you were there to see.

To remain vigilant you play mind games—if this happens you do that, if that happens you do this. You study the environment, alert to those areas where a target might slip past unseen. You watch birds and squirrels, hoping the birds will fly and the squirrels will run because that means something is moving.

The way I looked at it, surveillance was the same as hunting from a duck blind or a deer stand. You remained still, you watched, you waited. The problem was I had no idea what I was watching and waiting for. It was unlikely that a group of protestors carrying signs demanding the ethical treatment of tomatoes and jalapeños was going to convene in the parking lot. Nor did I have any reason to suspect that Erin's vandals would return to the scene of the crime. I was there only because of the possibility that something might happen.

And then it did.

A black and shiny car drove up the driveway. I recognized the make and model even in the low light because I used to own one just like it: an Audi S5 that retailed for about sixty-five grand. The value of the car made me ask myself, What does Salsa Girl drive?

Instead of heading for the front of the building, it pulled

around back, moved to the loading dock, and stopped. The flicker of rear lights told me that the driver had put the vehicle in park. I stared at it through the binoculars. The headlights were extinguished; personal experience told me that the driver must have turned off the engine. The dome light flashed on as the driver's side door was opened. For a moment I could see the driver's face. Not Erin but a man I didn't recognize, young, white. He slid out from behind the steering wheel and stood next to the car. He was wearing a long charcoal wool coat with the buttons undone and black gloves. That's all I could see before he turned his back to me, shut the door, circled the Audi, and headed toward the loading dock.

He climbed the staircase that led from the asphalt parking lot to the elevated dock and the door next to it. He unlocked the door. I couldn't tell if he was using a key or picks. I guessed a key because his body language didn't reveal a change in his demeanor from normal to nervous. Nor did he look around cautiously the way a thief might.

He entered the building, closing the door behind him.

Now what? my inner voice asked.

I figured I had two options.

One—move up on the scene and confront the driver when he left the building. I would have liked that idea better if I had thought to bring a gun.

Two—wait until the driver left the parking lot and follow him; try to get a good look at his license plate and take it from there.

I was debating the pros and cons when a third option presented itself: a black-and-white Ford Crown Victoria complete with light bar, push bumper, and the words POLICE CITY OF SAINT PAUL painted on the doors. It pulled in to the lot and approached the Audi, stopping only a few feet behind its rear bumper. An officer emerged from the patrol car. He did not turn off his engine. He did not extinguish his lights. Instead, he moved cautiously to the driver's side door of the Audi and shined a flashlight through the windows. He must not have seen anything that interested him, because he moved the light along the base of the building and along the loading dock.

Bobby, my inner voice said. *You would never reach out to the Western District patrol commander just to accommodate a friend. Of course not.*

The officer returned to his cruiser. Through the binoculars, I saw him speaking on his radio; I could almost hear his voice asking for a 10-24 on the Audi.

That's when the driver chose to leave the building. He backed his way out of the door, closed it tight, and turned. He was carrying a large box with both hands that he nearly dropped when he saw the police car. As it was, he paused for a long time as he stared at it.

The police officer slipped out of the car and spoke to the driver across the roof. Words were exchanged, yet the driver didn't budge. The officer gestured. The driver moved to the stairs and descended slowly. The box looked as if it suddenly weighed ten thousand pounds.

The officer didn't approach the driver; instead he remained behind the patrol car. He gestured for the driver to stop, and they began a conversation.

I left the Mustang and moved across the parking lot toward them. The driver's head came up when I crossed into the circle of light near the building. The officer caught the look in his eye and pivoted so he could watch me and the driver at the same time. He brought his hand to the butt of his Glock. He made sure I saw him do it.

I moved both of my hands away from my body so he could see that they were empty and continued approaching.

"Stop," the officer said.

I stopped.

"Who are you?"

"My name's McKenzie. I was asked by the owner to keep an eye on the place."

The officer gestured at the building. "This place?" he asked.

"Salsa Girl Salsa." I threw a thumb over my shoulder. "I was watching from over there."

"Licensed?"

"No. Just a concerned citizen."

"Uh-huh."

"Why were you watching?" the Audi driver asked.

"Because someone has been vandalizing the property."

"Salsa Girl never mentioned it to me."

"Why would she?"

"I'm her partner. No, really. Randy Sax. You can check."

I was close enough now to get a good look at his face. It was older than I thought when I saw it at a distance; the half moons under his eyes suggested that he didn't get much comfort from sleep. Yet he had a high, whiny voice that made him sound like a teenager questioning why everyone was picking on him.

"Okay," I said.

"What's your name again?" the officer asked.

"McKenzie. Call Erin Peterson. She's the owner. She'll vouch for me."

"Rushmore McKenzie?"

"Yeah."

"I remember you. You're the one who quit the department to collect the price on some embezzler a few years back. The insurance company paid you fifty cents on every dollar of the stolen money that you recovered."

"That's right."

"Damn."

From the way he cursed, I didn't know if he was envious or disgusted by what I had done. Believe me, I got both reactions from the cops in the Twin Cities.

"Let me see some ID." The officer made a gimme gesture

with his free hand; the other remained on the butt of his hand-gun. "Both of you."

While I reached for my wallet, Randy Sax set the box he was carrying on the trunk of the Audi. He dug into his pocket for his wallet, too. We both handed our driver's licenses to the officer. He returned to his vehicle and called in a 10-27, a driver's license check. Randy and I stood between the police car and the Audi where the officer could see us.

"You're a cop?" Randy said.

"I used to be a cop. Back when I was young and impression-able."

"I'd love to be a cop. Why'd you quit?"

"It seemed like a good idea at the time. Tell me something, Randy." I couldn't bring myself to call him Mr. Sax. "What's in the box?"

"Tomatoes."

Randy opened the box just wide enough to reach in and pull out a lush red tomato, then quickly closed it again. He held the tomato for me to see.

"I'm making a huge batch of my world-famous spaghetti sauce for my family Tuesday. It's my niece's birthday."

"Does Erin know that you're stealing her tomatoes in the dead of night?"

"Technically, ten percent of them are mine. I was on my way home from a party and decided—what's this about van-dalism?"

"Technically, I'm not at liberty to say."

"If you're working for Erin, then you're working for me, too." I held out my hand and gave it a little wag.

"You're making a mistake if you think you can treat me like some dumb kid," he said. "I not only own ten percent of the com-pany, my family owns Minnesota Foods. We distribute Erin's salsa. What do you think of that?"

"I'm sure it's a profitable relationship for everyone involved."

Randy's expression became that of a middle schooler who was being sent to his room for reasons that seemed unjust to him. I expected him to go off. Instead, he said, "No one tells me anything," and studied his tomato. Once again, I wondered about his age. According to the Salsa Girl origin story, he had invested in Erin's company about ten years ago. Assuming he was the age of consent at the time, he'd have to be at least thirty now, and I would say he looked a few years older. Yet Bobby Dunston's sixteen-year-old daughter, Victoria, seemed more mature.

By then the officer had decided that we were who we claimed we were and returned our driver's licenses.

"Thank you, gentlemen," he said. "Have a pleasant evening."

"We're good?" Randy asked.

"Yes, sir. Sorry to have troubled you."

"Not at all, not at all. Doing your job. That's great. Here. Have a tomato."

The officer took the tomato and gave Randy a casual salute with it. Randy opened the trunk of the Audi and put the box inside while we watched.

"McKenzie," he said, "you gotta come to the party, see what I do with all these tomatoes. Erin is always invited to family gatherings, only she never comes. Tell her to take you."

"We'll see," I said.

"Night-night." Randy climbed into his Audi and drove off. The officer and I watched him go.

"Where are you?" he asked.

I gestured at the corner of the parking lot where the Mustang was parked.

"Nice car," he said. "You buy it with the reward money?"

"Actually, my girlfriend gave it to me."

"Must be some girlfriend."

"I've always thought so."

The officer tossed the tomato into the air and caught it.

"It's not three million bucks," he said. "As long as we come out ahead, though, that's the main thing."

The officer climbed into his car and drove off. I returned to my Mustang, started it, rolled up the windows, and put the heater on high.

My inner voice asked, *Do you really believe that Randy stopped on his way home to steal a box filled with tomatoes?*

"I should have looked inside the box just to make sure," I said aloud.

I had left the parking lot and was heading west toward the entrance of a freeway that would take me home when my cell rang. Normally I would have ignored it; I don't like using my phone when I'm driving. Yet given the time of night, I thought it was probably Nina. I felt a tingle of concern as I pulled over and took the phone from my pocket. Only it wasn't Nina. It was Erin Peterson. I swiped right.

"This is McKenzie," I said.

"McKenzie, I just got a call from Randy Sax."

"He's kind of a dip, isn't he?"

"He's also irate."

"He didn't seem that way when he left."

"McKenzie, he told me that the police stopped him in the parking lot and all but arrested him, and then you showed up and started interrogating him, too."

"That's not quite how it happened."

"What did happen?"

I explained.

"You're right, Randy is a dip. McKenzie, what were you doing at Salsa Girl?"

"Keeping an eye on your building."

"You're taking this way too seriously."

"Or not seriously enough. Did Randy tell you that he stole a box filled with tomatoes?"

"Only after I insisted he tell me why he was there at this time of night. McKenzie, can you meet me?"

"Now?"

"Yes."

I glanced at my digital clock again. Knowing her habits, I figured that Nina was still at Rickie's.

"Tell me where," I said.

Like most women who take good care of themselves, Erin made it hard to guess her age. Thirty? Forty? Somewhere in there. I wasn't normally obsessed with age, but seeing her sitting at the bar in a joint not far from the Minneapolis campus of the University of Minnesota made me wonder. She seemed to blend in so nicely with the students. One of them was standing next to her chair and speaking earnestly. I didn't know what he was saying, although I could guess. Probably it was the same thing that I would have been saying to an attractive woman in a bar if I were his age. In any case, Erin kept smiling and shaking her head.

Finally Erin slipped off her chair and rested her hands on his shoulders. She leaned in and pecked his lips. Clearly he wanted a longer, more passionate kiss. It was just as clear that he wasn't going to get it. After some hemming and hawing, the kid left. Erin returned to her chair. She said something to the woman sitting next to her, and the woman laughed.

The woman raised her empty glass as I approached from behind. The bartender reached her in a hurry and refilled it. Afterward, he pointed at Erin's drink. She shook her head.

"Fancy seeing you here," I said.

"McKenzie." Erin's voice was high—at least higher than

usual—and her eyes were inordinately bright and shiny. *Saying no to another drink was probably wise,* my inner voice said. She rested her hand on my arm. "Thanks for coming."

"My, my," said the woman next to her. She spoke with a Hispanic accent that sounded second generation. "Aren't you a hunka hunka burnin' love?"

"Really?" I said.

"Down, girl," Erin said. "McKenzie is spoken for."

"Loudly?" asked the woman.

"I don't know. How loudly does Nina speak for you?"

"Pretty loud."

"See? She's so gorgeous, too, that you just want to run her over with your car. Her eyes are silver. I mean, they're blue, but they're so pale that they look silver. Silver."

"I take it you've been here for a while," I said.

"We started at—oh, McKenzie, this is Maria. Maria is my production manager. She's been with me eight years as of today. Maria, say hello to McKenzie."

"Hello to McKenzie," Maria said.

Both women giggled.

Oh my God.

"We decided to have dinner to celebrate after we closed up shop," Erin said. "Just the girls. Alice and the others have already gone home."

"Lightweights," Maria said.

"Is that why you called, because you need a ride home?" I said. "It's not a bad idea."

Erin lightly slapped my chest three times.

"Don't worry," she said. "I have that covered. I might be ever so slightly intoxicated, but I'm not ... I'm trying to think of a word."

"Out of control," Maria said. "That's three words, but if you say 'em really fast ..."

"No, that's not it. Injudicious. I'm not injudicious. A professor at DePaul University always used that word when he was scolding students for not paying attention to his lectures. It's my favorite word."

"DePaul, where's that?" Marie asked.

"Chicago."

"McKenzie, do you have a favorite word?"

"Yes, but I stole it from the Reverend Jesse Jackson. He once said, 'I not only deny the allegation, I deny the alligator.' "

"That's great. But which word? Allegation or alligator?"

"You need to use them both together."

"It's a favorite joke, then, not a word."

"I don't know what you want to talk about, but I suspect we'll be better off talking about it tomorrow."

"I wanted to tell you something important. Something that couldn't wait. What was it? Something about—oh yes, about the Bignell family. Randy Bignell-Sax is a member of the Bignell family, and we do not want to antagonize the Bignell family until I'm ready."

Until you're ready? my inner voice asked.

"Does that include Randy?" I asked aloud.

"Randy is—what's the word? Capricious."

"Ohhh," Maria said. "I like that one, too."

"I can control Randy. He's harmless. The rest of the Bignells, though, they are ruthless people, and I want to stay out of their line of sight."

"Randy invited me to a party for his niece tomorrow night," I said. "He said you should take me."

Erin thought that was funny.

"Absolutely not," she said. "That would be ... injudicious."

"Again, how about we talk tomorrow morning?"

"I'll be in the office at six thirty."

Looking into her shiny blue eyes, I didn't believe her.

FOUR

Eight A.M. The sun was shining, the birds were singing, and I was leaning against the doorframe with my arms crossed over my chest and looking into Erin Peterson's office. She was working her computer. Her eyes were clear, her hair was coiffed, what little makeup she wore was expertly applied, and her crisp white shirt and dark blue skirt and jacket were neat, businesslike, and sexy all at the same time.

"Don't you clean up nicely," I said.

Erin refused to look at me while she answered. "If you knew how much effort it took you'd be traumatized." Her voice had returned to its normal low register; once again it reflected her self-control. She stared at her computer screen for a few beats before she spoke again. "Should I tell you why I'm happy to see you?"

"I didn't know you were."

Erin swiveled her chair away from the computer screen, rose slowly, and circled her desk. There was a restlessness in her eyes that I hadn't seen before. She moved to the door and tugged my arm until I fully entered the office. Erin closed the door. She sighed heavily as she hugged me, her arms around my waist, her cheek pressed against my neck. It wasn't the welcoming hug of friends who have not seen each other for a while. It was stronger and filled with deep meaning.

I wrapped my arms around her shoulders and pulled her tighter against me. I could feel her breasts flatten against my chest. At the same time, a low charge of electricity rumbled through me that I hadn't felt since ... not since I first became involved with Nina Truhler.

Erin murmured my name into my collarbone. She stepped back and rested her hand against my chest. Her head came up and her eyes met mine. When she did that, I swear to God I nearly kissed her. I didn't because I knew Nina wouldn't like it. 'Course, she wouldn't need to know ...

Are you serious? my inner voice asked.

I took a step backward, putting distance between me and Erin's lips because yeah, for a moment there I was serious.

Erin tapped my chest. "Don't worry, McKenzie," she said. "That's not what this is about."

"What is it about?"

"Fear."

She returned to her desk.

"I arrive at six thirty every morning, always the first one here. My staff filters in between seven thirty and eight. We begin production sharply at eight fifteen and continue until six, six thirty P.M. Monday through Thursday. Nine thousand gallons of salsa. Most of my people have Fridays off, when our Upper Midwest shipments go out and my Texas truck returns with my jalapeños and other ingredients. That's the schedule."

"Okay."

Erin reached under her desk for a clear plastic sandwich bag. She held the bag for me to see. It was half filled with dark brown pellets about three-quarters of an inch long and one-eighth of an inch in diameter.

"This is what I found on my desk this morning," she said.

"What is it?"

"Rat excrement."

"Oh shit."

Erin chuckled as she dropped the bag into her wastebasket.

"You do have a way with words, McKenzie," she said. "I'll give you that."

"How bad is it?"

"If whoever left this on my desk had poured it into one of my mixing tanks instead, I'd have to shut down. Throw out any product that might have been contaminated. Clean and sanitize my equipment. Replace the ingredients that were wasted. Start mixing from scratch. Two days wasted, possibly three, without a chance of meeting my delivery dates. It would be injurious to say the least."

"Why didn't he, then? Why didn't he dump the rat droppings into your tanks?"

"I don't know. It's like whoever is doing these things wants to hurt me, but not too badly. McKenzie, please help me. Tell me what to do."

"My first thought—"

"Probably the same as mine."

"Randy Bignell-Sax."

"He has keys," Erin said. "I didn't know he had keys until last night—have no idea where he acquired them. He doesn't work here. He has nothing to do with Salsa Girl. Randy comes by every once in a while and I buy him lunch. That's the extent of his involvement."

"Does he want to be more involved? Has he ever mentioned taking an active role in running the company?"

"Randy doesn't want to run anything. He's concerned with having a good time, but not so much of a good time that his family will disown him, that's all."

I gestured at the baggie in the wastebasket. "Yet he did this," I said.

"We don't know for sure that that's true."

"Of course we do."

"McKenzie—"

"Erin, what does Randy want from you that he thinks threatening your business might get him?"

I thought I knew the answer. I was sure that Erin knew it, too. She sat in her chair and swiveled it so she could watch the traffic moving sporadically across the Pelham Boulevard Bridge through her window.

"He's not that kind of guy," she said. "The kind of guy who takes what's his, who collects what he thinks he's owed whether the woman agrees or not. No. Randy wants to be loved. If he's behind this it's so he can make himself a hero by riding to my rescue, saving the damsel in distress, all the while hoping I'll be appropriately grateful."

"It could work that way."

"*If* Randy is behind all this. I'm not convinced that he is."

"I'm open to suggestions."

"I was going to tell you the same thing."

"Surveillance. Originally I was thinking a four-camera setup watching the outside of your building. Now I'm thinking something more elaborate—and secret. We don't want any of your employees to know that they're being observed."

"My people are loyal, McKenzie."

"How many of them have keys?"

"They've been with me since—"

"How many?"

"Alice and Maria."

"Plus whomever they made copies for besides Randy."

"No."

"How else did he get a set?"

Erin stood up. I knew she wanted to walk off her anger, yet the office was too small. After a moment, she sat down again.

"You're wrong," she said.

"It wouldn't be the first time."

There was a knock on the door.

"Yes?" Erin asked.

The door opened and Alice Pfeifer peeked in. Unlike Erin, she looked like she was coming off a long night. Erin had said she had gone home early, and I wondered, how early?

"California is on line one," Alice said.

"Tell them I'll call back."

"Are you sure you want to—"

"Dammit, Alice."

Alice quickly pulled her head back and shut the door.

"I shouldn't have done that," Erin said. "Now she'll be pouting half the day. McKenzie, you might not know it to look at me, but I have a splitting headache."

"After seeing you last night, I believe it."

"I'd say you saw me at my worst, but the truth is this exact moment is my worst. I not only have a headache, I'm frightened. I haven't been frightened in fifteen years."

"Not even when you quit school to start your business?"

"You've been visiting my website."

"I notice that you haven't posted your photograph anywhere. Instead, you have the image of someone else representing your company."

"It's called branding. Who would you rather buy salsa from, a dark-haired, dark-eyed vixen with a Latin vibe or an immigrant from Sweden? I'm not Salsa Girl, McKenzie. There's no such person as Salsa Girl. There's no such person as Betty Crocker, Aunt Jemima, Joy Butterworth, Francesco Rinaldi, Juan Valdez, Lorna Doone, Uncle Ben, or Dr Pepper, either."

"How 'bout Baby Ruth?"

"Actually, she's real. The candy bar was named after Grover Cleveland's daughter."

"I didn't know that."

"Wendy's was named after Dave Thomas's daughter, who

was, and still is, represented as a pretty little girl in pigtails in the company's signage and marketing materials. When Thomas passed, they asked the real Wendy to take his place as the company's spokesperson. It didn't work out. You know why? Even though the real Wendy was a perfectly acceptable representative, she wasn't a little girl in pigtails. Image, McKenzie. Image. There's a reason why KFC is still using the image of Colonel Harland Sanders to sell chicken even though he's been dead for forty years."

"Okay."

"This is where I also repeat that I asked you to investigate the people who are vandalizing my property and threatening my business. Not me. Because you know what? I didn't do it."

"Okay."

"What do we do?"

"First, we go see a friend of mine. Under normal circumstances, I'd have him come to you, only I don't want anyone in your building to know what he's doing."

"Now?"

"Now."

I stood and opened Erin's office door. A moment later she passed through it, bag in hand, with me following behind. She walked to Alice Pfeifer's desk.

"I have an errand to run with McKenzie," Erin said. "It should take what? An hour?"

"About that," I said.

"Of course, *ma'am*," Alice said. She emphasized the last word like it was a curse.

"Stand up," Erin said.

"What?"

"Stand up."

Alice rose tentatively. While she did, Erin circled the woman's desk. Alice turned to meet her. Erin wrapped her arms around her and kissed her cheek.

"Don't you dare be angry with me," Erin said. "Some days I feel as if you're the only friend I have in the world, and today is one of those days."

"I'm not angry," Alice said.

"Not even a little bit?"

Alice smiled broadly. "No."

"Thank you. I'll be back soon."

Erin and I went to the closet for our coats. The phone rang. We put on our coats. Alice answered the phone. We headed for the front door. Alice called to us just as we reached it.

"Erin," she said, "you'll want to take this."

Erin paused. "California?" she said.

"Bruce Bignell."

"The old man himself?"

"Uh-huh."

"I'll take it at my desk."

Erin moved from the front door down the short corridor toward her office. I followed along until she gave me a look that asked "Where do you think you're going?" I stayed in the lobby. Alice smiled at me. I smiled at Alice. I noticed another woman working in a small office behind the reception desk. One of the part-timers that Alice had mentioned, I decided.

"Another day in paradise," I said.

"I have a terrible hangover."

I don't know why I laughed. Probably because of the offhand way she said it.

"It's not funny," Alice said.

"I'm sorry. I'm sure it isn't. When did you get home last night?"

"Early. Around eight thirty, nine."

A good hour and a half before you began your surveillance in the Salsa Girl parking lot, my inner voice reminded me.

"Three drinks and I had to call a friend for a ride home. It's embarrassing."

*She could easily have come and gone by the time you ar-
rived; dumped the rat excrement.*

"I don't think my girlfriend has ever had more than two
drinks at a time, and she owns a bar," I said aloud.

"It's just not the way I was raised. My mother—I'm not joking, McKenzie—she would sniff my breath when I came home
from a date. When I went to college she gave me a pillow em-
broidered with the words *Lips that touch wine shall never taste
mine.*"

"There are worse things that a parent could teach you."

"I have no experience at partying. Maria and the other
women in the production plant, especially the Hispanics, they
call me *la princesa virgen.*"

"There are worse things to be called than a virgin princess,
too."

"It isn't even true. Prom night, well, not prom night, but the
night after senior prom ..."

"Umm, Alice? A little too much information."

"Sorry."

By then Erin had returned to the reception area.

"Guess what," she said.

"What?" I asked.

"I've been summoned to the Bignell estate for a party this evening. Bruce won't take no for an answer. You know what else?"

"I'm afraid to ask."

"You're coming with me. You've been requested by name."

"I'm surprised Bignell would even know my name."

"Randy must have given it up. Randy is Bruce's grandson."

"I should tell you, Erin, I've been involved with seriously
wealthy people before. It has rarely ended pleasantly."

Marshall Lantry was wearing his uniform—blue sports jacket,
blue dress shirt, blue tie. On the pocket of his jacket, written in

script, was EASY CASH which was the name of the pawnshop he owned. He had just opened the doors when we arrived, and there was a line. Nearly everyone in the line had something to sell—jewelry, tools, electronics; one guy was carrying an electric guitar. Lantry greeted each in turn, directing them to specific spots in the store where his assistants were ready to start asking about proof of ownership and haggling over price.

He saw me and said, "McKenzie, long time, man." He saw Erin and added, "Are you selling today?"

I thought she might be offended by the suggestion, and maybe she was, but Erin said "Depends. Make me an offer."

"One million dollars."

"That's a little light. I'll have to think about it." She pointed at the huge posters of Jennifer Lawrence, Jon Hamm, and Angelina Jolie hanging above a kiosk in the center of the store where the cash registers were located. "What's that about?"

"It was McKenzie's idea. He said the posters would make the customers look up so the security cameras would get a good shot of their faces. What can I do for you?"

"Security cameras," I said.

"What are we talking about? You want to buy?"

"Rent. For a business location. Inside and out."

"Whose business?"

"Mine," Erin said.

"Oh, okay. So, not off the books."

"Marshall," I said, "have I ever asked you to do anything illegal?"

"Not for over a year now. Would you care to step into my office?"

Lantry led us across his well-lit store. To the casual observer it resembled a consignment shop that sold everything from clothes to lawn mowers; it didn't feel desperate at all. At the far end was a door that led to a metal staircase that led to a metal door in the basement. Lantry seemed to enjoy watching Erin descend the staircase in front of him. She seemed to sway with each step, and I wondered if she was doing it on purpose. At the bottom, he used a keypad to disarm the electronic lock. The door popped open and Erin entered; rows of fluorescent lights flicked on as she went.

Lantry whispered to me, "Very tasty. But I like the last lady you brought over, Nina. I like her better."

"I heard that," Erin said.

I punched Lantry hard in the arm.

"What'd I say?" he asked.

We stood in the middle of the room surrounded by metal shelf after metal shelf heaped with an amazing array of electronic gear, from satellite dishes to nanny cams. Nina had been astounded by it all when she first saw it and even now will tell acquaintances, "You wouldn't believe the stuff this guy had down there." Yet Erin didn't seem impressed at all. She glanced at cameras disguised as wall clocks and smoke detectors; she fingered the watches and black pens as if she had seen it all before.

I told Lantry what we were shopping for.

"If this is all legal, why come to me?" Lantry asked. "There are a lot of good security firms that can give you what you want for less."

"The cameras need to be placed in secret. No one can know that they're there."

"Mounting your cameras in plain sight makes for a good deterrent. People are honest as hell when they know they're being watched."

"We're not interested in deterring. We're interested in catching."

"Yeah, yeah, all right, I get it. But you know, it's gonna cost ya. Even if what you're doing is temporary, if you give the cameras back after you're finished." Lantry picked up a camera that looked like a thermostat and bounced it in his hand. "A setup like that ..."

Erin snatched the thermostat out of midair and examined it closely. She was still the same woman who had entered the basement, yet somehow her demeanor had changed, and with it her appearance. Her eyes seemed darker, her lips fuller, her posture straighter, her shirt and skirt tighter. She flicked her hair back as she tossed the thermostat to Lantry. Her voice conveyed a deep sensuality I had not heard from her before.

"Perhaps you'll take something in trade," she said.

Lantry was visibly agitated by the suggestion. He even licked his lips.

"What are you offering?" he asked.

"Salsa. I make six flavors of salsa."

It took us a while to map out exactly what we were going to do and when we would do it. It was decided that Lantry and his people would arrive at Salsa Girl at approximately seven thirty that evening after everyone else had gone. Alice Pfeifer would let them in. I didn't want her involved, but Erin reminded me that we were committed to attend the Bignell party. "I trust her," she said. I told her that we shouldn't trust anybody, but what else could we do? Lantry asked who would pay. I told him I would. Erin wouldn't hear of it.

"Just so you know, honey," Lantry said, "I deal strictly in cash."

Erin gazed up at me. "Did he just call me honey?" she asked.

"No disrespect," Lantry said.

Erin moved closer, invading his personal space. Her smile was purely carnal as she lightly stroked both lapels on Lantry's sports jacket. Her eyes stared deeply into his. Again her voice took on a smoky quality.

"Marshall," she said. "May I call you Marshall?"

Lantry hesitated before answering, "Yeah, sure."

"Do you prefer small denominations and nonsequential serial numbers?"

"Umm, just as long as it's American."

"Payable when I'm satisfied."

"Yes, sure. Satisfaction guaranteed."

"Men have said that to me before, Marshall, yet so few of them have kept their promise."

"I will."

Erin released Lantry's lapel and stepped back.

"We'll see," she said. "After the party tonight, McKenzie and I will drop by to check on your progress."

"Sure. All right."

We were back in my Mustang and nearing Salsa Girl Salsa when I said, "I enjoyed that very much."

"Enjoyed what?"

"The way you discombobulated Lantry."

"It wasn't too difficult. My greatest asset, any woman's greatest asset, has always been a man's imagination."

"Still, you did it so effortlessly. It must have taken years of practice."

"Remember the lecture I gave you earlier about branding? That's all it is, McKenzie. Branding."

We pulled in to the parking lot. I halted the Mustang near Erin's front door.

"The party starts at five thirty," she said. "The Bignells will expect us to be on time. That means you should pick me up at about four. We have a long way to go, and the traffic will be awful."

"Where are we going?'

"Cambridge."

"How should I dress?"

"Respectfully. What you need to remember, McKenzie, is that these so-called family gatherings are all about the Bignells. We're invited solely to admire them."

"In that case, maybe I'll have a few drinks before we go."

"Don't you dare."

"I was joking."

"Sometimes I can't tell."

"Sometimes I can't either."

"What will Nina think about this—you going out with me? Will she be angry?"

"She'll understand."

"More and more I'm growing to dislike that woman."

I was in my condo and sitting at my desk in the library area. The high-rise condominium in downtown Minneapolis that Nina and I bought together didn't have rooms. It was divided into areas: dining area, living area, kitchen area. The entire north wall was built of tinted floor-to-ceiling glass. From where I sat near the south wall, which was lined with floor-to-ceiling bookcases, all I could see was blue skies. Once again I reminded myself how lucky I was to have Nina, to have this condo, to have my friends.

I kept waiting for a knock on the door and a guy with a clipboard and thick glasses to say "Mr. McKenzie, Mr. Rushmore McKenzie? I'm from management. I regret to inform you that there has been a terrible, terrible mistake. This great life that you've been living? It was meant for someone else." Only the knock never came.

Instead, I received a phone call on my landline. The jangling bell startled me enough that I flinched. I glanced around to see if anyone noticed even though I knew I was alone.

"This is McKenzie," I said.

"McKenzie, this is Jones down at the security desk." Just

McKenzie, no "Mr." required; we had that kind of relationship. Since moving in, I had employed Jones and his partner Smith on a couple of cases—yes, I tease them about their names. They seemed to enjoy it. "McKenzie, we have a gentleman here who would like to go up and speak to you, but his name isn't on our list."

"Is he wearing glasses and carrying a clipboard?"

"No. What?"

"Who is he?"

"His ID reads Ian Gotz." His voice dropped a couple of octaves. "He looks like an accountant."

"He is an accountant."

"Oh yeah?"

"Send him up, Jonesie. Send him up."

A few minutes later, Ian knocked on my door. I opened it. He smiled at me. I smiled back and told him to come in.

"What are you doing here, anyway?" I asked. "In the middle of a workday."

"I was in the neighborhood."

"Sure you were."

"I was just wondering, you know, how Erin was doing."

"Call her and ask."

The expression on his face suggested that he couldn't think of anything more inappropriate.

"Ian?" I said.

"Erin was upset that I spoke to you. She said that what she tells me in private is supposed to stay private."

"She has a point."

"She told me to stop interfering."

"I doubt she thinks that way now."

"Why not? What happened? Did something happen?"

"I'm kind of caught in a difficult spot here, Ian. I'd like to tell you what's going on, but I can't without sacrificing client confidentiality."

"You're not a real private investigator, McKenzie. You're not bound by those rules."

"That's true. But I discovered a long time ago that it's better all around if I behave as if I were."

"You've told us stories in the past."

"Not all of the stories, and not the deep dark secrets that the people I help want hidden."

"We're friends, though."

"Ian, there are things I haven't even told Nina. My advice— if you want to know what's going on, ask Salsa Girl."

"I told you, Erin doesn't like that name. Anyway, she won't tell me. I'm afraid she'll become angry if I ask."

"What do you know about her, anyway?"

"I know I love her."

Ian flinched visibly. His eyes darted about as if he were searching the air for the words he had just spoken so he could snatch them back.

"I didn't mean to say that," he said.

I patted his arm. "It's okay," I said. "Everyone knows."

"Erin doesn't."

"I'm sure she does. Do you want a drink?"

I led Ian to the island in the kitchen area of the condo. He sat on a stool while I fetched the Summit Ale he requested. He was surprised when I didn't join him, pouring a glass of iced tea instead.

"Not drinking?" he asked.

"I'm going to a party tonight. Best to keep my wits about me."

"What party?"

"The Bignell family is having some sort of gathering."

"You're going with Erin, aren't you?"

"Yes."

"She's never taken me to one of those parties."

"It's strictly business, Ian."

"Are you sure? Just business?"

I gave it a couple of beats before I answered.

"Yes, I'm sure. And please don't ask me again, because it'll piss me off. And then you'll get pissed off. And then we'll be pissed off together. Why would you want that? C'mon. You need to remember, I'm not helping Erin because she's my friend. I'm helping her because you're my friend."

"I'm sorry."

"It's okay."

"It's just that—I see the way men look at her."

"They look at Nina and Shelby the same way. And Erica. And Bobby's daughter Victoria for that matter, and she's only sixteen. You can't let that bother you. It'll drive you nuts. What you need to notice is if the woman is looking back. Erin doesn't, does she?"

"No, not that I've ever seen."

"Well, then."

"That doesn't mean—"

"Stop it."

He took a long pull of his ale and wiped his lips with the back of his hand.

"I'm an idiot," he said.

"I don't know, Ian. Women always seem to make life more complicated than it needs to be. Not because they're dumb and foolish, but because they make us dumb and foolish."

For a moment, he stared at me as if he were trying to guess my weight. I knew what he was thinking. I said, "Go away, Ian."

"Yeah," he said. "I better."

I walked him to the door.

"See you around, McKenzie. Don't worry about me. I'm just being dumb and foolish."

"It's okay," I said again.

Only it isn't okay, is it? my inner voice said after he left.

It wasn't okay because while Ian was talking, I was remembering Erin's hug that morning, her arms wrapped around my waist, my arms wrapped around her shoulders, the look in her eyes, and how close I came to acting dumb and foolish myself.

Something rare for me: I felt a moment of panic.

I grabbed my smartphone and called Nina.

"Hey, you," she said.

"Hey. Listen, the Bignell family, which distributes Salsa Girl Salsa through Minnesota Foods, has insisted that Erin Peterson attend a party they're throwing tonight. I'm supposed to go with her, but I won't if you don't want me to."

Nina paused for what seemed like a long time before she said, "Why are you telling me this?"

"I just spoke to Ian, and he's not happy about it."

"That's because he's jealous."

"Yeah."

"Are you asking if I'm jealous?"

"No. I'm just—"

"Because I am."

"What? You are? Why?"

"Look at her."

"Look at you."

"McKenzie, I know who I am. I know who you are. I know the world is filled with temptation ..."

For some reason, I was reminded of the evangelist Billy Graham. I heard a story where he was supposed to meet with a female reporter, but instead of his suite, he chose to greet her in the hotel lobby. When asked why, he said it was because he wanted to avoid any appearance of impropriety that might harm his ministry. I always wondered, though, if that was the entire truth. One of Graham's most frequent sermons involved the psalm *Yea, though I walk through the valley of the shadow of death, I will fear no evil: for thou art with me.* I've always wondered if Graham met the woman in the lobby instead of his hotel room because, his faith in God notwithstanding, he understood that the best way to avoid impropriety was to stay the hell out of the valley.

"I don't need to go with Erin," I said. "I don't know if the Bignells have anything to do with her problems."

Nina paused again. She sighed as if she had come to a decision and said, "If you promised to help her—"

"It doesn't matter. If being with her causes you even a moment of anxiety—"

"I'm not anxious."

"I don't want this to be a thing between us."

"It won't."

"Just out of curiosity, I've been in close proximity to a lot of women since we became a couple, and you've never been jealous. Not once. Not even of Heavenly Petryk. Why now?"

"All those other women—none of them were even remotely your type. They were all too young or too old or too needy or too dumb or too married or too dishonest. But Salsa Girl ..."

"What about her?"

"She's a certain age, single, smart, and tough enough to build and operate her own business—independent minded, self-sufficient, and God knows she's beautiful."

"So?"

"McKenzie, she's me."

I started laughing.

"You think that's funny?" Nina said.

"Yeah, I do. A little. You are the most intelligent, most kind, most beautiful, most most most most most remarkable woman I have ever known or heard of. No one else is even on the same continent. You might not believe it, but I do. You know, Nina, talking to you always makes me aware of how great my life is."

You do *have a great life,* my inner voice reminded me. *And it won't be some nerd with glasses and a clipboard who screws it up. Only you can do that and you're way too smart, sure you are.*

"I feel better now," I said.

It was Nina's turn to laugh.

"So, do I," she said.

"It's an early party, supposedly for the Bignell niece. I don't expect to be out too late."

"Maybe I'll come home early myself. Make Jenness happy."

"Who's singing in the big room tonight?"

"Connie Evingson."

"I love her."

"Don't push your luck, McKenzie."

FIVE

Cambridge, Minnesota, was far enough away from the Twin Cities to be considered one of those small towns "up north." It was fifty miles from Salsa Girl Salsa, where I retrieved Erin, and took us over an hour to reach it because the first twenty miles of the drive were through heavy rush hour traffic. I asked Erin why the Bignell family lived way out there instead of Lake Minnetonka, Sunfish Lake, North Oaks, or any of the other areas of the Cities where the one percent tended to gather.

"They're simple folk," she said.

I didn't believe her, especially after I first saw the enormous family mansion. It was located northeast of town and surrounded by a vast field of tall grass—the only structure of any kind in sight.

"You're supposed to be impressed," Erin said.

"I am."

"Eight bedrooms, nine baths, four partial baths, over twenty thousand square feet, in-ground swimming pool, six-car garage, two hundred and seventy acres."

"You know these details because ..."

"It's my hobby. Stop the car."

I did, pulling to the shoulder of the single-lane road that led to the Bignell mansion and nowhere else. Erin stepped out of the car. I asked what she was doing. She answered by releasing the top three buttons of her white shirt; if she twisted her body just so it would open, and the casual observer would notice the lace bra she wore underneath. She pulled out the shirttails, rolled up the waistband of her dark blue skirt until the hem was inches above her knees, pushed back the sleeves of her jacket to her elbows, and pulled her hair into a loose ponytail, making sure that several unruly strands hung down along her cheek. She appeared younger; how much younger depended on your imagination. She slid back into the car.

"What are you doing?" I asked again.

"I told you before, it's called branding."

"You look like a student in an all-women's prep school flouting the dress code. All you need is a red tie with the knot pulled down to your cleavage."

"I'm just a naïve little girl, inexperienced in the ways of the world, who needs a strong man to advise and guide her as she attempts to grow her fragile boutique into a full-fledged business. Pretend that you're my big brother coming along to keep me out of trouble because you know how impetuous and flighty I can be."

"This is going to be fun."

"We'll see."

I continued driving toward the mansion. With nothing to compete with, it seemed to grow even bigger and grander as we approached—which, I'm sure, was the point. We parked next to a couple of dozen other cars, most of them a lot more expensive than mine. We didn't walk to the front door but instead circled the house to the back, where we found red, white, and blue bunting, folding tables and chairs, and plenty of white canopies. Under the canopies were bars and tables loaded with food and plates. Men and women attired in white catering outfits stood behind them. There was no one standing at the bars or eating the food, however. Instead, the guests mingled in small cliques around the canopies. Most of them were dressed for an Easter parade. The breeze coming off the fields made their clothes flutter.

"Who are all these people?" I asked.

"Family; a few friends, I suppose. Mostly they're business associates, though—people who are beholden to the Bignells for one reason or another. If you're involved in any way with the selling of food products in the Upper Midwest and Great Lakes Region, you're likely to be involved with the Bignell family."

"Speaking of food, I notice that no one is eating or drinking."

"It's not allowed until after prayers."

We moved among the other guests. Erin often received the once-over, that look most men and some women automatically bestow on pretty girls. The eyes of one man in particular grew wide with recognition when he noted her presence, yet he quickly looked away. He was in his midfifties with hair that was more salt than pepper. He was wearing a blue collarless shirt and black jacket. I noticed that he kept repositioning his body as he spoke to his companions so that he could track Erin's progress as she meandered through the crowd while pretending not to. I was going to ask who he was, except Randy Bignell-Sax interrupted.

"Erin," he said. "You're here."

He hugged his partner too tightly. Erin didn't seem happy about it yet said nothing. Once again I was impressed with how young he seemed compared to his physical age.

"I told Grandfather to make you come," he said. "I didn't think he would, though." Randy saw me standing behind Erin. "I remember you. What's your name? McKenzie. I'm still annoyed at you for the way you interrogated me last night."

"Is that what I did?"

"I'm not a child, you know. I suppose you were looking out for Erin, though, so I forgive you."

"I appreciate that."

"So, we're friends now?"

"Why not?"

"Randy, we need to talk," Erin said.

"You're not still mad because I stole some of your tomatoes?" he said.

Erin rested her hand on his arm. He seemed to like that.

"Of course not," she said. "You're my friend. Besides, like you said, ten percent of them were yours anyway. I just worry knowing that you're wandering the plant alone at night. What if you get hurt?"

"I'll be fine. I know my way around pretty well now."

You do? my inner voice asked.

"Ms. Peterson," a woman said. The three of us turned to face her. Another fifty-plus, I told myself, whose hair and makeup looked like they were done by professionals and not too long ago. She was wearing a body-hugging top with a long skirt that was tight around her hips and flared outward. She wore so many bracelets that when she moved her arms she sounded like a wind chime.

"Marilyn," Erin said.

"It's Mrs. Bignell-Sax."

"Of course."

I gave the woman the once-over. She seemed to enjoy the attention.

"I'm surprised to see you here," Marilyn said. "You don't usually grace us with your presence." She stepped back and gazed at Erin as if she were appraising her body. "Have you been dieting?"

"No. I prefer to look healthy."

"You do, too. As healthy as a horse. And you are?"

Since Marilyn was staring at me I answered, "McKenzie."

I offered my hand. She didn't seem to know what to do with it.

"And you are?" she repeated.

"An invited guest. Mr. Bignell insisted I attend."

"Which one?"

"How many are there?"

"Bruce invited us both," Erin said.

"I wonder why."

"He asked that I spare him a few moments to discuss a business matter. Perhaps you'd like to sit in on the conversation."

"I care nothing about your business."

"I didn't think you did."

"Seeing you two behave this way makes me sad," Randy said. "People I care about so much. I wish you liked each other. I wish you would be friends."

"I choose my friends very carefully," Marilyn said. "You should do the same."

"Mother, you're being rude."

"Am I?" Marilyn seemed jolted by Randy's remark, although she tried hard to hide it. It was as if she had never heard him speak up like that. It didn't stop her from speaking up herself, though. "I'm sorry, dear. But it's time you learned the difference between your friends and the people who are trying to take advantage of your good nature."

"Mother."

"Your grandfather is about to come down. You must be sure to greet him at the stones."

"I will, Mother."

"You should go now."

"In a moment, Mother."

Marilyn turned and walked away.

"That went well," I said.

"Fuck." Randy's eyes darted to Erin's. "Sorry."

She pressed her hand against his arm again. "It's okay. I've heard the word before."

"It's just that my mother has become so very cynical. I don't know why. She wasn't like that when I was young."

Erin moved her hand from Randy's arm to his chest and leaned in.

"Your mother cares about you," she said. "She doesn't want to see you hurt."

Randy covered Erin's hand with his own and gave it a squeeze.

"It's about time she let me grow up," he said.

"Go meet your grandfather."

"Will I see you later? I think there's going to be dancing."

"Then we'll need to dance."

Randy left, but he did it reluctantly.

"Why do I have the feeling that this is about more than a simple business arrangement?" I asked.

"I don't know what you're talking about," Erin said.

I was looking directly into her eyes and smiling when I said, "About thirty feet off your left shoulder there's a man dressed in a blue shirt and black jacket who has been watching every move you make."

Erin smiled in return and refrained from doing what most people would have done—she didn't look.

"He seemed especially interested when you were talking to Mrs. Bignell-Sax," I said.

"Short gray hair?" she asked.

"Yep."

"Brian Sax. Marilyn's husband, Randy's father; first in line to take over the company when Bruce steps down. Take my arm and lead me toward the house. Try not to make eye contact."

I did.

"What's going on?" I asked.

"What makes you think something's going on?"

Bruce Bignell had a full head of white hair; how much of it was real, I couldn't say. He was tall and thin and used a cane to help propel him along a stone path that sloped gently from the terrace in back of the house to where his guests were gathered in the leveled area at the base of the hill. He held the hand of a little girl dressed in one of those pink party dresses with a ruffled skirt that parents love but kids hate. The child wasn't smiling, but then neither was Bignell.

He halted at the edge of three carefully carved stones that served as a stage. An entourage consisting chiefly of family members and men dressed in gray and black suits clustered in front of him; they were careful to stand a few feet down the slope so that their heads were below his. The girl kept glancing to her left at a handsome woman who stood apart from the group. The woman wasn't smiling either.

Bignell introduced the girl as his beloved great-granddaughter, without mentioning her name. He said the party had been arranged to celebrate her tenth birthday and to impress upon her what it means to be a member of the fourth generation of the great Bignell family, which apparently began with him. He actually used the word "great." The girl curtsied. The people applauded.

Erin whispered, "They throw themselves a parade every Fourth of July. A high school marching band. Floats. The old man sitting like Santa Claus and waving to the crowd. I'm not exaggerating."

Bignell released the little girl's hand, and she dashed toward the handsome woman. They smiled once they were in each other's arms and wandered off together.

"Let us pray," Bignell said.

I thought he was going to pass the chore to a padre of some sort who would say a few words before leading the congregation in grace. But no, Bignell did the honors himself.

"Everything I have today comes from God. It is His. I own nothing. David said the world and everything in it belongs to God. I am not the owner of the things in my life. I am merely the manager whom He has trusted with His property. I must learn to think, therefore, like His manager. A manager oversees the Owner's assets for the Owner's benefit. The job of manager is to find out what the Owner wants done and then carry out His will. I am held accountable to God because He, as the Owner, has expectations of the manager. The Owner has complete right to full disclosure of what's being done with His property. As His manager, I will undergo a job performance review. So will those of His managers in government who are wasting God's money on bailouts and job stimulus programs, on healthcare bills and welfare subsidies, on food programs and housing assistance that rob God's children of ambition and drive and the gift of hard work. But as Christians, can we sit idly by and wait for God to judge these people who squander His gifts? The Lord helps those who help themselves. It is up to each of us to make sure that these elected officials face a harsh job evaluation on Election Day. It is our task to see to it that officeholders realize that the time and money they spend belong to God. That they must be managed according to His will. That is why I pray that all of you give much of the wealth that you manage in God's name to Christians for a Fiscally Responsible Government so that we can pressure these government officials to do what's good and right with the property that God has entrusted to them. Let us pray ..."

I looked around. The crowd was equally divided between those who nodded their heads in agreement and those who glanced surreptitiously at their wristwatches and cell phones. No one seemed outraged that Bruce Bignell was using prayer to promote a PAC but me.

"O God," he said, "You know my weakness and failings, and that without Your help I can accomplish nothing for the good of souls, my own and others. Grant me, therefore, the help of Your grace. Grant it according to my particular needs this day.

Enable me to see the task You will set before me in the daily routine of my life, and help me work hard at my appointed tasks. Teach me to bear patiently all the trials of suffering or failure that may come to me today. Amen."

There were plenty of "Amens" spoken in response to Bignell. Afterward, several people moved forward to seek audience with the great man. The rest of us turned and moved toward the bartenders and caterers under the white canopies, but slowly, as if no one wanted to be first in line.

"I thought you were supposed to have a conversation with Bignell," I said.

"He'll summon us when he's ready," Erin told me.

I surveyed the food tables. There was plenty of everything—beef, pork, chicken, fish, and an assortment of vegetarian and side dishes—yet no pasta and no spaghetti sauce. I filled a plate and sat with Erin and several other guests who seemed consumed with the weather. No one spoke politics. No one mentioned Bignell's prayer.

I had nearly finished my chicken when the man Erin had identified as Brian Sax appeared at the table.

"Excuse me," he said. Seven people looked up to see if he was speaking to them. "Ms. Peterson?"

"Yes, Mr. Sax."

"My father-in-law would like to have a word if you are finished with your dinner."

"Of course."

Erin stood. Sax turned toward me.

"Are you McKenzie?" he asked.

"Yes."

"You, too, then."

Erin and Sax strolled side by side to the stone path and then up the path toward the veranda. Sax walked with his hands clasped behind his back, and Erin crossed her arms over her chest, as if they were afraid they might reach out and touch each other. I followed several paces behind, close enough to listen to their conversation without looking like it.

"I've missed you," Sax said.

"You tell me that now with your entire family here to see?"

"It's torture when you're near and torture when you're not."

"I know."

"What were you discussing with my son?"

"Business."

"As long as that's all you talk about."

"I don't understand or appreciate this jealousy."

Sax's head snapped toward Erin. He quickly righted himself, but not before tossing a glance over his shoulder to see if I noticed. I pretended that I didn't.

"I have an early flight tomorrow," Sax said. "I'll be spending the night at the apartment in Minneapolis. Come see me."

"I don't know if I can."

"Please."

By then we were approaching Bruce Bignell. He was sitting on the veranda in a high-backed chair, the king on his throne. Why he didn't greet his guests inside his enormous house—I guessed it was because he wanted to be seen greeting them. He held his cane next to his leg like a staff.

"Good evening, Mr. Bignell." Erin's voice had a youthful bounce to match her appearance. "It's such a pleasure seeing you again." She crossed the stone floor in a hurry. Instead of offering her hand to shake, she rested it on top of the old man's hand, the one holding his cane, and squeezed. "How come all of us get old except you?"

"The Lord has been very kind to me. But Erin, sweetheart, how many times must I tell you to call me Bruce?"

"Oh, I couldn't, sir."

"Try."

Erin smiled brightly. She moved a chair so near to the old

man that when she sat their knees touched. Up close I noticed that he looked every minute of his eighty-plus years.

"Bruce," she said, followed by a girlish giggle. "Oh, Mr. Bignell, you're always teasing me."

Bignell glanced up at his son-in-law. There was a tightness around Sax's lips; other than that his face was impassive. Bignell dismissed him with a flick of his fingers. Sax bobbed his head toward Salsa Girl.

"Ms. Peterson," he said.

He turned and walked off the veranda toward the other guests. Give him credit, he never once looked back.

"Mr. McKenzie," Bignell said.

"Sir?"

"I am led to believe that you are our darling Erin's protector."

"In a manner of speaking."

"I want you to stay and listen carefully to what I have to say. Erin, I have been reliably informed that you are experiencing difficulties with your employees."

"Oh, I don't know about that," she said.

"How would you then explain the series of mishaps that have befallen you?"

"We're taking steps—"

"You brought this on yourself. You know that, don't you? Hiring Asians and Mexicans—"

"They're good people, Mr. Bignell."

"Don't interrupt, young lady."

"Sorry, sir."

"They all came to this country, or they're descendents of people who came to this country, looking for a handout, looking for a free ride; either way it's the same thing. I understand how it happened. They saw how good-natured you are, how kind and generous, and now they're taking advantage. Erin, there are a million swindlers out there, and if you are going to take your place among serious business people, you must learn to recognize and deal with them."

"It's so hard."

"I know it is, sweetheart. However, you must be firm. You. McKenzie. What are you doing about this situation?"

"What I can."

"It must not be very much if someone is pouring Krazy Glue into Erin's locks and dumping rat excrement on her desk. If you're allowing some welfare cheat who doesn't have the backbone to support himself and his family to tear down everything this young woman has built ..."

Wait. What? my inner voice said. *Welfare cheat?*

"What exactly do you think is going on at Salsa Girl?" I asked aloud.

Bignell refused to answer. Instead, he returned his attention to Erin.

"Say the word," he said, "and I'll have a management team down there by the day after tomorrow. Let me take care of you."

"No, Mr. Bignell. It's my company. I want to run it."

"I appreciate your ambition, my dear. The hard work you've put into Salsa Girl. That's one of the reasons I agreed to distribute your products. Only now your company has reached a size where it's too big for a young woman to control."

"But it's mine."

"It's also Randy's company. That makes you part of the family. You must understand, dear girl, this is not just about you anymore. Minnesota Foods has added a number of product lines to complement yours—tortillas, tortilla chips, taco shells, dried beans and rice. Your success is our success. Your failure—we simply cannot allow you to fail. Otherwise, we will need to reach out to someone else to anchor our Mexican brands, a different vendor, perhaps."

"Please, Mr. Bignell, I can fix this."

He was glaring at me when he replied, "We'll be watching." He looked back at her. "Erin, you must know how very much we care about you, about your welfare. Randy's, too. We would love to see your partnership grow even stronger. Please remember that we're here to assist you in any way that we can."

"Thank you, Mr. Bignell."

"Erin, please."

"Bruce. Thank you, Bruce."

He smiled. It was the first time I saw him do it, and it must have hurt, because it didn't last more than a second or two.

"You're such a pretty little thing," Bignell said. "You run along now and enjoy the party."

"Thank you, Mr. ... Bruce."

Erin smiled brightly and lightly caressed Bignell's hand, still gripping his cane. Then she and I walked back toward the party.

Halfway there she took my hand. She squeezed it so hard that I was afraid the other guests would notice the pain it caused me.

"I am not a screamer." Erin was again speaking with what I was beginning to recognize as her mature voice. "I do not engage in public displays of agitation."

"I, on the other hand, have been known to weep and wail in front of whole crowds of people."

Erin released my hand.

"Sorry," she said.

"Don't you think you've taken this 'helpless little girl lost' routine far enough?"

"As long as I get what I want."

"What do you want that's worth putting up with that asshole? I'm amazed you let him talk to you the way he did."

"Being an asshole isn't reason enough to make someone your

enemy. If you start doing that, pretty soon you'll be at odds with half the people on the planet. Besides, even assholes have their uses."

We returned to our table but didn't sit. Erin said she needed to mingle. I asked her if she wanted me to mingle with her. She said that would conflict with the brand. She was smiling when she said it, and in that moment I understood her more clearly than ever before. Erin used her sexuality like a Swiss Army knife. She had a tool that could be made to fit any task, to influence any individual, from the naïve sex kitten for Bignell to the caring older woman for Randy to the just-out-of-reach goddess for Ian Gotz to—how did she present herself to Sax, I wondered. A femme fatale, a full-blown "fatal woman"? She was the affectionate older sister for Alice, the rowdy drinking buddy for Maria, the sensual possibility for Marshall Lantry.

How is she playing you? my inner voice asked.

The honorable yet sorely tempted woman desperate to keep an alluring man at a distance for fear of betraying her friend, I told myself. Yeah, there was something enticing about that.

She's certainly got you thinking, hasn't she?

I went into one of the catering tents and built a steak sandwich out of the provisions I found there. After stopping in a bar tent for an ale brewed in Ireland—no domestic beers for the Bignells—I returned to the table. The sun was setting. Without it, the air turned cold and reminded me of winter. Lights went on, giving the party area a soft glow but no warmth.

I had nearly finished the sandwich when Marilyn Bignell-Sax arrived. She was wearing a cashmere sweater over the tight-fitting top.

"May I have a moment?" she asked.

She sat next to me without waiting for a reply.

"Mr. McKenzie ..."

"McKenzie is fine," I said.

She smiled. "You may call me Marilyn."

"Thank you, Marilyn."

"I wish to apologize for my behavior earlier. Randy was right. I was very rude."

"Fine. But I'm not the one you should be apologizing to."

Marilyn turned her head as if she were searching the crowd for Erin. I did, too. Neither of us could find her.

"How well do you know Ms. Peterson?" Marilyn asked.

"We've been friends for a long time."

"Yes, but how well do you *know* her?"

"What do you want, Marilyn?"

"I know you, McKenzie. I Googled your name." She held up her smartphone as if to prove it. "There are stories about you. Some of the people you've helped. Riley Muehlenhaus Brodin—I don't know her but I know the Muehlenhaus family. You seem capable."

I didn't respond. Instead I waited for the fabled shoe to drop, wondering where it would land.

"Now you're assisting Erin," Marilyn said. "But do you know anything about her?"

"Do you?"

"No. She's never told me anything about herself."

"Why would she?"

"McKenzie, my son is not a serious boy."

Maybe if you stopped calling him boy, my inner voice said.

"Randy lives only for the joy of the moment. He's what my father calls a wastrel. After he was dismissed from his fourth college in three years, Father insisted that we cut him off. No money. No sustenance of any kind. It was the only way he'd grow up, Father said.

"Then, out of the blue, this beautiful creature ten years his senior decides to make him her partner, decides that Randy is exactly the man she needs at her side as she builds her company.

Suddenly he's mature? Suddenly he's a sober businessman? He lends her the money to make her dream a reality. Her dream. Not Randy's. He never once talked about going into business. We don't even know where he found the money. The family had cut him off completely from financial assistance. My husband believes that he convinced a bank to make him a loan using the Bignell name as collateral. How else could he have secured the necessary funds?"

"However he managed it, Randy and Erin seemed to have done quite well," I said.

"Oh yes, I can't argue that. The company quickly made serious inroads throughout Minnesota and Wisconsin. Then it entered some competition in New Mexico and won best salsa of the year, or something like that. Based on that exposure alone, they were able to get Salsa Girl Salsa into stores there and in Texas. That's when Randy and Erin approached Minnesota Foods to distribute Salsa Girl throughout the Upper Midwest and Great Lakes Region. Both my father and my husband were delighted to partner with them. They were so pleased with Randy. By then Erin had repaid the loan, and he was a ten-percent owner of the company. I don't know how much that pays him, but it's enough that he no longer asks us for money. And Erin—she just charmed the socks off my father and Brian. They were so pathetic."

"What's the problem?"

"I don't believe it. McKenzie, I know I should be grateful. Randy talked back to me, today; you heard him. He's never done that until recently. I actually enjoyed it."

"Yes, I could tell."

"It's the stories that bother me. Or I should say, the lack of stories. McKenzie, who do you know that doesn't have stories to tell about their lives, their family; about where they went to school, their first job? Oh, Erin'll tell you things if you push, but nothing you can put a finger on, not one verifiable fact. I asked her once where she was raised and she said the suburbs, and I asked which suburb and she said, 'You wouldn't like it there. Too many people of color.' I'm not a racist, McKenzie. Erin answers questions that way so I'll stop asking."

"Have you shared these concerns with your people?"

Marilyn hissed dismissively. "They don't listen to me. They accuse me of being jealous. Jealous of my son's girlfriend even though she's not his girlfriend. Jealous because Erin's younger. They don't say prettier, but they mean that, too. They're so happy about her effect on Randy that I either have to shut up or become the enemy."

And that's how Erin played Marilyn, my inner voice said. *Nicely done.*

"I still don't know what you want from me," I said.

She seemed surprised by the remark.

"Nothing," Marilyn said. "I know that Erin is your friend. I was rude to her and to you earlier. I merely wanted to explain why. And to apologize."

Marilyn reached across the table and squeezed my hand just the way that Erin had squeezed Bignell's hand earlier.

"Enjoy the party," she said.

I watched Marilyn as she walked away. She was halfway across the lawn when she halted. I followed her gaze to where Erin and Brian Sax stood together. Marilyn shook her head sadly and kept walking. I kept watching. There was nothing untoward about their behavior; they could have been complete strangers asking directions, for all the emotion they displayed—which was exactly why I knew something was amiss. They'd known each other for a long time. Wouldn't they at least smile?

Finally he stepped closer. His eyes slid from side to side, making sure no one had come within eavesdropping range. She rested her hand on his chest . . .

She does that a lot, my inner voice said.

... and halted his advance. She stepped back and retrieved her cell phone from her jacket pocket. While she looked at the cell, he glanced at his wristwatch. They're synchronizing their clocks, I thought; I bet they're going to meet later.

Erin and Sax nodded at each other and walked off in separate directions. Erin came toward me. She was intercepted by Randy. He was smiling broadly. She became flirtatious and kept touching his arm and shoulder. He asked her a question. She shook her head. From his expression, I knew he was disappointed. Erin wrapped her arms around him, pulled him close, and kissed his cheek. It was a long kiss, and when it ended, Randy still appeared disappointed. Erin brushed his cheek with her fingertips where her lips had landed. He grinned. She pecked his lips, just like she had done to the kid in the bar the night before. Randy grinned some more. Erin left his side and made her way to where I was sitting.

"Let's go," she said.

We were in my Mustang and heading south on Highway 65 toward the Cities. Salsa Girl was leaning back against the seat, her eyes closed.

"You are a charmer," I said.

"Am I?"

"Old man Bignell, his son-in-law, his grandson—everyone except Marilyn."

"Afraid I'll turn my charms on you, McKenzie?"

"I was, but not anymore."

"Good. That's important to me."

"What would your mother say to all of this, I wonder?"

"My mother died a long time ago. I thought you knew."

"I'm sorry. I didn't."

"We talked about it once at a party Ian threw. Or was it Dave Deese? I knew your mother died when you were young just like my father had and then you lost your father like I lost my mother. We're both orphans, McKenzie."

"I don't remember."

"Maybe it was someone else I was talking to. McKenzie, about the Bignell family—can I trust you, I mean really trust you?"

"Sure."

"What about Nina?"

"What about her?"

"Do you tell Nina everything?"

"Nearly everything."

"What don't you tell her?"

"What my friends ask me to keep secret."

"Just between you and me, then. Our secret, okay?"

"Sure."

"The Bignells—I won't go into details right now, but just so you know, I intend to screw them over before they do it to me."

"Okay."

"Okay? That's all you have to say?"

"I noticed that the Bignells didn't serve Randy's world-famous spaghetti sauce at the party as promised."

"It was probably meant for family only."

"Probably."

"You sound skeptical."

"Who knows about the rat shit that was dumped on your desk? Besides you and me and the person who did it?"

Erin's eyes snapped open, and she turned her head to look at me.

"No one," she said. "I didn't even tell Alice."

"Yet Bruce Bignell knew all about it."

"Yes, he did."

"I wonder how."

She diverted her attention to the traffic outside the window as we gobbled up the miles on the way home.

"That's a very good question," Erin said.

I noticed she didn't attempt to answer it.

It was well after 9:00 P.M. when we reached Salsa Girl Salsa. Alice Pfeifer and Marshall Lantry were sitting in the office foyer. She was behind her reception desk. He was perched on a chair across the room from her. If they were enjoying each other's company, I hadn't noticed.

Lantry glanced at his watch when we walked in.

"It's about time," he said.

"I thought you'd still be hard at it," I said.

"I know my business. Come with me."

Lantry rose from the chair and led us down the short corridor to Erin's office. He circled the desk and sat in Erin's chair. If she was annoyed by the snub, she didn't show it. We all crowded around him. He moved the mouse, and Erin's computer screen came alive.

"Here," he said. "This icon brings up the outside cameras."

He clicked on the icon, and the screen was immediately divided into quarters. Each displayed one side of the building.

"This gives you a real-time view of what's going on outside," Lantry said, "but it's also recording on a seventy-two-hour loop. After seventy-two hours, it starts recording over what was recorded before—so every three days. Now, if you want to erase in case you filmed something you don't want the USDA to know about—"

I slapped him upside the head.

"Oww. What?"

I gestured at the screen.

"If you want to erase something in a hurry, you can do this ..."

Lantry manipulated the recording bar.

"Okay?" He was asking me, not Erin. I didn't say a word.

"I understand," Erin said.

Lantry closed the icon and clicked on another. This time the screen was divided into eight equal boxes.

"Same thing as before except this is inside," Lantry said. "We have two cameras in your production plant, and one each in your prep room, recipe room, finished-goods cooler, inside loading dock, front office, and lunchroom. I was going to mount a camera in your office, but sugar lips here wouldn't let me do it."

I whacked him on the head again.

"Would you stop doing that?" Lantry said.

"Would you stop insulting my friends?"

Lantry looked up at Alice. She was standing off to the side with her arms crossed over her chest.

"No disrespect," he said. "Now, if you want to take a closer look, this is what you do." He clicked on the box showing the prep room. It suddenly filled the entire screen. I could clearly see the shelf where the box of tomatoes that I had been reaching for when Hector Lozano slapped my hand should have been resting, only now it was empty. "If you want sound ..." Lantry right-clicked on the image, and a volume-control bar appeared. He moved the cursor along the bar, and we heard a hissing sound. "We couldn't manage it in the production plant. Too much interference. All the other rooms, though, you'll be able to listen in." Lantry clicked on the image a second time, and once again the screen was divided into eight boxes. He spun in his chair toward Erin.

"So, hon—Erin. Are you satisfied?"

Erin reached past him to her desk drawer, pulled it open, withdrew a thick envelope, and closed the drawer. She handed the envelope to Lantry. He held it up for everyone to see.

"I'm not even going to count it," he said.

"I'd be insulted if you did," Erin said.

"That's why I'm not going to count it. I don't want McKenzie to hit me again."

Lantry left. Alice continued to stand there with her arms crossed.

"Is there something you want to say?" Erin asked.

"It's impermissible to use video cameras to monitor employees unless you notify them about the surveillance."

"You learned that in business school, did you?"

"As a matter of fact, I did. Erin—"

"Alice, it's okay if you're trying to counter theft, violence, or sabotage. I looked it up."

"So did I, and you must notify your employees first or you could be open to legal action for invasion of privacy. You might even be violating federal wiretapping laws."

"It's temporary—just until we find out who's trying to sabotage the company. We have enemies, remember? You said so yourself."

"I still think it's wrong."

"Don't ever change, Alice. McKenzie, thank you for everything. I have one last errand to run. Alice, please lock up. I'll see you tomorrow."

Erin left the building.

Alice dropped her arms to her sides.

"That woman," she said.

"Alice, do you know Randy Sax? Bignell-Sax, I guess it is."

"Yes."

"Have you ever seen him hanging around the place when Erin wasn't here?"

"What do you mean?"

"Has he ever dropped by unexpectedly? Has he ever wandered over to the production plant? Gone into the prep room, maybe, to steal some tomatoes?"

"No. No, I don't think so. He knows some of the guys back

there. On the rare occasion when he does stop in, he'll joke with Hector and Tony Cremer and some of the others, but it's not a regular thing by any means."

"Thank you. Have a good night, what's left of it."

I stepped out of the building and moved to the Mustang just in time to catch the taillights of Erin's BMW 530i as it pulled out of the lot onto Pelham Boulevard. At the same time, I saw the headlights of a second vehicle snap on. It was parked down the street. The car quickly pulled away from the curb and went in the same direction as Erin.

What are the chances? my inner voice asked.

I dashed the remaining distance to my Mustang. I had all the latest electronic gadgets, so I didn't need to fumble for a key. The fob in my pocket unlocked the door from three feet away, and all I needed to do was press a button to start the ignition. I pulled out of the parking lot in a hurry. Soon I was on the tail of a blue Toyota Camry. I hoped it was the right car.

The Camry crossed Pelham and jumped on the I-94 freeway heading west. I was relieved when up ahead I could see Erin's Beemer under the freeway lights. The Camry trailed about five car lengths behind it. I followed six car lengths behind the Camry and one lane over. The traffic was sparse at that time of night, and I wasn't afraid of being cut off.

When the BMW and the Camry took the Seventh Street exit I had to wonder—were they going to my place? I felt a thrill of recognition when both cars turned right on Eleventh Avenue South and continued on to Washington. That was my corner. I relaxed, though, when they each hung a left and sped past the coffeehouse where Nina and I sometimes hung out, moving west.

Erin took a right on Park Avenue and a left on South Second Street. The Camry followed her. I followed the Camry. I got close enough to finally read its license plate and dropped back again.

The Guthrie Theater had just let out, and there were plenty of empty spaces on the street. Erin claimed one in front of a tall apartment building with a view of both the Mississippi River and downtown Minneapolis. The Camry drove past her, which is what I would have done if I'd been driving it. I pulled my own car into a space half a block back. The Camry turned off Second Street, and I lost sight of it.

Erin stepped out of the BMW. Once again she pulled the tails of her shirt out from her skirt. I couldn't see if she had undone any of her buttons, but she draped her jacket over her shoulders like a cape and walked into the apartment building's foyer. I left my Mustang and moved quickly down the street, using the parked cars for cover, to get a better look through the building's windows.

Inside the foyer, Erin walked directly to a desk staffed by two security guards dressed in blue jackets. She spoke to them. One of the guards retrieved a phone and made a call. A moment later, he returned the receiver to the cradle and gestured toward a bank of elevators. The doors of one of the elevators were open. Erin stepped inside and pressed a button, and the doors closed. When they did, the two security guards laughed and slapped hands if it were one of the most entertaining things they had ever seen.

I wondered if Erin had made this trip before—and how often.

While I was wondering, the sound of a heel scraping sidewalk caused me to turn my head.

I heard it before I felt it, the sound of heavy impact as metal met bone with a wet crack followed by an electric shock that raced down my spinal column and loosened all of my extremities.

I collapsed to my knees with the brief recognition that someone had just hit me very, very hard. My torso bent forward until both elbows rested against the concrete. I bowed my head between them.

I didn't think I had lost consciousness. Yet when I looked up, the sidewalk was empty. I explored the side of my head and found a knot the size of a microwave oven. It was warm to the touch and throbbing, but there was no blood.

I stood.

My head ached so much I was convinced I had brain damage. *Think anyone would notice?* my inner voice said.

I stumbled my way back toward my Mustang, using the cars parked on the street for support. A pair of theatergoers saw me; they probably thought I was drunk.

"You okay, mister?" one of them asked.

"I'm fine," I said. Only I wasn't. I doubted I could spell the word if you spotted me both the *f* and the *n*. I made my way to the Mustang and climbed behind the steering wheel. Probably I shouldn't have. My place was only about five blocks away, yet somehow walking seemed harder than driving.

I started the car. Fifteen minutes later, I was standing inside the condominium. Swear to God, looking back I couldn't tell you how that happened.

I swallowed a couple of aspirin and ibuprofen, pulled off my clothes, and climbed into the shower. Washing my hair around the knot was painful, yet when I finished I felt better. I threw on a pair of shorts and wandered into the kitchen area. I didn't think a drink was a good idea no matter how badly I wanted one. Instead, I poured an iced tea. Afterward, I pulled out a gel ice pack that I kept in the freezer for just such occasions and pressed it against the knot.

I made my way to the sofa in front of the HDTV to watch *SportsCenter* and wait for Nina. I was out before the first commercial break.

SIX

I opened my eyes, yet I couldn't see. And then I could. The sorrowful blackness became dark gray; I could make out shapes and figures. There was light slipping between the drapes and light emanating from the clock on the nightstand next to the bed. I sat up. A lightning flash of pain made me moan. It also cleared my head. The dark gray softened; the clock light became numerals—11:17 A.M.

That's plenty late even for you, my inner voice said.

"Good morning, sleepyhead," Nina said. She was carrying a bed tray. On the bed tray were two mugs of coffee, buttered English muffins, and a pile of sausage links. She set the tray on the bed next to me and went to the floor-to-ceiling windows. She pressed a button, and the drapes parted to reveal the curve of the Mississippi River as it approached St. Anthony Falls, the lock and dam, Nicollet Island, and the Stone Arch Bridge. The sunlight nearly blinded me. I shielded my eyes with my hand. Nina was wearing a silver-blue nightgown that matched her eyes; the light behind her exposed the shadow of her body beneath the silk. I lowered my hand and watched her.

"You must have had a rough night," she said.

"How did I get here?"

"What do you mean? Home?"

"In bed."

"I found you sleeping on the sofa when I got back from Rickie's. I said, 'Hey, McKenzie, go to bed.' You did. Don't you remember?"

"No."

"A very rough night, then."

"You have no idea."

"Sounds like a story."

Nina crawled onto the king-size bed and sat cross-legged next to the tray. She picked up a sausage with her fingers and ate it while I told her everything that had happened, starting with the Bignell gathering.

"Should we take you to the hospital?" Nina asked. "It sounds like you suffered a concussion."

"I've had 'em before."

"McKenzie ..."

"No, I'm fine. F-I-N-E. See?"

I fingered the spot on my skull where I had been hit. The swelling had gone down, and while the pressure I applied caused some pain, it wasn't much.

"A couple of ibuprofen and I'll be as good as new," I said.

"Who do you think Salsa Girl had a rendezvous with?" Nina asked.

"I'd only be guessing."

"From what you told me about seeing them together at the party, I'm guessing—do you think Erin and Brian Sax are having an affair?"

"I honestly don't know, but I intend to find out. In the meantime, if you would keep it to yourself ..."

"Do I ever tell anyone the things you tell me?"

"No, you don't. You have no idea what that means, having someone I can trust like I trust you."

Nina raised and lowered her eyebrows Groucho Marx–style and sipped her coffee. She set her mug back on the tray. She bent forward to do it, and the top of her nightgown opened; I could see the swell of her breasts underneath. The ache in my head moved to my lower extremities. I took a bite of English muffin just to have something to do with my hands.

"You said you don't know who hit you, either," Nina said.

"No, but I'll find out who he is, too. I have his license plate number."

"If it was the man in the Camry. If it was a man. You don't even know that for sure."

"I'll find out."

"Then what?"

"That depends on what I find out. I might decide to crawl back under the covers and never leave my bedroom again."

"There's a thought."

"I noticed you haven't dressed yet."

Nina ate another sausage.

"Why would I?" she said. "I don't have anywhere to go."

I reached for her. She caught my hands.

"What do the commercials say, 'Ask your doctor if you're healthy enough for sex'?"

"That which does not kill us makes us stronger."

It turned out that Nina was lying when she said she had nowhere to go. There was Rickie's, always Rickie's.

After she left, I put myself back together and dressed in gym shoes, shorts, and a shirt. I sat at my desk and used my landline to call Sergeant Billy Turner, who ran the SPPD's Missing Persons Unit. He worked out of the James S. Griffin Building, named after the African-American deputy chief who helped desegregate the department back in the day. Turner, who was also black, played hockey, didn't hold it against me that I exchanged my badge for the reward, and wasn't afraid of Bobby Dunston, which made him a true minority in my book.

We exchanged pleasantries, and he asked, "what do you need, McKenzie?"

"Can you run a license plate for me?"

"Not now, but if you give it to me, I can get back to you later this afternoon."

I recited the number.

"Is this going to get me in trouble with the bosses upstairs?" Turner asked. "Bobby D gonna come down here and give me shit about what we can do and can't do for civvies like you?"

"Not if you don't tell 'im."

"You guys still playing?" Turner asked.

"Nah. Our season ended the final week of March. You?"

"We have games till the last week of April, and I'm thinking that's too long, man. I know guys who play hockey all year round, but when summer comes, I just can't do it."

"Neither can I."

"It seems abnormal to play puck when it's eighty degrees outside. There's a time for everything, you know what I mean?"

"I know exactly what you mean."

I decided to head down to the second-floor gym and get in an hour's work. I don't exercise just to look fit, although I do—a fine figure of a man, trust me on this. Occasionally, though, I've been required to perform vigorous activities, like those I had planned for the driver of the Toyota Camry, and taking a brisk walk around the park wasn't going to cut it. Especially at my advanced age. I was also a member of a martial arts academy in St. Paul where I'd go from time to time to spar, but my headache had disappeared at about the same time Nina had removed the tray from our bed and I didn't want to risk a recurrence.

First I took the elevator to the ground floor and approached the security desk. The guards were wearing blue suits with name tags that read SMITH and JONES.

"Gentlemen," I said.

"McKenzie," said Jones.

"What's going on? Anything exciting?"

"No, it's been very quiet."

"We wouldn't mind changing that, though," Smith said.

They had both made it clear when Nina and I first moved in that they knew who I was and wouldn't mind at all if I found ways to alleviate their boredom.

"I've got two things for you," I said. "First, keep an eye out for a blue Toyota Camry." I recited the license plate number. "Let me know if you see it on the street."

They both glanced down at the monitors on their desk that gave them a clear view of the perimeter of the building as if they expected it to appear right then and there.

"Something else," I said. "You guys don't actually work for the owners of the building, do you?"

"No," Smith said. "We're employees of the security firm that works for the owners of the building."

"Your firm supplies security for a lot of places in downtown Minneapolis."

"It does."

"What about the apartment building on Second Street on the far side of the Guthrie? I noticed the guys over there were wearing the same kind of jackets as you do."

"Yeah, that's us."

"I'm hoping you can do a favor for me on the down low."

They both smiled.

"I know it's against the rules," I said. "I wouldn't want to get you guys in trouble."

They kept smiling.

"If you could reach out to your colleagues," I said.

"We can do that," Smith said.

"There was a woman, five-six, one-twenty, blond, blue eyes, dressed in a white shirt and dark blue jacket and skirt. She entered the building at about ten fifteen last night. Ask your colleagues who she went over there to see."

Smith and Jones glanced at each other. They seemed disappointed.

"Is that all?" Jones said.

"Don't you want to know who the woman is?" Smith said. "What she was driving?"

"I already have that."

"Oh. Well, yeah, we can make a call."

"I appreciate that. It's too bad your firm has a policy that forbids you from accepting gratuities."

"We've always thought so," said Smith.

"Tell me, though—did you ever find out who left that case of Irish whiskey in the hallway that I turned in to the lost and found awhile back?"

"We didn't," Jones said. "But the night shift must have, because you know what? It disappeared right after."

"Hmm."

I didn't hit the gym as hard as I had intended. I just didn't have the energy. I blamed Nina and not the events of the previous evening. Afterward, I showered again and dressed. I finished off what was left of the breakfast sausages Nina had made and went to my TV. It was Wednesday afternoon, and the MLB Network was broadcasting a get-away day game out of Camden Yards in Baltimore. I got in two innings before my landline rang.

"McKenzie," Sergeant Billy Turner said.

"Billy," I said in reply.

"The guy you're looking at, his name is Darren Coyle." Billy added an address in Columbia Heights. "You could've found that out by yourself, though."

"Yeah, but it would have required a little work, and you know how much I like to avoid that. What can you tell me about him?"

Over the phone line I heard a sudden chill followed by a cheerful "Not a damned thing."

"Is he in the system?"

"Nope."

I might have believed him, yet Billy answered so quickly that I was sure he was lying. He didn't say he anticipated my question and ran Coyle after learning his name and address, for example. That told me Billy knew exactly who Coyle was. There were only three reasons why he wouldn't say so.

Coyle was the target of an investigation.

Coyle was an asset, a CI perhaps.

Coyle was a cop.

Why would a cop whack me on the head? I asked myself.

Why wouldn't he? my inner voice answered.

"Thanks, Billy," I said. "I owe you."

"Take care, man."

I hung up the phone and looked at my watch, which, in addition to telling time, counted the steps I took, the miles I walked, the calories I burned, and the beats of my heart. Right then my heart rate was higher than usual.

I was convinced Billy only told me Coyle's name and address because he knew I could find them on my own. In Minnesota, civilians are no longer allowed to run the license plate of someone else's vehicle, but there are ways even if you don't have friends with legal access who are willing to bend the rules.

The question was—why were the police watching Salsa Girl?

If they're watching Erin, my inner voice said.

I figured I'd find out soon enough. If the cops now knew that

I knew what they were doing, I estimated it would take about two hours before someone reached out and told me to back off.

Unless whoever is running Coyle is smart enough not to confirm Coyle's status by calling you.

Unless Billy is telling the truth and Coyle really isn't in the system, which means he isn't a cop, which means he's working for someone else.

Unless Coyle knocked a screw loose when he hit you and now you're jumping to conclusions.

"We'll see," I said aloud.

I returned to the ball game and settled in to wait. My landline rang during the seventh-inning stretch. I glanced at my watch.

That didn't take long at all, my inner voice said.

I answered the phone. However, instead of a menacing voice threatening my life unless I listened to reason, I heard a far more chipper voice say, "McKenzie, it's Smith from downstairs."

I was actually disappointed.

"Hey, Smith," I said.

"I have what you wanted. At exactly ten seventeen—the guys over there are sticklers about noting when people come and go. So are we. Anyway, at ten seventeen Ms. Christine Olson arrived to see Mr. John Ripley—"

"Wait. Christine Olson?"

"That's the name she used. I thought you knew who she was."

"I thought I did, too. Also, Ripley?"

Not Brian Sax like Nina thought, my inner voice said.

"John Ripley, yeah. A company based in California called Central Valley International owns the apartment. It's used by its executives whenever they're in town on business. I guess it's a lot of business if the company is willing to spring for a luxury apartment with a view of the river."

"Thanks, man."

"McKenzie, we've been talking it over ..."

"Oh yeah?"

"We hate to be presumptuous, but the Red Sox are coming to Target Field this weekend, and if you were to find some tickets lying around ..."

"You never know."

I went to my computer and Googled Central Valley International. It was a ninety-seven-year-old consumer goods and farm products company located in one of the most productive agricultural regions in the world, California's Central Valley. It packaged and distributed mostly freshly prepared food products made from the fruits, vegetables, and nuts grown in the valley to restaurants, stores, and other customers worldwide through three separate divisions. It was credited with helping to establish the California avocado industry in the mid-1920s, as well as markets for limes, coconuts, kiwis, mangos, persimmons, and papayas. Two different investment research groups ranked the company's stock as "a great value pick."

John Ripley was listed as an executive vice president for fresh products sales.

When I finished with Central Valley, I went to the Minnesota Twins website, bought four tickets for Saturday's Red Sox game, and printed them out. I folded the sheets neatly and slipped them into my pocket. I promised myself I'd stop at the security desk while on my way to the underground parking garage to deliver the tickets to Smith and Jones, keeping up the charade by telling them that I found the tickets in the elevator and asking that they be placed in the building's lost and found. That's what you're supposed to do with recovered property, right? And I'm a guy who always does what you're supposed to do.

Before I left the condo, I went to my secret room. Yes, I said secret room. It was hidden behind a bookcase between the fireplace and the south wall and was the major reason why I let Nina talk me into moving to a high-rise condominium in Minneapolis (and haven't my friends across the river in St. Paul been giving me grief about it ever since).

I do like my gadgets, and you have to admit, this one was pretty cool. To access the room, you needed to nudge the corner of the bookcase just so until you heard a click and then swing it outward to reveal an eight-by-ten carpeted chamber. I tripped a sensor when I entered, and a ceiling light flicked on. There was hockey equipment in there, plus golf clubs, bats, balls, and a baseball glove I hadn't used in over a decade. A safe was filled with $40,000 worth of tens and twenties, credit cards, and a driver's license and passport with my picture and someone else's name. A few years ago I had to disappear for a while, and it was difficult because I wasn't prepared; now I am.

There was also a gun cabinet with six weapons, four of them registered. I retrieved a nine-millimeter SIG Sauer and holster, made sure it was loaded, and positioned the gun and holster off my right hip beneath my sports jacket. I knew it wouldn't have done me any good the night before when Darren Coyle attacked me from behind. I promised myself the next time I met the man, it would be face-to-face.

I left my Mustang in the underground garage. Instead I drove a beaten-up Jeep Cherokee that I had owned since long before I became a millionaire; Coyle hadn't seen the Cherokee. I drove to Salsa Girl Salsa. This time, though, I tried to be clever about it. I entered from the east side of the industrial park and wandered up and down the various side streets searching for a blue Toyota Camry and didn't find one. Nor was Coyle parked on Pelham Boulevard. I left the Cherokee in the back lot, used the Salsa Girl loading dock entrance, and made my way to the office.

Alice must have been getting used to seeing me around, because she gave me a wave when I marched down the corridor, followed by a "Good afternoon, McKenzie." A woman I hadn't seen before, another part-timer, I decided, looked up when I passed her desk and smiled, too. Erin was less charitable.

"What are you doing here?" she asked.

I sat in a chair in front of her desk without being asked.

"John Ripley, executive vice president in charge of fresh products sales for Central Valley International," I said.

She responded with the same calm, unruffled voice that I had come to admire, yet I could tell by the way she leaned forward and fixed her eyes on me that the woman was furious.

"You followed me last night," she said.

"No, I wouldn't do that."

"Oh?"

"I was following the blue Toyota Camry that was following you last night."

Erin leaned back in her chair.

"Oh," she said.

"It picked you up when you left the parking lot."

"I hadn't noticed."

"Why would you?"

"I'm usually pretty observant about those kinds of things."

You are? my inner voice asked.

"Perhaps you were too preoccupied with your late-night meeting," I said aloud.

"I don't suppose you know who was driving the blue Toyota Camry?"

"Mr. Darren Coyle. He has an address in Columbia Heights. Do you know him?"

"No."

"He was either very upset that I made him or very protective of you."

"Why do you say that?"

"He hit me in the head with something hard and heavy, left me on the sidewalk along Second Street."

"Are you all right?"

"I've been better. Erin, tell me about John Ripley, executive vice president—"

"Close the door, please."

I did. By the time I returned to the desk, Erin had her Woodford Reserve out and two glasses. She filled half of one glass with the bourbon and glanced up at me.

"Thank you," I said.

She filled the second glass to the same depth and slid it across the desk. I took a sip. I felt it in both my head and my toes.

"You've asked me a question, McKenzie," Erin said. "Knowing you, though, I presume you already have the answer."

"I didn't investigate as thoroughly as I'd like, but based solely on its website and Wikipedia page, I'd say Central Valley International must be three or four times larger than Minnesota Foods."

"Closer to ten, but go 'head."

"You're looking to change distributors. You told me that you wanted to screw over the Bignell family before they did it to you. This is what you had in mind."

"More than that. Salsa Girl was never a hobby with me, McKenzie. I never meant for it to be a boutique. I wanted a national presence and all that it entailed. Central Valley can deliver it to me. Minnesota Foods can't. It's as simple as that.

"More and more, people are buying healthy, they're buying fresh. There are chains like Whole Foods that exist solely to tap into that market. Even so, it's very difficult to get into the stores when you only have one product to sell. The big retailers don't want to buy from you. They want to buy from distributors—one delivery, one bill, one payment, easy administration. That's why I needed Randy. Otherwise, Minnesota Foods probably wouldn't have even bothered to take a meeting with me. My success there opened the door to Central Valley. Not only do they have a national presence, they sell a wider range of complementary products such as guacamole, pico de gallo, cheeses like queso fresco and asadero, panela ..."

"You can dump Minnesota Foods just like that?"

"It's their own fault. When they negotiated our contract, the Bignells insisted on a clause that would allow them to opt out anytime they chose for any reason. I insisted on the same option, and they agreed. They could think of a hundred reasons to part company with the inexperienced little girl, yet couldn't imagine that I would cut ties with them. I would tell you that it's just business, McKenzie, only it's not. I've had it with those sanctimonious, self-aggrandizing, misogynist bitches. I put up with them while they were useful to me. Now they're not. At least they won't be."

"What's the deal with Central Valley?"

"If it goes through, they'll buy sixty-five percent of the company. I'll retain thirty-five percent and management responsibilities for three years. After three years, Central Valley has the option to buy me out entirely."

"You would sell your company?"

"In a heartbeat. Take the money—and it's going to be a helluva lot of money, McKenzie. Take the money and become a philanthropist. See if I can buy my way into heaven."

"Do your employees know all this?"

"Just Alice."

"Randy or the Bignell family?"

"God, I certainly hope not. Only Alice is supposed to know.

I want to keep it that way, too, until the deal is consummated. Otherwise, I could lose ... I'm all in, McKenzie. Actually, it's kind of exciting. You probably understand what I'm feeling. From the stories I've heard, you're a gambling man."

"I am, but your boyfriend will tell you that I'm not very good at it."

"You mean Ian?"

"Does he know what you're up to?"

I barely noticed when Erin shook her head.

"He's your accountant," I said. "How can he not know?"

"He keeps such good books that I was able to give CVI what it needed without involving him."

"Don't you trust Ian?"

"Of course I do."

"Well, then?"

"There are things I can't tell him."

"What things?" I asked.

"It's complicated."

Which I took to mean that Erin wasn't going to tell me.

"At least we now have a better understanding of why Salsa Girl has been targeted," I said.

"What do you mean?"

"What would happen, Erin, if during negotiations with Central Valley, while the company was doing its due diligence, Salsa Girl Salsa started experiencing unexpected difficulties, such as, I don't know, missing delivery dates because of problems with your trucks, or if you were forced to shut down your operation for a few days?"

Erin closed her eyes. This time, if she was counting to ten, she did it very slowly. She opened her eyes and took a long sip of her bourbon.

"Hmm," she said.

"Perhaps your employees don't want you to sell the company for fear they'll lose their jobs."

"That's ridiculous."

"What's the value of your company?"

"What do you mean?"

"What is Central Valley buying?"

"The brand. The recipes."

"Not the physical plant, though."

"They get that, too."

"What I mean is, Central Valley could just as easily make Salsa Girl Salsa in California as here, am I right?"

"Yes."

"So what's keeping it from moving the operation?"

"I am."

"For three years, at least. Anyway, do your employees know that?"

"They don't know anything about Central Valley."

"What happens to Randy Sax?"

"He'll receive ten percent of the sales price, which is a great deal more than he deserves."

"He'll no longer be a business owner, though. He'll lose Mommy and Daddy's respect, not to mention Grandpa, who stands to be plenty pissed off when you drop the hammer on him, especially after adding all those Hispanic brands to complement yours."

"You heard him yesterday. He'll replace me easily enough."

"Except retailers prefer the status quo. They don't want change unless they're the ones that make the change. It annoys them when they have to explain to customers why the products they want to buy are no longer available."

"You know more about how this works than you let on, McKenzie."

"What about your vendors, the guys across the river who supply your tomatoes, and those guys down south with the jalapeños? I'm guessing Central Valley has its own suppliers."

"It has its own farms."

"In any case, that's four groups that might like to kill your deal with Central Valley without permanently damaging your company."

"I told you, none of them are aware of what I'm trying to accomplish."

"Someone knows."

"I just don't ... I'm having a difficult time getting my head wrapped around that, McKenzie. It seems so—"

"Injudicious?"

"Yes."

"You're a smart woman, Erin. You must have thought it through."

"In your head it's merely ruminations. Spoken out loud gives it a different reality."

"Which returns us to Darren Coyle of Columbia Heights."

"Who does he work for, do you know?"

"Besides himself?"

"Himself?"

"He could be a sex maniac fixated on beautiful blond entrepreneurs."

I thought I was being funny, but from the expression on her face, Erin didn't agree.

"A couple of thoughts come to mind," I said. One that included the cops, but I decided to keep that theory to myself. If the police really were interested in Salsa Girl, I didn't want to interfere; she wasn't that good a friend.

"For example?" Erin asked.

"Like I said, someone must know what you're doing. The incidents of sabotage; the threat of greater sabotage pretty much proves it, don't you think?"

Erin stared for a few beats before calling, "Alice."

Alice Pfeifer knocked briskly on the door and opened it.

"Yes?" she said.

"Do we have any employees who live in Columbia Heights?"

"No."

"No?" I said. "You can say that off the top of your head?"

"Columbia Heights is a North Minneapolis suburb. Everybody who works here is from St. Paul, mostly the East Side. A lot of them take the Green Line and get off at the Raymond Station, then walk the three blocks here. There's no reason why that is. We don't discriminate against Minneapolis or anything. It just worked out that way."

"Okay."

"Thanks, Alice," Erin said.

Alice continued to stand there. She seemed confused. At least I know I would have been confused.

"I'll explain later," Erin said.

Alice retreated from the office, closing the door behind her.

"So," Erin said. "Not an employee, not a husband or brother of one of my employees. There's no personal relationship."

"We don't know that. Could be a friend of a friend."

"I suppose."

Erin finished her bourbon and stared out the window at the Pelham Boulevard Bridge. I finished mine and did the same thing. She didn't make a move to refill either of our glasses.

"Christine Olson," I said. "Why did you use the name Christine Olson when you went to meet Ripley?"

"The meeting was supposed to be a secret, remember?"

"But why Christine?"

"It's just a nice innocuous Scandinavian name that"—she waved her hand in front of herself—"that fits my appearance. What difference does it make? McKenzie, I told you before—don't investigate me. Investigate ..."

Her eyes met mine. I saw so many conflicting emotions in her face—anger and composure, fear and confidence, fragility and determination—that it was difficult to grab hold of any one. Yet her voice hadn't altered a decibel during the entire conversation. It remained quiet and unruffled. I used to date a

911 operator who could do that, but only on the job. Off the clock she was a mess.

"Two weeks, McKenzie," Erin said. "Help keep Salsa Girl alive for two weeks and I'll buy you another Mustang. I'll buy Nina a Mustang."

Since it didn't look like I was going to get any more bourbon, I stood up.

"It's like what Shelby Dunston told me the other day," I said. "If you want to know something about a person, just ask."

"What does that mean?"

"Darren Coyle—I know where he lives."

Only I didn't need to go that far.

I left Salsa Girl Salsa through the rear entrance. The plant must have been on break, because Hector Lozano and Tony Cremer were back there chatting while sucking on heaters.

"Gentlemen," I said.

They replied with silence and hostile stares.

I took the stairs down from the loading dock and walked to the Jeep Cherokee. The vehicle was too old for electronics, and I had to unlock the door with a key. I half expected the lock to be jammed with super glue, only it wasn't.

I worked the Cherokee out of the rear parking lot through the industrial park and onto Pelham Boulevard and hung a left on Wabash Avenue. That's when I saw a blue Toyota Camry parked down the boulevard with an unobstructed view of Salsa Girl's front entrance. Coyle wasn't looking for a Jeep Cherokee, so he didn't see me.

Not a cop, I told myself. If Coyle had been a cop, he would have known that I had made him; my call to Billy Turner would have confirmed it. The police would have pulled him off surveillance and replaced him with someone smarter. Probably an entire team of someone smarter.

Why didn't Billy tell me who he was, then? my inner voice asked.

"One question at a time," I answered out loud.

I circled the block and parked a good hundred yards behind the Camry. I moved across the seat so I could depart the Cherokee from the passenger side. Coyle was leaning against his car door; he would have detected movement in his driver's side mirror. I approached the Camry from his blindside. There were no pedestrians on the sidewalk and little traffic on the boulevard, so I felt comfortable drawing the SIG Sauer from its holster and holding it against my thigh.

Coyle did nothing to indicate he was aware of my presence, and I wondered if he had zoned out. Remember what I told you about surveillance—it's a lot harder than it looks.

I took a chance that the passenger door was unlocked; it was. I yanked it open, squatted down, and pointed the SIG at Coyle's head. He was jolted, but his hands had been comfortably tucked under his arms, and now they were of no use to him.

"Remember me?" I said.

He didn't say if he did or didn't.

"Put your hands on the steering wheel," I said.

Coyle slowly unwrapped his arms and did what I asked.

"Move and I'll shoot you right in the head," I said.

"Why are you doing this?"

"Pound of flesh."

"What's that mean?"

"If you prick us, do we not bleed? If you tickle us, do we not laugh? If you poison us, do we not die? And if you wrong us, shall we not revenge?"

"Huh?"

I crawled into the car and shut the passenger door, making sure the muzzle of the gun never wavered.

"Shakespeare," I said. *"The Merchant of Venice.* Act three, scene—I forget the scene. Are you carrying?"

He didn't answer, so I shoved the muzzle against his right ear.

"Yes," he said.

"Where?"

He told me. I switched hands, shoving the SIG against his ribs with my left while I reached across his body with my right. I found his weapon, a .38 wheel gun in an old-fashioned shoulder holster. I plucked it out and waved it in front of his face.

"Is this what you used?" I said. "You suckered me and left me in the fucking gutter after hitting me with this? You're lucky I don't put a bullet in your spine."

I dropped the .38 into the pocket of my sports jacket and leaned back. He turned his head to look at me. I told him to look straight ahead.

"What are you doing here, Coyle? Why are you following Erin Peterson? Who are you working for?"

He refused to answer any of my questions.

"Coyle, you should know I have a volatile personality."

"You won't shoot me. Not like this."

"Who says?"

He glanced at me out of the corner of his eye and then looked forward again.

He knows you, my inner voice said.

I jammed the muzzle of the SIG hard into his ribs again. He winced at the pain it caused, and for a moment Coyle's expression suggested that he didn't know me at all.

I worked my free hand over his body until I found a wallet. I yanked the wallet free and leaned back again. I opened the wallet. My eyes flicked from Coyle to the contents and back to Coyle again. Minnesota has rules about the IDs that private investigators must carry. Along with name, address, head shot, and date issued and expired, they must also in really big letters disclose the name of the firm the PI is working for.

"Are you fucking kidding me?" I said.

Coyle didn't answer.

I slipped the wallet into my other pocket and opened the car door. I slipped out cautiously, once again refusing to let the business end of the SIG leave my target.

"Call your boss," I said. "Tell the sonuvabitch I'm coming to see him."

Schroeder Private Investigations was a cop shop. Every field operative who worked there had been an investigator for one law enforcement agency or another—local police, sheriff's department, state cops, even the FBI. I say "field operative" because the company also employed a platoon of computer geeks that ran skip traces, conducted background checks, hunted identity thieves, vetted jurors, uncovered hidden assets, and conducted cyber investigations without ever leaving the comfort of their workstations.

I walked into the office without knocking and made my way around the reception desk. The receptionist was named Gloria, and she knew who I was. Instead of trying to stop me, though, she smiled and said, "He's in his office."

I made my way to a corner office with a splendid view of the new U.S. Bank Stadium in downtown Minneapolis. There was a desk in the center of the office. A man was sitting behind it. I dumped Coyle's wheel gun and wallet on the desk blotter in front of him.

He slowly swept them both into his drawer before looking up at me.

"Let me guess," he said. "You've come to file a complaint."

"What the fuck, Greg?"

Greg Schroeder was a trench-coat detective, or at least he tried real hard to maintain the image. He actually wore a gray trench coat over his rumpled suit when the weather allowed, along with a pinstripe fedora. He drank his coffee black and his whiskey neat and liked to sneer while he ran his thumb across his chin, which was exactly what he was doing while I sat in a chair across from him. For all I knew, he carried photographs of Humphrey Bogart and Robert Mitchum in his wallet. Mostly I liked him. 'Course, he did save my life, after all. Twice.

"Did Coyle call?" I asked.

"Yeah. He's pretty embarrassed."

"Did he tell you that he laid me out last night?"

"No."

"Sonuvabitch is pretty loose with his hands, Greg. I thought you didn't condone that kind of behavior from your people."

"I'll talk to him."

"Talk to him? You know what? Fuck you. I'll go talk to him."

"Don't you think you're being a little sensitive about all this, McKenzie?"

"How 'bout I smack you on the back of your head with a .38 and we'll see how sensitive you feel?"

"I'm sorry, okay? I'm sorry it happened. How can I make it up to you?"

"Where did you even find this guy, anyway?"

"He was on the job in St. Paul, same as you."

"Oh, crap."

"What?"

"Missing Persons?"

"That was one of his assignments. Why?"

That's why Billy Turner didn't give him up, I told myself. He was protecting one of his own.

Do you think he'd ever do the same for you? my inner voice asked.

Probably.

"Coyle is following Erin Peterson," I said. "Why?"

Schroeder spread his hands wide as if he didn't know what I was talking about.

"You asked how you could make it up to me," I said. "Tell me who your client is."

"You know I'm not going to do that."

"Are you going to make me guess?"

"You know how it works, McKenzie. You don't carry a license, but you know how it works."

"Fuck you, Greg."

"Jesus, you're cranky today."

"A concussion will do that."

Greg stared at me. I stared at Greg. I had an ace in my hand, and I decided to bet it. I stood up.

"Where are you going?" Schroeder asked.

"Cambridge—but only after I stop to pick up my lawyer so we can both threaten Bruce Bignell with a lawsuit over the reprehensible behavior of his employees."

Schroeder shook his head slowly. "I wish you wouldn't do that," he said.

"Okay, I won't."

I sat down again.

"It's not Bruce Bignell, by the way," Schroeder said. "Our client."

"Who is it?"

Schroeder sighed as if he had made a difficult decision and now had to live with it.

"In the fifties and sixties, divorce investigations were a major revenue stream for most PIs," he said. "That changed in the seventies when more and more states started adopting a no-fault approach to divorce. Minnesota is a no-fault state, for example. That means if you or your spouse believe your marriage is broken so badly that it can't be saved, and a judge agrees, the court will issue a divorce. You don't necessarily have to prove infidelity, except to yourself, of course. As a result, divorce work dropped off. But things have changed lately, because more and more couples are signing prenuptial agreements. The majority have fidelity clauses. To beat them, well, sometimes now you do need evidence of adultery. Do you understand what I'm telling you?"

I stood again.

"Thanks, Greg."

"You're welcome."

"See you around. Oh, and tell Coyle to stay the hell away from me."

"Love to Nina."

SEVEN

I looked for Coyle, but couldn't find him or his Camry when I drove back to Salsa Girl Salsa. I was hoping to catch Erin before she left. Some of her employees were already heading to their cars in the parking lot when I arrived, while others were making their trek to the light rail train station—the end of a long ten-hour day. Hector Lozano was walking toward me when I got out of the Cherokee, as if he wanted to talk, so I walked toward him. We met in the middle of the lot. He spoke very slowly as if he thought that would help me to understand his language. I wasn't offended. Americans do it all the time.

"*¿Tú McKenzie?*" he said.

"*Sí.*"

"*¿El amigo de La Señorita?*"

"*Sí.*"

"*¿Qué haces para por ella?*"

I didn't completely trust my Spanish, though, so I answered in English; I knew he could speak it because I heard him when Alice Pfeifer first introduced us. "I'm trying to help Miss Peterson find out who wants to ruin her business."

"*Tony Cremer, él dice que eres policía.*"

"Tony's right. I used to be a cop, but not anymore."

"You arrested Tony."

"Ambos éramos personas diferentes en ese tiempo"—at least I hoped we had both become different people since then.

"La Señorita—ella es muy amable con nosotros," Lozano said.

"From what I've seen, Ms. Peterson is kind to everyone."

"Nadie quiere verla herida."

"Someone wants to hurt her. Do you have any idea who?"

He shook his head and said, "Tell *La Señorita* we all sorry."

"Voy a decirla."

I watched Lozano turn and cross the parking lot to his car. That's when I saw Tony. He was sitting behind the steering wheel of his own vehicle and watching us both intently. I gave him a little wave. He started his car and drove off. A moment later, Lozano followed, leaving the parking lot empty. I walked toward the entrance of Salsa Girl Salsa. I glanced at my watch—6:45 exactly.

That's when the bomb went off.

I saw it first—a red-orange flash beneath the hood of the truck Erin used for local deliveries, painted with the name, colors, and smiling face of Salsa Girl. The explosion lifted the hood off the truck and smashed the engine to pieces.

Then I heard it—a lightning strike close enough to make my head ring, never mind my ears.

Finally, I felt it—a shock wave that lifted me off my feet and threw me to the hard asphalt the way a linebacker might. I felt an intense pain in my shoulder. I rolled to my hands and knees and sat up. I breathed in shallow panting breaths, my hands on my thighs, as I looked at the remains of the truck. The engine compartment and cab were demolished, the front tires melted, yet the trailer part seemed undamaged. Whoever had planted the bomb did as much damage as he had wanted and no more.

I stood and forced myself to breathe slowly and deeply. Erin and Alice sprinted out of the building to where I was standing. It was an interesting study in contrasts. Alice viewed the smashed, smoking truck with amazement and terror. Erin's face expressed curiosity. It was as if she were thinking, "My truck exploded. I wonder how that happened."

Alice chanted, "Oh my God, oh my God, oh my God," and dashed back inside the building to call 911.

Erin said, "McKenzie, your shoulder."

I brought my hand up and gingerly explored it. Something was sticking through the material of my sports jacket. A chunk of metal or a sliver of glass. I pulled on it. The pain—I must have blacked out, but only for a moment. When I came to, I was on my knees again and Erin was holding me upright. I was shaking. The sound of sirens filled the air. Men in yellow slickers and boots surrounded us.

"Easy there, miss," one of them said. "Move away. I've got this."

I nearly cried when Erin released me; I don't know why. But someone else's arms soon replaced hers, and I felt better.

"What the hell is that in his shoulder?" someone asked.

"Shrapnel. Get him an ambulance."

"On the way. No, it's here."

Two pairs of gloved hands scooped me up and carried me across the parking lot. A walkie-talkie squawked; cell phones rang; a hose was drenching the engine of Erin's truck. I don't know why. It wasn't on fire. Both firemen and police officers stood in small groups and talked. I heard one of them ask, "Is that McKenzie?" I was laid on an ambulance gurney and strapped down. The gurney was lifted, and I was shoved inside the ambulance.

A voice asked, "Miss, would you like to go with him?"

Erin said, "Yes."

Doors were shut. The ambulance left in a hurry, its siren

blasting. If I shut my eyes I felt sick to my stomach. When I opened them I felt dizzy. I went with dizzy.

Erin held my hand with such tenderness that if she had asked me to marry her, I would have answered yes.

"Don't tell Nina," I said.

We swooped in through the ambulance entrance to Regions Hospital. I recognized the place instantly. I had been there before.

The triage nurse was asking me a lot of questions that I tried to answer as best I could. I somehow got my wallet out of my inside jacket pocket without passing out and gave it to Erin. She found my insurance card and passed it to a woman with a clipboard who was also asking a lot of questions. "Who's your doctor?" was one of them.

I told her that I didn't have one even as I wondered, How is that possible? I have a lawyer. I have a financial adviser. I have an auto mechanic. An IT guy. A man who sharpens my hockey skates. Why don't I have a doctor?

"I'm his doctor," a woman said.

I turned my head. I recognized the name on her picture ID before I recognized her.

"Lilly," I said.

Dr. Lillian Linder, emergency medical specialist, leaned over me and did something unexpected. She kissed my cheek. Someone else stuck a needle into the back of my hand. The needle was attached to a thin hose attached to a clear heavy plastic bottle with LACTATED RINGER'S printed on it

"How are you doing, McKenzie?" Lilly asked.

"I've really missed you."

"You know, I'm available for lunch. You don't have to keep coming to the ER to see me. We're going to have to cut away your clothes."

"All of them?"

"You wish."

They started working on my sports jacket. There was a collective gasp when they discovered my SIG Sauer. I passed it off to Erin.

"Put that someplace safe," I said.

Only she didn't have anyplace safe; she had left her coat and bag at Salsa Girl. She wrapped the gun in a towel and tucked it under her arm. Someone told her that she needed to go to the waiting room.

Erin said, "I'll be right outside."

I said, "This will only take a minute."

After she left, Lilly said, "She's new."

"Friend of a friend."

A nurse handed Lilly a syringe with a hypodermic needle. I thought she was going to stick it in me, but instead she inserted it into a valve in the hose that was attached to my hand. When she finished, she leaned over me again. I pursed my lips, looking for another kiss. She opened my eyes with her fingers and looked into them.

"McKenzie," she said, "what's the capital of Madagascar?"

I thought about it and said, "Is that a trick question?"

A moment later I was being wheeled into a recovery room. I was surprised enough to ask, "What happened?"

"Surgery happened," the orderly said.

There was still a throbbing pain in my shoulder, but nothing was sticking out of it. Believe me, I looked. I found only a bandage, and it wasn't that big. I dozed off. I woke at 11:27 when the resident came in to check my vitals. They had left my all-purpose watch, so I knew the time. I just didn't know if it was morning or night, so I asked.

"Night," Nina said. She had been standing near the window and looking out. Her eyes were puffy, but I knew it wasn't from a lack of sleep.

"I'm sorry about all this," I said.

The RN left the room. Nina moved near the bed. I tried to reach for her but was hampered by all the cables that attached me to a monitor. Wavy red, green, and blue lines and ever-changing numbers were keeping track of my vital signs.

"When the truck exploded, a piece of the frame shot into your shoulder like an arrow," Nina said. She held up a thin six-inch-long slice of metal. "Want to keep it?"

"No."

Nina was staring directly at me while she dropped it into a wastebasket.

"I really am sorry," I said.

"We've had this discussion before. You are who you are."

"Where's Salsa Girl?"

"She's being interviewed by Bobby and his people."

"I'd pay money to see that. Bobby caught the case, huh?"

"We don't get that many bombs going off in St. Paul. Apparently, he thinks it's a major crime. Alcohol, Tobacco, Firearms, and Explosives is interested, too."

"Nina, I really am sorry to put you through all of this."

"Again."

"Yeah, again."

Dr. Linder came through the door. She stopped at the base of the bed and studied the colored lines and numbers on the monitor.

"We're going to send you home now," she said.

Both Nina and I were surprised.

"Really?" I said.

"Out of surgery into an Uber. It's the way we practice medicine these days. If there's nothing more we can do for you or to you, the insurance company says you're outta here. It's basically just a puncture wound anyway. There was some muscle damage, but we managed to take out the shrapnel without nicking any arteries. It should heal nicely. We'll give you a sling. Wear it, McKenzie. Is it possible for you to get some rest for a day or two?"

"Yes, it is," Nina said.

"Don't let the dressing get wet for a week. Come back next week and I'll change the bandage and see how you're doing."

"Isn't that a little bit below your pay grade?" I asked.

"It's a service I provide only for regular customers. Nina."

The two women hugged.

"We need to stop meeting like this," Lilly said.

The resident signed my discharge papers and wrote out prescriptions for painkillers and an antibiotic used to treat bacterial infections. We arranged to send it to a pharmacy near the condominium. Nina had brought me a change of clothes. After I dressed and slipped my arm through the sling the hospital provided, a nurse pushed me to the hospital lobby in a wheelchair. Bobby was waiting there along with his partner, Detective Jean Shipman. She was young, beautiful, and smart as hell—at least that's how Bobby once described her to me, although I couldn't see it. She had been Bobby's partner before they made him a commander, and she remained his cohort of choice on those occasions when he stepped away from his role as a practicing bureaucrat and actually did some investigating.

"Hey, Jeannie," I said.

"That's Detective Shipman to you."

Did I tell you—she doesn't like me one bit.

Erin stood behind them, the white towel pressed against her breasts with both hands.

I stepped out of the wheelchair, and the nurse swept it away.

"How are you?" I asked. "Are you okay?"

"Yes," Erin said. "Just worried about you."

"Apparently I'll live to fight another day. They don't even want me hanging around overnight."

"Nina, I am so sorry."

"People keep saying that to me," Nina said.

"Let's talk," Bobby said.

"Anyone know a good bar around here?"

"You're going home," Nina said.

I thought about arguing with her for about two seconds.

"I guess I'm going home," I said. "You guys know the way."

"I don't have my car," Erin said. "I came in the ambulance."

Bobby offered to drop her off at Salsa Girl Salsa so she could retrieve her BMW. It was a nice gesture, I thought, because God knew Nina wasn't about to do it.

Erin handed me the towel. I unwrapped it to reveal the SIG Sauer. I dropped the weapon into my pocket. Both Bobby and Shipman glared at Erin, probably, I thought, because they had been interviewing her all that time without realizing she had it.

"Guys," I said. "You act like you've never seen a gun before."

Because of the side trip to Salsa Girl, it took Bobby and Shipman longer to reach Minneapolis. While we waited, Nina said, "I don't know what to do."

"What do you mean?"

"Half of me wants to take you to bed. The other half wants to beat the hell out of you."

"Do I get a vote?"

"No, you don't. In fact, it would be better if you didn't talk to me for a while."

"Okay."

I sat on the sofa across from the fireplace that we hardly ever used and held my damaged arm close to my body. The sling pulled at my neck, and I adjusted it. Nina rummaged around in the kitchen area; I had no idea what she was doing. Drawers were opened and shut; cabinet doors were slammed. I turned my head to look.

"What the hell were you thinking?" Nina asked.

"I wasn't thinking. I was walking across a parking lot. I didn't know there was a bomb. If I had known there was a bomb, I wouldn't have been walking across the parking lot."

"You're always walking across a parking lot."

"Ahh ..."

"You know what I mean."

Yes, you do, my inner voice said.

"I'm sorry," I said aloud.

"Stop saying that."

"What do you want me to say?"

"Say you're going to stop walking across parking lots."

"I will. I promise."

I stared at Nina. She stared at me. She started to smile, although clearly she didn't want to.

"Shut up," she said.

A few minutes later, Bobby and Shipman arrived. They had already heard Salsa Girl's account of events and sent her home. Now they wanted to hear my version, see if I corroborated or contradicted her. Before they asked their questions, though, I had a few of my own.

"Tell me about the bomb," I said.

"I already have a preliminary from the ATF. Chad Bullert, remember him?"

"He owes me a favor."

"Who doesn't owe you a favor?" Shipman asked.

"You two. You're all paid up."

"Bullert said it was the real deal," Bobby said. "Not an IED, but good old-fashioned dynamite. Two sticks."

"Timer or remote detonator?"

"Timer."

"Meaning the bomber wanted it to go off after the Salsa Girl employees cleared the area. He didn't want casualties."

"Doesn't mean I like him any better. We know Peterson's side of the story. Tell me yours."

I did. It took some time. While I spoke, the anesthesia in my system kept pulling at me. One moment I was alert, the next I felt myself drifting off. At first, both Bobby and Shipman kept challenging me, interrupting every few sentences to demand greater explanation. Eventually they just let me tell it all my way. I might have left out a few parts, but it wasn't by design and nothing essential, I don't think. I certainly wasn't attempting to hide anything. They both seemed satisfied when I finished.

"What do you guys have?" I asked.

"It's a little early in the investigation," Shipman said.

I glanced at my watch—1:14 A.M.—and did the math.

"You've had nearly six and a half hours," I said. "What have you been doing?"

"Are you trying to be funny or obnoxious?" Shipman said. "I can never tell."

"What did the cameras show?"

"Cameras?"

"What cameras?" Bobby asked.

"McKenzie," Shipman said. "There are cameras?"

"Didn't I tell you?"

Shipman jumped quickly to her feet. She walked away from us, her cell phone pressed against her ear.

"How are you feeling?" Bobby asked me.

"I'm fine."

"You look like you're in pain."

"No." I adjusted the sling for the thirtieth time since I sat down. "Just uncomfortable. Tell me about Salsa Girl. I take it she didn't mention the cameras either."

"No. Erin ... most people would be in hysterics if this happened to them. Erin behaves like it's just another day in the life, you know?"

"Poise in the face of adversity."

"I don't think so. I think it's something else."

"Like what?"

"Experience."

"I don't know what you mean."

"Walk up to anyone on the street and punch them in the mouth. Nine out of ten times, the vic will cover up and back away ask, Why are you doing this to me? One out of ten, he's going to stand his ground and hit back. You know why? Because he's been hit before."

"I just spoke to Peterson," Shipman said. "She apologized about the cameras. Said she's only had them for less than a day and forgot about them. Said she'd be happy to meet us at Salsa Girl. Said she'd like to see the footage herself."

"When?" Bobby asked.

"Right now."

"I'm going with," I said.

Nina didn't like it. But she didn't try to stop me.

Erin was waiting for us outside her building when we arrived at about one forty. I was disappointed by how quiet it was in the empty parking lot. I don't know what I was expecting. An army of techs examining every inch of the bombed-out truck under bright work lights while armed law enforcement representatives held their collective breath, I suppose. What I got was the shadow of twisted wreckage surrounded by yellow tape printed with words I couldn't read at a distance and the sound of light traffic on I-94.

I slipped my hand beneath the sling, rested my hand on my damaged shoulder, and moved toward the truck. I don't know why. I stopped when Bobby called out to me.

"Where are you going?" he asked.

"Revisiting the scene of the crime."

"You can take a selfie tomorrow. We have things to do."

"I don't even know why you're here," Erin said. "Shouldn't you be in bed or something?"

"Something," I said.

"McKenzie is one of those guys who always think someone else is having more fun than he is," Shipman said. "It kills him."

Erin unlocked the building's doors, flicked on a few lights, and led us down the short corridor to her office. More lights were turned on. She accessed her computer and adjusted the monitor so we could all see comfortably. Icons were clicked and ...

"What's going on?" Erin said. "McKenzie? It's not working."

I hovered over her shoulder while she operated the controls.

"Am I doing it right?" she said.

"I think so."

I leaned in. The pain in my shoulder became acute, and I hissed at it.

"The cameras are on, but they're not recording like they're supposed to," Erin said.

The computer screen was divided into quarters. Together the four cameras gave us a real-time view of the perimeter of the building; we could see the remains of the truck in one box and our parked cars in another. Yet when Erin clicked on the camera that was aimed at the rear of her building, she discovered that it had not recorded a second of film.

"Try the other cameras," Shipman said.

Erin did. The cameras in front and on the sides of the building worked fine, but not the one that would have recorded vehicles entering and leaving the parking lot. I glanced at Bobby. I knew him well enough to know exactly what he was thinking—

"How inconvenient."

Erin switched to her inside cameras. The two cameras in her production plant had stopped recording, and so had the camera that was pointed at the reception area.

"Five cameras failed," Erin said. "Five out of twelve. How much did I pay your friend for this?"

"They were working before."

"They're not working now, McKenzie."

"Lantry." I said his name like it was an obscenity.

"I'm sorry, Bobby." Erin's voice was filled with regret. So were her eyes. "Detective Shipman, I don't know what to say."

"Next time hire a company that's a little more trustworthy," Bobby said.

"I'm sorry," Erin repeated.

"I still can't believe this is about who's going to distribute your salsa," Shipman said.

"That's McKenzie's theory," Erin said. "I'm not so sure myself. I'd appreciate it you kept it to yourselves, though, about my negotiations with Central Valley International."

"What's your theory?" Bobby asked.

"It seems silly. I didn't even think about it until I was driving home and I saw the protest signs in one of my neighbor's yards."

"What protest signs?" Shipman said.

"It wasn't about that. The signs just got me thinking."

"Erin," Bobby said.

"When I first moved here—I don't know why I didn't tell you this before, but there were several neighborhood groups that opposed the construction of the industrial park. They organized, they protested; they were demanding that the area be rezoned from light industrial and office to accommodate low-income housing. I think it was because of the new light rail and the Raymond Station—they thought this would be the perfect place for it. The St. Paul City Council sided with the residents, but the Ramsey County District Court judge said the developers could proceed with the industrial park. Some protestors had a sit-down strike in front of bulldozers and stuff like that, but eventually the park was built. This location, the facility, it was perfect for Salsa Girl, so we moved in after construction was completed. We were the first tenant. People didn't like it. They paraded on the street in front of the building with protest signs, but that only lasted a few days. Besides, it was three years ago, and nothing's happened since. I've tried to be a good neighbor. But now—I don't know. Some people can hold a grudge for a long time."

"It's something to look into," Bobby said. He was gazing at his watch when he said it, though, so I don't think he meant he was going to look into it at that exact minute. He proved it by leaving with Shipman a few moments later. Erin said she'd give me a ride home.

"Call Shelby tomorrow," Bobby told me. "Let her know you're still alive. She worries."

"God knows why," Shipman said.

A few minutes after they left, Erin and I climbed into her BMW and started off.

"I'm sorry," Erin said.

"About what?"

"You've been injured on my account. Twice. Nina hates me."

"No, she doesn't."

"Yes, she does. I saw it in her eyes tonight. I'd hate me, too, if I were her."

"Don't worry about it."

"I don't want to come between you and her."

"That's not going to happen. By the way, that was quick thinking tonight."

"What do you mean?"

"Blaming the bombing on protestors. It'll play well in the media."

"I'm hoping they've already jumped on it. Google 'Salsa Girl Salsa,' and stories about the protests are the only remotely controversial items that'll pop up. I don't know exactly what kind of questions the media has been asking, though; what it's reporting. Alice was dealing with that for me while I secreted myself at the hospital."

"Here I thought you were deeply concerned about my health."

"I am deeply concerned about your health, at least as much as I'm allowed to be."

Let it slide, McKenzie, my inner voice said. *Let that last remark just slide on by.*

"One of the reasons I appreciate the protestor angle," I said aloud. "The story won't be about what you're doing, but rather where you're doing it. The developer becomes the bad guy, not you. It'll probably save your deal with Central Valley, although it might also encourage them to move your facilities."

"I'll talk to them tomorrow, hear what they have to say. McKenzie, why were you in my parking lot when the bomb went off?"

"I came to tell you what I learned about Darren Coyle."

"What about him?"

"He's a private detective working for Schroeder Private Investigations in Minneapolis. I know people over there."

"Why was he following me?"

"The people I know over there wouldn't tell me, although I can make a pretty good guess."

"What?"

"Marilyn Bignell-Sax."

"I don't understand."

"Yes, you do. I saw and heard you and Brian Sax at the party, Erin. So did Marilyn."

"I stopped being that woman a long time ago, McKenzie."

You were that woman? my inner voice said.

"Does Marilyn know that?" I asked aloud. "Does Sax?"

"What are you going to do?"

"Go to Cambridge and ask her about it."

"I wouldn't bother. I'll bet you a thousand dollars that the entire Bignell family will descend on me tomorrow. The old man likes to hold court in the morning after his prayer meeting. He always has a prayer meeting; he's one of those guys who believe faith and business should mix. 'Course, his faith forbids unions, universal healthcare, or paying his low-level employees a living wage. In any case, if he holds to his usual schedule, I expect he'll drop by after lunch—after lunch because he wouldn't want an incompetent female to spoil his meal."

"I'd like to sit in."

"I wish you would."

"Bignell might not like it."

"My office, my rules. Besides, when you're a naïve, innocent little girl like me, you need a big, strong man to lean on."

"I've noticed that about you."

"Ian has called twenty times since the bomb went off. I don't know what to tell him."

"Tell him that you're alive and well, Erin. Tell him that you miss him. Tell him that his unending devotion is what sustains you during your hour of trial."

"McKenzie, please."

"The man loves you."

"You don't have to be a jerk about it."

"Neither do you."

By then Erin had stopped her BMW outside of my building. She leaned against her leather steering wheel as if she needed a hug and it was the only thing nearby that she trusted.

"Not everyone gets a happy ending, McKenzie," she said. "Not everyone deserves it."

"Ian does."

"I should have told him years ago I wasn't interested in a relationship. I should have told him he was too good for me. I should have told him I liked him as a friend, but ... I should have fired him as my accountant."

"Why didn't you?"

She paused before answering. "I need to go home, McKenzie. I have to get up in four hours."

I slid out of the Beemer, and Erin drove off without looking back.

EIGHT

Alice Pfeifer proved to be an astonishingly effective spokesperson for Salsa Girl Salsa. At least I was astonished. Never mind that her big brown eyes gave off an innocent, I-can't-believe-this-is-happening vibe. The young lady managed to answer all of the media's questions as succinctly as possible and yet told them nothing at all. It's exactly what the media wanted, too. Good storytellers know that it isn't the answers that keep the audience engaged, it's the questions.

From the questions they asked, you could tell which story the reporters wanted to pursue. One asked about disgruntled employees in a down economy. Another asked about the number of immigrants and people of color employed by Salsa Girl Salsa. Yet most of the outlets were clearly interested in the protest angle. I don't know if Alice had planted the seed off camera, if they had been tipped by a source at the SPPD, or if they had come to it on their own. Alice rebuffed the suggestion, however. While she had no idea who would engage in such a terrible crime as bombing the truck, she was pretty sure it wasn't one of their neighbors. Besides, she said, the company was apolitical. It didn't pollute the environment, hire illegal immigrants, promote gun control, oppose minimum wage, or tell people how to educate their children.

"All we do is make good salsa," Alice said.

I used the remote to silence the TV.

"I like her," I said.

"Do you think sales will go up because of all of this or go down?" Nina asked.

"Go up. Absolutely. At least locally. People will want to know what the fuss is about. My question: Why isn't Erin speaking for herself?"

"I doubt she'd appear as sympathetic as Alice."

"I think Erin can make herself appear any way she wants."

"How's your shoulder?"

"Hurts like hell."

I was tired. I had gone to bed soon after Salsa Girl dropped me off in front of the condominium, but I had slept fitfully, the pain in my shoulder jerking me awake every time I turned in my sleep. I gave it up at eight A.M. and took a shower. It wasn't easy, because I was keen to obey Lilly's instructions about keeping the dressing dry; I ended up wrapping a plastic trash bag over the bandage. I dressed and put on the sling. Its off-white color clashed nicely with my gray sports jacket. Breakfast was a couple of English muffins with cream cheese and coffee. Nina joined me at about ten. She ate yogurt. Afterward, she went out to get my prescriptions filled while I watched a rebroadcast of *On the Fly* on the NHL Network. She returned just as I switched over to watch the local news at noon.

"Take your pain pills," Nina said.

"They'll make me nauseous and lethargic at the same time."

"You know this because ... ?"

"Remember the last time I was in the hospital?"

"Vividly."

"Because of that."

"Why didn't you tell the doctor?"

"Lilly has enough to worry about. Besides, I can take it."

"McKenzie, are all men as dumb as you?"

"Just hockey players."

"How's your head?"

"F-I-N-E."

"That's debatable."

"Usually you're off to Rickie's by now. I hope you're not hanging around on my account."

"Of course I am."

"That's sweet of you, Nina, but it really isn't necessary. I can take care of myself."

"That's debatable, too."

"I need to run over to Salsa Girl in a little bit anyway."

"C'mon, McKenzie. Give yourself a break."

"Let us, then, be up and doing, with a heart for any fate; still achieving, still pursuing, learn to labor and to wait."

"Henry Wadsworth Longfellow. For a guy who claims he doesn't like poetry, you seem to know an awful lot of it."

"I'm just saying lying around here isn't going to make me heal any faster."

"Yes, it will."

"In any case, Erin wants me to sit in on her meeting with Bruce Bignell. It shouldn't take long. Afterward, I'll come back home and crash."

"Promise?"

"I promise."

"I'll be home early."

I liked the sound of that. Only when I twisted my body without thinking and felt a stiletto of pain slicing through my shoulder I thought, Maybe not. On the other hand, what was it my first hockey coach used to say—no pain, no gain?

Nina was the first to leave. As she was heading for the door she spoke to me.

"Don't forget to call Marshall Lantry and have him fix Salsa Girl's cameras," she said.

"Oh, sweetie," I said. "There's nothing wrong with the cameras."

I read somewhere that Mary, Queen of Scots, wore a bright red dress when she climbed the scaffold to meet her executioners. Erin Peterson wore dark blue as she waited for the Bignell clan. It was an attractive dress, and while you could argue that it was office appropriate, if the workday included a cocktail hour, no one seeing her in it would believe for a moment she was an innocent little girl. It made me think that Erin had decided to draw on a tool in her Swiss Army knife to deal with Bruce that was different than the one she used before.

We were sitting in Erin's office, her chair swiveled so she could look out her window at the parking lot and the bridge beyond. She was drinking coffee. I would have asked if she had mixed it with anything besides cream but thought it would be impolite. Instead, I asked her about Central Valley International.

"They take their own sweet time when dealing with these matters," Erin said. "Apparently Ripley has to bring it to a committee that meets every two weeks. He doesn't think what happened to my truck will be a problem. CVI has had incidents of its own to deal with over the years. The way he looks at it— you were right about that, by the way. The way he looks at it, if we can't make Salsa Girl Salsa here, we'll make it somewhere else. We'll decide that later, though. In the meantime, I have to wait eleven days before we get a final decision. Not the way I would run a business, but hey, I'm just a naïve little girl from—"

"Stop it."

Erin's head snapped toward me.

"You're the least naïve person I've ever met," I said. "In fact,

I look at you and I think—what's the antonym for naïve? Clever? Cunning? Devious?"

"Sophisticated. The antonym for naïve is sophisticated. Look it up."

"What was on the camera, Erin?"

"Nothing. You saw. There was a malfunction of some sort."

"Or you could have watched the footage late last night after Bobby and Shipman dropped you off before heading to my place and erased it. When I told them about the cameras later, you agreed to meet them here, waiting in your parking lot instead of your office so you could feign surprise when we all saw that the memory was empty."

"That's one explanation, I suppose."

"I'm open to alternatives."

"I like you, McKenzie. You have a broad-minded worldview."

"Is that what it is?"

"Also, I can trust you. You're one of the few of Ian's friends who haven't hit on me."

"Seriously?"

"Yep. Some were more straightforward than others, but— Bobby Dunston doesn't like me, does he?"

"He's never said. I take it he's also among the few who haven't approached you."

"I almost wish he would. The man has a suspicious nature. I suppose it comes from being a police officer all those years."

"Nah. He was the same way when we were kids."

"He wasn't here this morning, but his partner was."

"Jean Shipman?"

"*Detective* Jean Shipman. She and a couple of other investigators with the St. Paul Police Department were here early this morning. They interviewed every single employee I have. Most of them were pretty upset."

"The detectives?"

"No, my workers. Some of them are immigrants, some of

them—I don't blame them for being suspicious of the police or the government, especially the way things have been going on in Washington lately. It didn't matter how courteously the detectives behaved, my people were left feeling that they're being blamed for what happened, for setting the bomb. I had to call a meeting to explain that it wasn't true."

"You said they were upset. Any one employee more than the others?"

"Don't you start, McKenzie—here we go."

A black Buick Regal pulled in to the lot and parked in the handicap zone closest to the door even though it carried no handicap sticker.

Erin called, "Alice."

Alice Pfeifer appeared at the office door seconds later.

"The Bignells are here," Erin said. "When they say they want to see me, ask if they have an appointment. They'll say they don't need one. When they do, you call my phone. Okay?"

"Okay."

"Off with you now."

I watched as the driver's side door of the Buick opened. Marilyn Bignell-Sax slid out from behind the wheel. Apparently Bruce didn't have a chauffeur, unless that was Marilyn's daytime job. Randy came out of the front passenger side of the car while Marilyn opened the rear passenger door. I saw Bruce Bignell's cane before I saw him. He tapped it against the asphalt parking lot as if he were claiming it for the Crown. Marilyn helped him from the car and then he shook her hands away.

The three Bignells approached the front entrance. I lost sight of them. Erin sipped her coffee, leaned back in her chair, and closed her eyes.

"Anyway, I don't think Bobby likes me," she said. "Shelby's a sweetheart, though. So are her girls, Victoria and—what's the other one's name? Karen?"

"Katie. Well, Katherine, but everyone calls her Katie."

Erin's phone rang. She let it ring three times before she answered.

"Yes."

I leaned close enough to hear both sides of the conversation.

"Bruce Bignell to see you," Alice said.

"Tell him I'll be out in a moment. Alice? I'm going to wait exactly seven minutes. It will seem longer. Bruce will become impatient. If he says anything, and he will, tell him that I'm very busy and remind him that he didn't make an appointment. Okay?"

"Yes, ma'am."

Erin hung up the phone and leaned back again. She glanced at her watch.

"Are we having fun yet?" she asked.

"I think we were discussing naïveté."

"You know how many men have done this to me over the years? Kept me waiting and waiting and waiting because they were too busy to see me, even though they're the ones who scheduled the meeting? Including Bignell. Especially Bignell." She glanced at her watch again. "It's not that they're all misogynists, although there's a lot of that. They need to make sure you know who's important, who's in charge. They need you to know that they have the power. Well, now I do."

"You do?"

Erin glanced at her watch yet again.

"Yes," she said. "For the first time in a long time."

What exactly did the security cameras catch, anyway? my inner voice asked.

After exactly seven minutes passed, Erin stood up.

"Wait here," she said.

I loitered near the open doorway so I could hear what was going on in the foyer.

"Mr. Bignell, a pleasure to see you," Erin said. "Randy. Mrs Bignell-Sax."

"Never mind them," Bignell said. "No one keeps me waiting, young lady."

"I appreciate that it can be very annoying, sir, especially if you had scheduled an appointment. Oh, wait. You didn't. You just barged in and expected me to drop everything to accommodate you."

"Erin," Randy said. His voice sounded nervous. "Please."

"Please what?"

"We need to talk."

"Yes, we do. If you care to follow me to my office ..."

I was leaning against the wall and hugging my damaged arm against my body when they trooped in, Erin first. She circled her desk and sat down while Bignell moved to a chair in front of the desk. He seemed offended that Erin sat before he did.

"Have a seat, Bruce," she said. She gestured at the chairs. There were only two of them. Bignell took one and Randy took the other, leaving Marilyn to stand next to me in the suddenly cramped office. "You all remember McKenzie."

Bignell and Randy both glanced at me but said nothing. Marilyn said, "Good afternoon," followed by, "McKenzie, your arm."

"It's okay," I said.

"Were you hurt—" Her eyes grew wide. "The bomb?"

"It's okay."

Bignell tapped his cane vigorously against the floor. Because it was carpeted, all he could generate was a dull thud-thud-thud.

"The bomb," he said. He tapped some more. "The bomb."

"What about it?" Erin said.

"Certainly you must be aware of the ramifications."

"Ramifications?"

"I was afraid of this. I told you that the company had become too big for a young woman to control. I told you that—"

"How dare you?"

From the expression on his face, I got the impression that no one had ever asked Bignell that question before.

"Salsa Girl belongs to me"—she pointed her finger at her partner across the desk—"and Randy. You have no standing here whatsoever, yet you come into our place of business and presume to dictate to us? You can cease distribution of our product anytime you like. You have that option. If you wish to exercise that option, then by all means do so. But don't tell us what to do. Don't tell us how to run our business unless you wish to make an offer. Let's say sixty-five percent of Salsa Girl. We retain thirty-five percent and management responsibilities for three years. After that time, you may have the option to buy us out entirely, payments spread out over three years. Yes? No? Maybe?"

I was surprised by Bignell's reaction. He had been in business a long time, built his empire from scratch, and from what I saw of his guests at the party the other day, he had imposed his will on a lot of people. Yet he seemed both confused and disconcerted by what Erin had to say, as well as the eerily calm manner in which she said it. It made me wonder how much of himself he had lost as he'd grown old.

"I don't know what you're playing at, young lady," he said.

"I'm not a young lady and I'm not playing. McKenzie." Erin looked up at me. "Perhaps you will be kind enough to escort Mrs. Bignell-Sax to the employee lounge while my partner and I discuss *business* with Mr. Bignell."

No, no, no, my inner voice chanted. I felt like a child told to leave the room because the film his parents were watching was rated R. I wanted to stay to see what happened.

"Please," Erin said.

I nodded at her and then at Marilyn. She stepped out of the office, and I followed her.

"Close the door," Erin said.

Marilyn and I followed the corridor to a large room with plenty of tables and chairs, vending machines, cabinets, a refrigerator, several coffeepots, and three microwave ovens. I knew there was a camera and microphone in there, too, but I couldn't find them.

"Do you get the impression that the adults don't want the children to see them arguing?" I asked.

"Actually, I thought you planned it to separate me from the others so we could speak privately."

"Why would I want to do that?"

Marilyn went to a hot plate where a half-filled pot of coffee stood warming and poured herself a mug. She took a sip.

"Oh my God," she said. "That's awful."

"It's probably been sitting there since this morning. Let's brew a fresh pot."

I went about making that happen while Marilyn found a chair at a nearby table.

"I received a call from Schroeder Private Investigations early this morning," she said. "Mr. Schroeder told me what had tran-spired the evening before. He was very apologetic."

"I'm sure he was, but only about getting caught following Salsa Girl, not about his man whacking me on the back of the head with a .38."

"He didn't mention that, the whacking. I believed he called only because he feared you would confront me."

"Would I do a thing like that?"

"I don't know. You're a bit of a mystery to me, McKenzie."

By then I had put all the pieces together and hit the START button. Water was heated and began pouring through the grounds into the glass pot. Voilà, coffee. I managed to fill two mugs without spilling much and handed one to Marilyn. She took a sip.

"It's still pretty bad," she said.

"You're spoiled."

"That's very true."

"Why did you have Erin followed?"

"The usual reasons."

"Why not have Schroeder follow your husband, then? It seems to me your issues are with him, not her."

"I did. Should I tell you what he found out?"

"What's between you and your husband is none of my business."

"I'm not talking about Brian. I'm talking about Erin Peterson."

"What about her?"

"Nothing."

"I don't understand."

"Schroeder couldn't find out anything more about her past than I did. Don't you think that's strange, McKenzie?"

Yes, my inner voice said.

"Not necessarily," I said aloud.

"She's left a very tiny footprint. That's what Schroeder told me."

How tiny?

"Erin's a very private person," I said. "She lives for her company. If you investigated my girlfriend, Nina, I bet you wouldn't learn much more about her."

I bet we would.

"Why do you care, anyway?" I asked aloud.

"I'm jealous, though not for the reasons people think. Yes, Erin's pretty, but I was pretty once, too. She's young, but so was I. I'm jealous because she's doing what I wanted to do. Did you know that I went to the Carlson School of Management at the University of Minnesota? Graduated summa cum laude. Do you know how many students earned that honor the year I gradu-ated? Six. Yet when I took the degree to my father and told him I wanted to become involved in the family business, he told me that business is no place for a woman. He even quoted Bible verses at me. My mother agreed with him. So did my two sisters. Because that's what they were taught. If that's what you truly believe, I asked him, then why did you allow me to attend Carl-son in the first place? My father said he thought the school would do more to discourage women from entering the business world so he wouldn't have to; he was disappointed that it hadn't. That's when I did a stupid, stupid thing, McKenzie. I did noth-ing. What I should have done was leave home and find a job working for someone else, prove myself that way. I don't know why I didn't. Was I a coward or too conventional?" Marilyn held up her coffee mug and stared at it for a moment. "Or too spoiled?"

She drank the coffee without complaining about it.

"I was encouraged to marry," Marilyn said. "I was encour-aged to bring forth male heirs because dear old Dad was loath to leave his businesses to his daughters. I chose Brian Sax. He was one of my father's up-and-comers at the time."

"Why him?"

"Because I loved him. Unfortunately, all he loves is Minne-sota Foods."

"You signed a prenup," I said.

"Yes, I did."

"Now you're looking to challenge it. That's why you hired Greg Schroeder."

"My father hates divorce, thinks it's an affront to God. Do you know what he hates worse? Adultery. That, after all, is a violation of one of the Ten Commandments. Number six, if I remember correctly."

"Do you think that your husband is sleeping with Erin?"

"No. I wish he were. Instead, he's been sleeping with one of our reps in Chicago. That's where he is now."

"Your father actually hired a female to represent his company?"

"No, he didn't."

"I don't—oh."

"Apparently Brian likes to play for both teams." Marilyn chuckled at the reference. "I heard a comedian say that once— both teams. I don't know why I thought it was funny."

"What are you going to do?"

"I decided on the what a long time ago. Now it's just a matter of when and how. My father's not only a misogynist, he's a raging homophobe. With Brian out—and he will be out—I'm hoping I can convince my father. McKenzie, Bignell Bakeries and Minnesota Foods is a privately held company, one of the biggest in the state. I think we're only a couple of billion dollars behind Cargill." Marilyn laughed at her own joke. "We have no debt and no outside investors. Even so, my father assembled a diverse independent board of directors many years ago. He wanted objective input into the direction of his company as well as other corporate matters. Whatever you think of Bruce Bignell, he's a good businessman. What I need to do is convince him to make me chairwoman of the board when he steps down. My mother passed ten years ago, and my sisters have all escaped to domestic bliss with husbands who are decidedly not businessmen. That leaves me. Dad will need to make a decision soon. He's still very robust and very active, but for only about four hours a day."

"What if he taps Randy for the job?"

"What if? McKenzie, you're Salsa Girl's friend. I need you to know that I'm not interested in hurting her or her business. Truth is, I love her salsa, especially the new fire-roasted tomato flavor. All I'm trying to do is protect my son, my family's business, and me."

Not necessarily in that order, my inner voice said.

"I think you can help," Marilyn said.

"How?"

"Are Erin and my son ... intimate?"

I tried not to laugh. "No," I said.

"But they could be."

"No."

"Are you sure?"

"Yes."

Are you?

"She seems to have some kind of hold on him," Marilyn said.

"She seems to have some kind of hold on most men. She's good at that."

"Including you?"

I wagged my hand.

"Randy doesn't listen to me the way he used to," Marilyn said. "He does listen to Erin, though. He seems devoted to her."

I wagged my hand some more.

"There are many things that Minnesota Foods can do to promote Salsa Girl Salsa that it's not necessarily doing now. Provide funds to develop sales and marketing campaigns. Establish more favorable terms with customers such as discounts, stock levels, selling prices. Expand distribution to include smaller outlets and not just the larger chains. A lot of things."

"What would Erin need to do in exchange for this favorable treatment?"

"All I ask is that she remember who her friends are."

"Okay."

"Okay?"

"I'll deliver your message."

"Can I rely on your discretion?"

"I wouldn't if I were you."

Bruce Bignell's words rolled down the corridor to the employee lounge where Marilyn and I were sitting. "Marilyn," he said.

"Where are you, woman?" There was distress in his voice that caused her to jump up from her chair and move quickly toward it.

"Dad?" she said.

I followed her down the corridor. Bignell was standing outside Erin's office. He was looking right and left as if he didn't know where he was. He seemed smaller than before, as if someone had removed all the padded linings from his clothes. Randy reached for his arm.

"Grandfather," he said.

Bignell pulled his arm away. He waved his cane; the tip struck both walls.

"Don't ever talk to me again," he said.

"Grandfather," Randy repeated.

Bignell tried to hit Randy with the cane and missed. The momentum propelled him forward. Marilyn caught him before he fell.

"What's going on?" she asked.

"Marilyn?" Bignell said.

"What is it?"

"Take me away from here. Take me home."

"What happened?"

"Did you not hear me? Take me home."

"Grandfather," Randy repeated.

"You, you ..."

Bignell looked as if he wanted to strike at Randy with his cane again. The younger man backed away. Marilyn took Bignell's arm and spun him until he was facing the correct direction.

"This way," she said.

Marilyn led Bignell down the corridor and into the foyer. Alice Pfeifer watched as if it were the most amazing television show she had ever seen. Marilyn held open the front door and helped Bruce pass through it. Randy followed behind.

"Will you at least let me explain?" he said.

"No, you, you bastard," Bignell said.

They stepped outside and moved to the Buick.

I went into Erin's office. She was still seated behind her desk. Her Woodford Reserve was out and she was pouring a glass.

"Want some?" she said.

"Sure."

She filled a second glass while I watched the scene unfolding outside her window. Marilyn helped Bignell into the back seat on the driver's side and closed the door. Randy was on the other side of the Buick. Marilyn said something to him. He shook his head. She pounded the roof with the flat of her hand and shouted. I couldn't hear her words, but I was enough of a lip-reader to know what she said—"Get in the goddamn car."

He did. Marilyn opened the driver's door, slipped behind the steering wheel, and closed the door. It took longer for them to drive off than you would have supposed.

"What just happened?" I said.

Erin held up her glass up to the light and examined the rich brown liquid inside as if she had never seen it before.

"We have reached a mutually satisfying conclusion to our negotiations," she said.

"Bruce didn't seem to think so."

"After being top dog for how many years, to suddenly lose that position seems degrading to him."

"Does that mean you're the top dog now?"

"Hardly. In any case, I want to thank you for everything you've done for me."

"What have I done for you, Salsa Girl? I'm not entirely sure."

"I asked you not to call me that."

"Sorry."

"Tell me about your conversation with Mrs. Bignell-Sax."

"She's trolling for allies. She thinks you're just the girl she needs."

"Allies?"

Erin stared at my face as if it were an equation written on a chalkboard in a physics lab. It took her about ten seconds to figure it out.

"Marilyn's going to make a move on Minnesota Foods," she said. "She thinks I can help by asserting my influence on Randy."

"You never cease to impress me."

"Bignell will never cede control of his company to a woman. But Randy ... No, Brian Sax is the designated successor."

"Brian is on his way out. He just doesn't know it yet."

"Huh. That's an angle I hadn't considered."

This girl has so many angles they should name a new branch of geometry after her, my inner voice said. *Like Euclid and Pythagoras.*

"Well, that's somebody else's problem," Erin said.

"You're not interested?"

"I'm not that greedy, McKenzie. I'm going to sell Salsa Girl and poof, I'll be gone."

"I like a girl who keeps her eyes on the prize."

"Woman. I'm not a girl. I'm a woman."

"Yes, you are."

"I think my problems are behind me, but you can never be sure. I'd appreciate it if you hung around for, say, eleven days."

For a moment I felt like I had on Saturday night when I moved my last chips into the center of the table, betting my ace-high against Bobby Dunston's full house.

"Sure," I said.

I went home as I had promised Nina, had a bite to eat, sat in front of my TV, and crashed. My aching shoulder wouldn't allow me to get comfortable, though, so fifteen minutes later I sat down in front of my computer. I Googled "Erin Peterson" and found doctors, teachers, financial advisers, communications directors, scientists, productivity experts, and one woman who was a victim of the Virginia Tech massacre in 2007. I had no idea that it was such a common name. As far as I knew, I was the only Rushmore McKenzie in the world. I didn't find Salsa Girl until the fourth page, and that was only because she was mentioned in a couple of magazine articles that I had already read.

What exactly are you looking for, anyway? my inner voice asked.

The answer was I didn't know. I was intrigued by the idea that Erin had such a "tiny footprint," according to Schroeder, and that she has revealed so little of herself to Marilyn Bignell-Sax. And me.

I Googled "Erin Peterson University of Wisconsin" and was surprised again by the number of women that popped up—twenty-seven in all. I clicked on IMAGES and went down the list again, this time checking out the blondes one by one. I found a financial officer, music director, teacher, health support worker, nursing student, senior epidemiologist, lab assistant, materials planning specialist, and events planner, yet no one who made salsa. One woman that intrigued me was a horticulturalist who took a summer internship at the Boerner Botanical Gardens near Milwaukee thirteen years ago. They liked her so much that they offered her a job when her internship expired. She left the University of Wisconsin shortly after starting her junior year, like Salsa Girl had, to accept it, although she took night courses at Wisconsin-Milwaukee to finish her degree years later.

Her story forced me to ask two questions that I realized I didn't have answers for. One—when did Erin leave Wisconsin to start Salsa Girl out of her mother's kitchen? Two—how old was she? Marilyn said Salsa Girl was a full decade older than Randy. Randy was at least thirty, which would make Erin forty. Except then the dates didn't match up, I reminded myself. Let's say Erin was twenty when she left Wisconsin and that she spent two or three years working the farmer's markets before she met Randy. That would make her thirty-three-ish.

By then Nina had returned home.

"How old do you think Salsa Girl is?" I asked.

"About our age. Maybe a little younger. Say forty."

"Not thirtyish?"

"Please. I mean, she looks great: perfect petite figure, not a ripple of fat. You could bounce quarters off her backside. I'm not saying she had work done, either. But thirty? No. Men might believe it. But women—I think we have a better sense of age. Why? Does Erin say she's thirty?"

"I've never heard her mention how old she is. I've never heard her mention a birthday."

"Why is that a thing?"

"Let's say that Salsa Girl is forty years old. That means she met Randy when she was thirty years old. She was developing Salsa Girl Salsa for three years before that. She left school in her junior year when she was twenty or twenty-one. When you do the math, that leaves a seven-year hole in her story."

"So?"

"So what did she do during those seven years?"

"Maybe she married a man who abused her and she doesn't want anyone to know because she's embarrassed and ashamed even after all this time."

Like Jason Truhler had abused Nina, my inner voice said so I didn't have to.

"Maybe she finally freed herself of the bastard and found the strength to not only rebuild her life but to build a thriving business as well," she added.

Again like Nina.

"In that case, she would be a remarkable woman," I said. "And I would love her with all my heart."

To prove it, I left my place behind the desk and went to where Nina was standing. I slipped my damaged arm out of the sling, wrapped both of my arms around her, and pulled her tight against me. She sighed into my collarbone. I kept holding her.

"This can't be doing your shoulder any good," Nina said.

"It's not. In about thirty seconds I'm going to start whimpering because it hurts so much."

"Let me go."

"Never."

"Boy oh boy."

Nina wrestled out of my grip and pushed me away. She watched as I winced while slipping my arm back into the sling, stepped forward, and gently cupped my face with both of her hands. She kissed me.

"Boy oh boy," she said again.

"Yeah, I think so, too."

"Should I tell you what I think? I think Erin did what she did when she was young and *then* went back to school and started Salsa Girl Salsa. Her origin story remains intact—it's just that we all assume she started college when she was eighteen like most of us did, and she never bothered to correct the assumption. Why would she?"

"That still leaves those seven years."

"Why are they important?"

"Someone has been sabotaging her business, blew up one of her trucks. We all assume that it's connected with her attempt to sell Salsa Girl to Central Valley International. But what if it isn't? What if it's all about revenge? A vengeful ex-boyfriend like you once suggested. How 'bout a vengeful ex-husband?"

"Like mine?"

"Like yours."

"You asked her about it once before and she said no, remember?"

"Yes, but I didn't believe her."

"So now what?"

"Keep looking, I guess."

I did, too, and discovered exactly what Marilyn Bignell-Sax and Greg Schroeder had discovered—nothing. I thought about giving it up and decided that would be injudicious.

Injudicious? my inner voice asked. *How would Salsa Girl, a student at the University of Wisconsin in Madison, know what a professor at DePaul University in Chicago tells his inattentive students?*

I Googled the DePaul yearbooks and discovered that the *Minerval* served as a journal and chronicle of life at the university until it was replaced by the *DePaulian* yearbook in 1924. Unfortunately, it ceased publication in 1997. The entire yearbook was posted online, though, and I went through it page by page looking for an image of Erin Peterson. I found several women who could have been her, but her name wasn't listed anywhere.

I decided to stop wasting my time and go to the source. I picked up my landline and dialed the number that I found on the DePaul website. I told the woman who answered that I was checking on a resume I had received from a job applicant who claimed she had attended DePaul University.

"What year did she graduate?" I was asked.

"You tell me."

The woman sighed as if I were being overly dramatic and put me on hold. I was bounced from one phone to another until a man with a young but earnest-sounding voice told me that Erin Peterson graduated from DePaul with a degree in business administration in June 1988. Unfortunately, that would have made her over fifty unless she was some kind of prodigy, which I wouldn't have put entirely past her.

"I don't believe that could be my job applicant," I said. "Too old."

"Just a moment, sir."

The young man returned to the phone five minutes later. He

said, "The only other Erin Peterson to graduate from DePaul did so in 1966."

"Yeah, not her, either. Could you tell me if there was an Erin Peterson who attended classes at DePaul but who did not graduate?"

"No."

"No you can't or no there wasn't?"

"No, there were no other women named Erin Peterson who attended DePaul."

That surprised me. Not because there was no record of Salsa Girl attending the school, but because there were only two Erin Petersons altogether. Wisconsin had a boatload.

"Is there anything else, sir?"

"If it's not too much trouble, could you check on the name Christine Olson?"

"Just a moment."

As it turned out, three women by that name had attended DePaul, only none of them fit my timeline. I thanked the young man and went back to my computer. I Googled the name. Wow, there were a lot of Christine Olsons in the world, and Salsa Girl had been right: At least half of them had a Scandinavian appearance.

I clicked on some of the names at random, including a Christine Elizabeth Olson who was last seen in Chicago fifteen years ago. Her physical description was close enough to Salsa Girl: RACE white, GENDER female, HGT 5′6″, WGT 115, HAIR blond, EYES blue. But the three separate photographs of her posted on the Illinois State Police missing persons web page bore no resemblance to Erin Peterson at all.

After four hours I came away with exactly what I had started with—an aching shoulder.

NINE

I returned to Salsa Girl Salsa early the next morning. Alice Pfeifer was behind her desk, speaking softly into a microphone attached to a headset with one earpiece as she worked her computer. The two women I had seen earlier but not met were each in their own small office and wearing identical headphones. They also were speaking softly while they typed on the keyboards of their computers. I hung around the foyer waiting for someone to take a moment. Only none of them did, each moving from one call to another *just*like*that*.

Erin entered, using the door that led to her production plant. She was dressed in a lab coat and a hairnet.

God, my inner voice said, *she even makes that look good*.

"What are you doing here?" Erin asked.

"I know Fridays are important to your company. This is when your saboteur first struck, remember?"

"I remember."

"I thought I'd hang around to see if I can be of some help."

"I appreciate your concern, but I'm going to be awfully busy for a few hours, and I'm afraid you might get in the way."

"I can watch the entire operation on your office computer."

"Be my guest, although I don't know what you think you'll see."

"I'm looking for anything out of the ordinary."

"What's out of the ordinary in a plant that makes salsa? Do you even know?"

"I'll take note of what I think is suspicious activity and ask you about it later."

"There's not going to be much to see anyway. Most of my staff has Fridays off. The rest of us load the reefers and unload the Texas truck. After that we're pretty much done for the day, although the office staff will be taking orders for the coming week until three P.M. We increase or decrease production based on demand. The NBA playoffs begin next week, so that will give us a nice uptick in sales. 'Course, it won't be as big as March Madness. Or the Super Bowl. The Super Bowl is the second-highest food-consumption day in the United States, behind only Thanksgiving. People will eat something like eight tons of tortilla chips, not to mention 41 million dollars' worth of salsa. But okay, All right. I'm happy to see you, McKenzie. I appreciate that you're looking out for me. There's coffee and donuts in the break room. Help yourself. I'll see you later."

Throughout the entire conversation, Alice kept working the phones and her computer.

Erin had bought assorted treats from Bignell Bakeries for her employees, and I wondered if it was a daily thing or just Fridays. I grabbed a couple of custard-filled Long Johns and a cup of coffee and retreated to her office. I called up her external cameras first and then her internal cameras. I flicked through them one at a time with one hand while holding my tender arm in its sling against my chest. Salsa Girl had been right; all I could see was people going about their business. They could have been building a nuclear bomb and I doubt I would have known.

By midmorning the reefers appeared. One by one, the refrigerated trucks were loaded with pallets stacked with plastic-wrapped salsa. One by one, they drove off without incident until the finished-goods cooler room was empty except for the salsa that would go out Monday morning on the local trucks. Everyone seemed relaxed, including Salsa Girl. 'Course, she always appeared that way, even when I knew she was agitated beyond words.

Eventually the truck that Erin had sent to Texas on Monday morning returned. I could hear the beep-beep-beep it made as it backed up to the loading dock. Its huge door was opened and Hector Lozano and Tony Cremer began moving boxes of fruit and vegetables from the trailer into the prep room. I remembered the driver's name was Jerry. I figured there must have been union rules forbidding him from lending a hand, because Hector and Tony didn't seem to mind at all that he just stood there and watched.

. When they were halfway through, Hector stopped unloading and began rummaging through the boxes inside the prep room. His back was to the camera, so I couldn't see what he was doing—and then he shifted his position and I could: loading various fruits and vegetables into a single carton. When he finished, he put the box on the shelf nearest the door. It looked exactly like the box I had reached for when he slapped my hand earlier in the week.

Tony came in, moving his load to where the other boxes were stacked.

"S'okay?" he asked.

"*Somos buenos,*" Hector said.

We're good? my inner voice asked. *What does that mean?*

Afterward, Hector rejoined Tony, and the two of them finished unloading. Jerry pulled away from the dock and parked the truck near where its bombed-out sister was sitting, still surrounded by yellow tape—POLICE LINE DO NOT CROSS.

Back on the loading dock he asked Tony and Hector, "What the hell happened?" Hector explained. His English was a helluva lot better than my Spanish.

"That's fucked up," Jerry said. "I don't wanna work no place where I could get blown up."

Tony and Hector thought that was funny. Tony slapped Jerry's shoulder.

"Who's gonna waste a bomb blowing up a guy who sits on his fat ass all day?" he said.

"Better sittin' than standin' all day, amigo. Get to see some of the world, too. What do you see all day?"

"*La Señorita*. Now *she* has a nice ass."

"*Es perfecto*," Hector said.

The boys joked around some more. Instead of Erin, though, they seemed more impressed with the attributes of Maria Serra, the production manager. Apparently Erin was too skinny for their tastes.

Salsa Girl appeared a few minutes later.

"Gentlemen," she said. "Are you still here? Go home."

"*Señorita*," Hector said, "Jerry is worried about the bomb."

"All the more reason for you to get out of here. Listen, I don't understand what is happening or why any more than you do, but I'll talk to the police and by Monday maybe I can tell you something more, okay?"

Her employees agreed with Erin's plan and they all wished each other a pleasant weekend. The three men left. I watched Erin cross from one box on her computer screen to another as she made her way back to her office. Eventually she appeared in the doorway.

"Well, that's done," she said. "See or hear anything interesting?"

I flashed on Tony's and Hector's opinion of her backside, but kept it to myself.

"Nothing, I'm sorry to say," I said.

"Sorry to say?"

"I was looking for clues."

"Get out of my chair."

I did, sliding past her as she made her way behind her desk. She sat in her chair, clicked the camera boxes off her screen, and pulled up something with a lot of numbers. I sat in the chair in front of the desk.

"I'd offer you a drink," Erin said, "except as soon as I'm done here, I'm going home to take a nap. I'm just exhausted. I have a date tonight, too."

"Anyone I know?"

"Ian's taking me to the Twins game."

"Ian never takes me to the ballpark."

"I can't imagine why not."

Alice appeared at the door. "Ma'am," she said.

"Alice, you can't still be mad at me."

"I have to go."

"What?"

"I need to leave. I'm sorry."

"Alice?"

Alice wasn't listening. She was down the corridor and gathering up her bag and jacket before Erin could leave her office.

"Alice, what's wrong?" Erin asked.

By then Alice was out the door and jogging to her car. She drove off in a hurry.

"Family emergency?" I said.

"Her family lives in South Dakota."

Families in South Dakota have emergencies, my inner voice said.

Only I didn't believe it.

Erin stepped around Alice's desk and donned the headset.

"No rest for the wicked," she said. Into the headset she said, "Salsa Girl Salsa, how may I help you?"

I drove back to the condo using both hands. My shoulder still ached, but not nearly as much as it had. Besides, you can't baby yourself. Well, you can, but if you do your hockey-playing pals will make fun of you. I'd rather take the pain.

It was pushing two o'clock. I had just enough time to pop the cap off a bottle of Summit Ale and wonder what I was going to make for lunch when my cell phone rang.

"McKenzie," Alice Pfeifer said, "I need help."

"What's wrong?"

"You can't tell anyone."

"Tell anyone what?"

"Can you come to my apartment?"

"Where are you?"

She told me.

"I'm on my way," I said. Before leaving, I went to the secret room for my SIG Sauer. Time and experience had taught me that when a pretty girl calls out of the blue asking for assistance, you'd best be prepared for anything.

I wasn't prepared for this, though. I stepped inside Alice's apartment after she opened the door and discovered Randy Bignell-Sax sitting on the sofa. The left side of his face was swollen, and he had a gel ice pack not unlike the one I used pressed against it. He was wearing a black sweater over a dark blue shirt; the collar of his shirt and the shoulder of the sweater seemed wet from the condensation off the ice pack.

"Let me guess," I said. "You ran into a door."

"McKenzie, please," Alice said. "He's hurt."

I didn't care that Randy was hurt. In fact, it gave me pleasure to see it. But Alice's voice was filled with anguish that she was working hard to keep to herself.

"What happened?" I asked.

"I don't know how to say it," Randy said.

Alice sat by his side and wrapped an arm around his shoulder. He leaned against her. That gesture alone told me a great deal.

"Tell me more," I said.

Randy tried to reply but didn't do a very good job of it, just a lot of "what happeneds" and "you sees."

"Randy was attacked by a drug dealer when he said that he was going to stop working for him," Alice told me.

"Oh."

I sat down in a chair opposite the sofa and adjusted my sling. I had the feeling this was going to be a long story.

After settling in, I watched the couple across from me. Alice still had her arm around Randy and he was resting his head against her. I thought "*La Princesa Virgen* and the Wastrel." It sounded like one of those movies Harry's wife watched on the Hallmark Channel. Not that I would know.

"Explain," I said.

"Where should I start?" Randy said.

"*Begin at the beginning and go on till you come to the end: then stop.*"

They both stared at me like they had heard the line before but didn't know where. I could have told them it came from Lewis Carroll's *Alice's Adventures in Wonderland*, impressing them with my literary expertise, only I wasn't in the mood.

"Just talk," I said.

"New Mexico," Randy said. "I guess it all began in New Mexico. Albuquerque. We went down there, Erin and I, to enter Salsa Girl Salsa in a contest. This was a long time ago. Eight years at least. Nine. The Scovie Awards. I guess it's like the Oscars of the hot sauce world. And we won. First place in the fresh salsa category. Erin thought it would be good publicity for Salsa Girl, and it was. She thought it would open doors for us, and it did. We were contacted that very day by a distributor who wanted to sell Salsa Girl Salsa throughout New Mexico and Texas. The business was on its way because of that. We were able to negotiate a deal with Minnesota Foods because of that. Erin did all the negotiating because I wasn't very good at it. She represented the company, ran the company, because—I'm not good at anything. Grandfather was right. I'm just a fuckup. I fuck up everything I touch."

"No, you don't," Alice said.

"Yes, I do. Now I'm screwing up your life by involving you in all of this. I'm so sorry, Alice."

"Don't worry."

Part of me was impressed by Alice's loyalty toward her boy-friend. *I wonder when that happened*, my inner voice said. The rest was disgusted with Randy's apparent disloyalty toward Alice. *Wasn't he trying to be all lovey-dovey with Salsa Girl just three days ago?*

"How exactly did you fuck up this time?" I said aloud.

"McKenzie," Alice said.

"I was approached by a man, a Mexican, Colombian, I don't know, Hispanic," Randy said. "In Albuquerque. This was five years ago. Erin sent me down there. She said I should make my-self useful because—I never really did have much to do with running the company. My name was on the door, but that was all. I went down there—all I had to do was sign some papers for our distributor. We could have sent them through the mail, used FedEx, but looking back I realize now that Erin thought it would please my family to think I was actually involved with running the business even if I wasn't. Anyway, his name was Alejandro Reyes. He said he had a deal for me. I told him that Erin did all the deals. He said that he and his people didn't do business with no *putas*. *Puta* means—"

"I know what it means."

"He said he would only deal with me. An *hombre inteligente y fuerte*."

Playing to his vanity, my inner voice said.

"Go on," I said aloud.

"He said he was willing to sell Salsa Girl all the jalapeños, all the other chilies and bell peppers we'd ever need. The price he quoted was half of what we paid in Minnesota. Plus"— Randy looked down and away—"he said there would be a little something extra in it for me. For me personally. All we'd have to do is supply the truck, pick up the fruits and vegetables in Delicias, Mexico, and take them to the Cities. Since we were already sending a truck down there once a week, it didn't seem like a problem. I took the offer to Erin. She was impressed. My family was impressed, too, when I told them, especially because I kind of embellished the story a little." Randy smiled, but only for a moment. "Erin agreed to accept the deal. 'Course, she never knew about the kickbacks. Anyway, now what we do, we deliver our salsa to the distributor in Texas, and our driver crosses the border, loads up the fruits and vegetables in Mexico, and brings them here. It's a good arrangement."

"When do we get to the drugs part?"

"McKenzie, you have to understand. I never made enough money from Salsa Girl to support myself, to pay for what I need. I'm a Bignell. I can't live like ordinary people. My family wouldn't give me anything, though. They cut me off years ago because—because I'm a fuckup."

That's already been firmly established. Get on with it.

"They were waiting for me to prove myself, prove myself worthy," Randy said.

"What happened?" I asked.

Randy moved slightly away from Alice and adjusted his ice pack. That's when I noticed that Reyes had not only slapped him around, he had used a knife. I crossed the room and sat on the sofa next to him. I pulled the ice pack down to take a closer look. There was a straight cut from the middle of his ear to his cheekbone. The wetness I had thought was caused by the melting ice pack was actually blood.

"Is it bad?" Randy asked. "It took forever to stop bleeding."

"It isn't very deep," I said. "Not deep enough for stitches, anyway. It's going to leave a mark, though. Think of it as a dueling scar. The chicks dig that."

Randy smiled weakly. Alice didn't look like she dug it at all.

"You were telling me what happened," I said.

"Reyes came to me after we had been doing business for two, three months," Randy said. "I was in a coffeehouse here in the Cities and I looked up and Reyes was standing there and smiling like he had been expecting to meet me all along. I asked him what he was doing there. He said he had another deal for me. A big deal just between me and him. One not involving the *maldita puta*."

"I'm getting real tired of you calling my friend a whore."

"Not me. It wasn't me, McKenzie. It was Reyes."

"What was the deal?"

"That he would, that we would ... Reyes said he was moving his operation to the Cities. He said that I already proved I could be relied upon because we had been doing business for three months. I asked what kind of business. He said he was opening up a ... he used the word 'franchise.' "

"Selling what?"

"Heroin."

I left Randy's side and returned to the chair. Instead of looking at him, though, I leaned my head against the back of the chair and stared up at the ceiling.

C'mon, McKenzie, my inner voice said. *You didn't buy a ticket for this ride. All you agreed to do was help a friend of a friend keep the glue out of her locks.*

"Oh, Randy," Alice said. "Heroin?"

"When I said I was assaulted by drug dealers earlier, what did you think I was talking about?"

"I don't know. Marijuana?"

"Look, Alice, I don't sell it. I don't. All I do ... all I do is what Minnesota Foods does. I take the product from one place and transport it to another. That's all. I don't know these people. I don't associate with them. McKenzie, Reyes said if I didn't do what he asked, he would tell Erin about the kickbacks I was accepting. I had to do what he said, you see?"

"No, I don't," I said. "But go on."

"The driver, Jerry, he doesn't know anything about it. Reyes said that way he never looks suspicious when he passes back and forth across the border. The customs people get used to seeing him. The drugs are mixed in with the jalapeños and other stuff. He drives the truck up here. We unload the truck—I don't. I don't do it. Hector does. I pay him. And Tony Cremer. I hired Tony because Hector can't always be there week after week."

Week after week. Five years' worth of week after week.

"They unload the truck, sort out the heroin, and put it in a box," Randy said. "They put the box on the shelf. I take the box and deliver it to wherever Reyes tells me to. A man comes and looks in the box and gives me an envelope. That's all I do. It's not like I hurt anybody."

"I gave you a key to the building," Alice said. The way she said it, I was sure she now considered herself an accomplice.

"I told you, I'm a partner," Randy said. "I should have a key."

"Why are you doing this?"

"I couldn't live on what I get from the company. Honey, it was only temporary, until I could prove to my family that I wasn't—"

"A fuckup?" I said.

This time Alice didn't object.

"I didn't hurt anybody," Randy said. "It's just business."

People have used those words since the beginning of time to justify all manner of bullshit, my inner voice reminded me.

"If people are stupid enough to use drugs ..." Randy said.

I would have gotten up and punched him in the mouth, but I didn't have the energy. Besides, my shoulder was starting to throb.

"I'm just a middleman," Randy said.

"Sure," I said.

"Look, I'm doing the right thing now, okay? I'm trying to quit."

"Except Reyes won't let you. Will he?"

"No. I told him what happened. He doesn't care."

"What happened?" It was about the thirtieth time I had asked that question, though I was less concerned than I was earlier. Now I was just curious.

"I found out that Erin was trying to sell the company," Randy said.

He glanced at Alice. Alice had removed her arm from around his shoulder and was now looking away. I had a feeling she was in the midst of reevaluating her current situation.

"I told Reyes," Randy said. "Partly he was afraid if Central Valley International sent productivity experts to study the operation, they might learn what we were doing. Mostly, though, he was afraid CVI would move the entire operation out of the state, or insist Salsa Girl use their suppliers, and he would need to find another way to move his product across the border and up to the Cities. He said we should damage the company enough to kill the deal without putting it out of business. That's why I poured the glue in the locks, why I dropped the rat pellets on Erin's desk. I could have done worse, McKenzie. Much worse. All I wanted to do was make her think about what she was doing. When that didn't work—"

"You bombed the truck," I said.

"That was Reyes's idea. He's the one who gave me the dynamite. I timed it so—McKenzie, no one was supposed to be hurt. I'm sorry you were hurt."

"Yeah, me, too. I take it you didn't know you were being filmed at the time."

"No." Randy glanced at Alice again. "I didn't know about the cameras."

Alice left the sofa and began pacing.

"I'm glad," she said. "I'm glad I didn't tell you. This has got to stop."

"Alice . . ."

"You said you loved me."

"I do love you. I love you with all my heart."

"How can you do these things and still love me?"

"Please."

"Erin is my friend. She's more than a friend. She's—McKenzie, you need to believe me. I didn't know what Randy was doing. I would have told someone if I had known."

An innocent bystander blinded by love, my inner voice said. *Her eyes wide open now.*

"Randy, tell me about Erin," I said. "What happened at the meeting yesterday?"

"She told me and my grandfather she had film that showed me putting the bomb in the truck. Erin doesn't know about the heroin. She thought I was just trying to kill the deal with CVI, that I was working with my grandfather to bring down the market value of the company and force her to sell it to us instead. She said we were idiots because if we really did want to buy Salsa Girl all we had to do was make a fair offer. My grandfather said she was crazy. Erin said crazy or not, she was going to keep the film to herself as long as we left her alone. Grandfather said he would not submit to blackmail. Erin said he was right, she was way out of line. She brought out her cell phone and asked if she should call the police or if he wanted to do it. My grandfather was—"

"Yeah, I saw how your grandfather was."

"Erin also said that if she ever saw me anywhere near Salsa Girl again she'd make sure I spent the next twenty years in prison. But that was just because she was angry. After she has time to think about it—I know things about her. I know plenty."

What do you know? my inner voice asked.

"Anyway, I didn't tell them the truth because I figured the truth was much worse than what Erin and my grandfather thought I did," Randy said. "I was right. When we went home to Cambridge that day, my grandfather was more upset that I got caught than with what I did. He kept saying there were smarter ways to take over a company than using bombs. He blamed my parents for not teaching me better."

Probably there's something in Scripture explaining how it should be done, my inner voice said.

Alice moved against the wall as far away from Randy as she could get and still be in the same room with him. I thought of her ultrastrict mother, the one who didn't want her daughter to drink. I wondered what she would think of all this.

"I called Reyes this morning," Randy said. "I couldn't leave Cambridge last night, so I called him this morning and arranged a meeting. I told him what happened. I told him that he couldn't use Salsa Girl to ship his drugs anymore. I told him that I was out, too. I should have told him over the phone, because he said I was out when he said I was out. He said he was going to keep using Salsa Girl and he didn't care if Erin knew about it or not—that was my problem. He had his men do this to me." Randy pointed at his cheek. "He did it to prove that he was serious. Now I don't know what to do." He looked across the room at Alice. "I don't know what I'm going to tell my mother."

Alice shook her head as if she didn't know either.

"I have a more important question," I said. "What are you going to tell the police?"

"No," Alice said. "No police. We can't."

"Alice, I think we're way past protecting your boyfriend."

"It's not about Randy."

"You don't mean that," Randy said.

"What he did was awful, but the police? McKenzie, if we go to the police, Erin will lose everything."

"Think it through," I said. "It's heroin."

"Erin would lose the deal with CVI. Minnesota Foods would cut her loose. All the stores—who would stock her salsa if this got out? That her company was involved in drugs? She'd be back to working farmers markets in a week. She'd be all the way back to where she'd started. And the others—what about all the others? Her employees? People who have been with her for years? They'd be out of work. Some of them, it would be hard for them to get new jobs. We can't let that happen. Can we? McKenzie, you said you wanted to help her. This isn't helping."

"To hell with Erin," Randy said. "What about me? They'll want revenge. Reyes will come after me. He'll come after my family. My mother."

"Don't play that card," I said. "You didn't care about your family before, did you? You expect me to believe you care about them now? Besides, your family has all the resources in the world. They can surround themselves with an army out there in Cambridge. They'll be fine."

"But then they'd have to know what I did. You know my grandfather. They'll disown me."

"Do you honestly think I care? This is all on you, man."

"Erin. What about Erin? Alice is right. If this gets out, Salsa Girl is finished. And not just the company. Erin, too. You don't know these people, McKenzie. Revenge is part of their business plan."

Don't listen to him, my inner voice said. *He's just using the threat to Erin to protect his own ass.*

Except there is a threat to Erin, and it's very real, I told myself. Erin is your friend. You can't just allow her life to be shattered like this.

What are you going to do, McKenzie? You're the one who had better think this through.

"How do you communicate with Reyes?" I said.

"Cell phone," Randy said. "I never actually see him. Well, I saw him today, but that was the first time since he moved up here."

Meaning there's no direct evidence linking Randy to Reyes or Reyes to the heroin, I told myself. Just Randy's word. That'll mean next to nothing in court.

So what?

"Give me the number," I said.

"I can do better than that."

Randy handed me a classic burn phone, one of those prepaid flip-phones available at Target for $19.99 that you can use and then dump along with the phone number when it becomes too risky to use. I had about a dozen of them in my secret room.

No, no, no, McKenzie. Don't you dare. This is way bigger than Salsa Girl, and you know it. Bobby told you about the heroin epidemic in the Cities. Now we know where it's coming from. If you want to call someone, call him. Imagine how happy he'll be.

Alice crossed the room to where I was sitting. She knelt next to the chair and took my hand in both of hers.

"Can you help her?" she asked. "Help Erin? And Randy, too." She turned her head to look at him. He seemed so damned pathetic sitting on the sofa. "Usually he's very caring."

"I know some people," I said.

Hell yes, you know some people. Bobby in Major Crimes. Harry in the FBI. Chad in the ATF. You know agents who work for the Bureau of Criminal Apprehension. And cops in the Minneapolis Police Department. You know the assistant U.S. attorney, for God's sake. Call them.

"When are you supposed to deliver the heroin?" I asked.

"Tuesday, as usual," Randy said.

"Why Tuesday? Why not tonight? Why not sometime over the weekend?"

"I don't know. That's just the way Reyes does things."

"That gives us some time, at least."

To do what?

"Just so you know," I said. "Whatever happens, there will be no more deliveries. None. You are officially out of the drug trafficking business. If you contact these people in any way, shape, or form from this moment forward, I'll send you over. Do you know what I mean by that?"

"You'll tell the police on me."

"I might do it anyway. If I can't figure out a way to get Erin and you out of this mess by Tuesday when Reyes expects his drugs, we'll be forced to contact the cops to protect you, protect Erin from them. You'll have to tell them your story and let them take it from there. Do you understand?"

"I understand, but no. I won't do that."

"Won't do what?"

"Tell them about—I don't want to go to jail."

"Well, then we'll just show them the film of you planting the bomb in Erin's truck. That's a federal crime, by the way. There's no parole for federal crimes. Erin was right. You could get a twenty-year jolt in prison, not jail, and you'll serve every damned day, so how 'bout it? Do you want to cooperate or not?"

"Please ..."

"It's time for you to grow up, Randy. It's time for you to man up." I pointed at Alice, who was watching her boyfriend with a mixture of encouragement and hope. "Be the person she needs you to be."

Randy thought about it for a moment. "I'll try," he said. He was smiling at Alice when he said it. I wasn't sure she believed him. I knew I didn't. 'Course, the real question was whether he believed himself.

"Give me your key," I said.

"What?"

"Your key to the Salsa Girl building. I need it."

Randy stood. He fished his keys out of his pocket and took one of them off the chain. He gave it to me.

"McKenzie?" Alice's voice was low and calm. For a moment, she reminded me of her boss. "Do you have a plan?"

I tossed the key into the air and caught it.

"First do no harm," I said.

I excused myself from the apartment. Alice followed me outside to where my Mustang was parked. She hugged herself against the April chill.

"This is all my fault," Alice said.

"None of this is your fault."

"McKenzie, do you need to tell Erin about this?"

"About Randy? Yes, I think so."

"Do you need to tell her about me? About what I did?"

"What did you do, sweetie?"

"I lied to her. Erin asked me not to tell anyone about Central Valley International, and I promised her I wouldn't, but I did. I told Randy."

"Why did you tell Randy?"

"Because we ... we started seeing each other just before Thanksgiving. We kept it a secret; Randy said that Erin might not like it. He's older than I am and charming. He wasn't like the person in my apartment. I had never met the person in my apartment until today. He cared about me, too. McKenzie, he did. I told you, I started to tell you about my prom, about the night after my prom. McKenzie, there hadn't been anyone else between him and Randy. I was never confident enough to be with anyone else. My mother—I don't want to blame my mother. I blame me. But McKenzie, Erin ... I never meant to hurt Erin. She's the best friend I've ever had. More than a friend. She taught me ... I would never have had the nerve to be with Randy if it wasn't for Erin. Please don't tell her."

"I won't, but I think eventually you will. You're not the kind of girl who can carry something like this around with her. Sooner or later you'll blurt it out because that's the way you're wired."

"No, I won't. I'd be too afraid."

"You're a good person, Alice." I gestured at the apartment building. "Don't let that jerk turn you into something you're not."

"I don't know what to do, McKenzie. Tell me what to do."

Kick him to the curb, my inner voice said.

"All I know is that the guy up in your apartment has nothing to give you, and he'll squander whatever you give to him."

I unlocked my car door and slipped inside. I rolled down the window. Alice continued to stand there, staring at her apartment building.

"For whatever it's worth," I said, "I'm on your side. I'd bet quite a bit that Salsa Girl is, too."

Alice nodded her head as if she believed me.

I left Alice standing in the parking lot of her apartment building. My intention was to find Erin, either at Salsa Girl or at her home in Prospect Park. I didn't think the kind of bad news I had was something that should be delivered over a cell phone. When I reached the intersection, though, I hesitated.

Did I really want to disturb her nap? Did I really want to ruin her date with Ian?

You're kidding, right? my inner voice answered.

Besides, what was I going to tell her?

The truth.

I'll need to tell her everything eventually, but why now? Besides, as a wise man once said, don't bring me problems, bring me solutions.

Call the cops, call Bobby Dunston—how's that for a solution?

Erin might choose that answer, too, I decided. But Alice was right; it could ruin everything she'd worked for. Besides, I had an idea that would keep her out of it. If it worked, great. If not, it would be on me and not her.

Are you sure about this?

I turned right.

I drove to Salsa Girl Salsa and parked on Pelham Boulevard where I knew the cameras couldn't spot me. It was well past three in the afternoon, and the parking lot was empty. I sat watching the place for ten minutes anyway.

Eventually I popped the trunk and got out of the Mustang. Inside the trunk was a hoodie with the logo of the Minnesota Wild hockey team. I removed my sling, put on the hoodie, and pulled the hood up over my head. I walked a big circle around the building so the cameras wouldn't see me until I approached the loading dock. I knew Randy's key worked on the door next to the loading dock because I had seen him use it earlier in the week. I kept my head low so the cameras would record my figure but not my face.

I unlocked the door and stepped inside. I knew the inside cameras could now see me, so I kept my head down as I made my way to the prep room. Just inside the prep room was a shelf. On the shelf was the box that Hector Lozano had placed there. I picked it up. It was heavier than I had expected, and pain shot through my shoulder. I pretended it didn't hurt.

I retraced my steps as I carried the box out of Salsa Girl,

again keeping my head down. I stepped onto the loading dock and took the stairs to the parking lot.

Now what, I asked myself. I didn't want the drugs found on me any more than I wanted them found in Salsa Girl. The bombed-out truck was sitting in the corner of the parking lot, yellow police tape still surrounding it.

Why not, I decided. I carried the box to the truck. I knew the cameras were now filming my back. I ducked beneath the yellow crime scene tape and moved to the wreck. I set the box down and opened it. The heroin was in the bottom of the box beneath the jalapeños, bell peppers, and tomatoes. It was sealed inside four reusable, resealable plastic bags. I bounced one in my hand and guessed its weight at a couple of pounds. Make that a kilogram since, unlike America, Mexico was on the metric system. A key equaled a thousand grams of heroin with a street value of approximately fifteen to twenty dollars a gram depending on how it was cut. The content of the bags was white, not brown or black, which meant the heroin was high grade. I was sure it went for top dollar. Multiplying four kilograms by $20, I estimated the shipment was worth approximately $80,000. That's $80,000 a week, every week. Four million a year plus change. Twenty million bucks' worth of heroin sold on the streets of the Twin Cities since Randy started five years ago. Unless ... I wondered if, like Salsa Girl's, Reyes's shipments increased or decreased according to demand. People who don't use drugs call marijuana dope. People who smoke grass call heroin dope. How much dope did America use on Super Bowl Sunday, I wondered.

I returned the heroin to the box, repacked the vegetables, and sealed it. I shoved the box behind the burned-out tire and stood back. You couldn't see it unless you were looking for it, and I doubted the truck would be moved anytime soon; both the feds and cops were reluctant to disturb even old crime scenes.

I left the wreck and moved in a straight line until I knew I was outside the range of the cameras. I pulled down the hoodie and pulled out Randy's burn phone. There was only one number attached to it. I clicked on the number and pressed CALL.

A man answered. He spoke in a vaguely Hispanic accent. "What?" he said.

"Let me speak to Alejandro Reyes."

He hesitated, probably realizing that I wasn't Randy.

"Who?" he said. "You sure you got the right number?"

"I don't have time for this. Tell your boss that Nick Dyson called. Tell him that I just jacked his heroin shipment."

"You did what?"

"Four keys separated into baggies. Tell him I'll call later to ask what he wants me to do with it."

"Wait."

I ended the call and deactivated the phone. On the way to the condominium I nearly stopped the car on the Franklin Avenue Bridge and tossed the cell into the Mississippi River but decided, Where's the fun in that?

TEN

There really was a career criminal named Nicholas Dyson. If you surf the right websites, you'll discover that he specialized in robbing banks, jacking armored cars, and burglarizing the occasional jewelry store. What those files will not tell you, though, is that Dyson is currently doing time in the United States Penitentiary in Terre Haute, Indiana. And what they absolutely will not tell you is that the photographs that accompany each of the files are not of him but of, well, me. In one I'm clean-shaven; in the others I'm wearing long hair and a scraggly beard.

What happened, a couple of years back I was coerced by both the FBI and the ATF into going undercover as Dyson to search for weapons along the Canadian border that had been stolen from the U.S. government during a botched sting. The operation was off the books. The Feds were desperate to avoid the embarrassment of public disclosure, which is why they wanted a civilian to take it on, a civilian that could later be disavowed if things went sideways—you know, like in the *Mission: Impossible* movies. That's how I met Assistant U.S. Attorney James R. Finnegan and why he now owed me a huge favor that I had been hoarding ever since. Although the case had long been closed and forgotten, the Feds neglected to update the files or take down the pictures. I never said anything about it because I figured there were times when a fellow might want to pretend to be someone else. In fact, I had used the Dyson disguise with some success just fourteen months ago.

I unlocked the door to my condo. Nina wasn't home; no surprise there. It was Friday, and Fridays were as big at Rickie's as they were at Salsa Girl.

I swung open the door that led to my secret room and stepped inside. I exchanged my IDs for those with Nick Dyson's name, replaced the SIG Sauer with an unregistered nine-millimeter Taurus, and counted out the $40,000 before shoving the cash into a small soft-sided gym bag. I grabbed one of my burn phones and punched in a number. I recognized the voice that answered my call; he recognized mine.

"You busy?" I said.

"Naw, man. Not for you."

"How 'bout for Nick Dyson?"

"Fuck."

"Is Herzy around?"

"I'm lookin' right at 'im."

"I'll be there in fifteen minutes."

Thaddeus Coleman, aka Chopper, was an entrepreneur. When I first met him he was running a small but lucrative stable of girls around Selby and Western, a neighborhood in St. Paul that used to be rich with prostitution until patrons became bored with it, as they eventually do with any so-called trendy hotspot, and moved elsewhere. Afterward, he moved to Fuller and Farrington and dealt drugs. Sometimes he sold the real thing; sometimes he passed laundry soap and Alka-Seltzer tablets crushed to resemble rock cocaine to the white suburban kids who drove up in Mommy and Daddy's SUV. I busted him for that—representing and selling a substance as a drug, whether it is or not, is a felony—only the judge threw the case out. I blamed the prosecutor.

The court might have been lenient with Coleman, but the Red Dragons not so much. They objected to his activities and pumped two rounds into his spine as a way to express their displeasure. I'm the one that scooped him off the sidewalk and got him the medical attention that saved his life. We've been friends ever since, even though six weeks after he was shot, Coleman wheeled himself out of the hospital in a stolen chair. A couple of days later, we discovered the bodies of three Red Dragons under the swings at a park near the St. Paul College of Technology. We never did find out who did the deed, although the ME reported that the bullet holes had an upward trajectory as if the Dragons were shot by someone who was sitting down.

It was the wheelchair, which Coleman drove with the reckless dexterity of a dirt-track biker, that earned him the nickname Chopper. As Chopper he ran a crew of shoplifters that operated in the Twin Cities malls until the security guards began greeting him by name. Later, he smuggled name-brand cigarettes out of Kentucky and sold them to independent convenience stores, making a hefty profit by dodging the state's cigarette tax. Now he was involved in the less criminal if not less reprehensible business of ticket-scalping, working out of a small office in a converted warehouse with a view of Target Field, where the Twins played baseball.

I carried the gym bag into his office. He smiled at me from the other side of his desk. There was a computer on the desk and half a dozen more arrayed on tables along the wall. Chopper would have associates sitting at every terminal to grab concert and sports tickets when they became available online. Or he would use bots and other computer gadgetry to circumvent security systems to buy bundles of the best seats. Or he would hire guys to stand in line at the on-site ticket booths. Or he would tap insiders who had access to the events. Or, usually, all four simultaneously. That's why he could get $700–$850 for tickets with a face value of $39–$147 for the Adele concert at the Xcel Energy Center.

I asked him about that once.

"Face value—what does that mean?" Chopper said. "It's just an arbitrary number. What we do, we let the fan dictate the market price. You know, if people refused to pay what I charge, I'd have to charge less. Am I right? It's called capitalism, the backbone of America."

He had me there.

"McKenzie, you sonuvabitch," Chopper said.

He rolled his chair out from behind the desk and greeted me in the center of the office. We engaged in an elaborate handshake dance that didn't end until I messed up. Chopper laughed when I did. Not Herzog. He just looked at me and shook his head like he felt sorry for me.

"Herzy," I said.

"Fuckin' McKenzie," he said.

"Good to see you, too, man."

Herzog was sitting in a chair along the wall, the largest man I had ever met in person; you could roller-skate on him. He was also the most dangerous. He had done time for multiple counts of manslaughter, assault, aggravated robbery, and weapons charges. He'd been out on parole for the past three years, with two more to go, and had been working for Chopper ever since they released him from the halfway house.

He tolerated me because we both liked old movies and listened to jazz, and because I had arranged through Nina to get him and his date the table closest to the stage when Cécile McLorin Salvant sang at Rickie's.

"What you doin' here?" he asked.

"I thought I'd take you guys to dinner. Pick a spot. Any spot."

"Dinner," Chopper said. "Dinner means you want somethin'."

"What are you talking about? We're old friends. Can't a man take his friends to dinner?"

"You maybe," Herzog said. "But Dyson? Chop said you mentioned Dyson."

"I did."

"Last time I saw Dyson people was shot."

"Yes, but neither you nor I did the shooting, so ..."

"Don't matter. I told you before, McKenzie, do I have t' tell you again? I ain't doin' nothing that'll break my parole. I ain't hurtin' nobody no more."

"There's a few bucks in it."

"I'm doin' just fine workin' for Chopper."

I turned toward Chopper. He was smiling.

"You was the one who got all hot and bothered when I took the man on," he said. "A stone killer, you called him. Now you tryin' to git him to go back to the life?"

"I ain't doin' it," Herzog said. "If it wasn't that I like your girlfriend, I'd kick your ass outta here."

"You guys have me all wrong. I'm not looking to hurt anyone. I'm just trying to avoid getting hurt myself."

"Looks like you already there," Chopper said. "What's with the sling?"

"That's part of the story."

"You on another one of them fucking crusades, ain't ya?" Herzog said. "Gonna save the world from itself."

"There's this girl—"

"Shit. That's exactly what you said the last time."

I explained, making Salsa Girl sound a lot more innocent and vulnerable than she really was, ramping up Randy Bignell-Sax's duplicity, exaggerating both the explosion and my injury, and tossing in Alice's story of love and betrayal for good measure. The thing about Herzog, and Chopper, too, for that matter, is that despite their career paths, they both have kind hearts.

When I finished, Chopper was laughing. Herzy said, " 'Kay, you tell a good story, but goddammit, McKenzie."

"I'm not asking for a lot," I said.

"If everything goes 'cordin' t' plan it ain't a lot. But if it don't ..."

"I don't know this Alejandro Reyes," Chopper said. "Him or his crew."

"Would you?" I asked.

"Man workin' the drug trade here in the Cities for half a decade, yeah, you'd think I'd at least heard of 'im."

He has a point, my inner voice said. *The man has more connections than Xfinity.*

"Tells me he know how to keep a low profile," Chopper said. "Tells me he's smart."

"I'm counting on him being smart," I said. "Smart means he'll listen to reason."

"I know a lot of smart people up at Oak Park Heights," Chopper said. "Know a lot of smart people fuckin' dead, too. Don't you?"

"When did you become so negative?"

Herzy snorted at me.

"I'm thinkin', though, there might be another way t' git rid of Alejandro wit'out takin' the risk," Chopper said.

"I'm open to suggestions."

"Drop a dime on 'im."

"I told you before, I'm trying to avoid police involvement."

"No, no, no, man. Not the po-lice. The Red Dragons."

"Your old friends—those Red Dragons?"

"Dragons been dealin' OxyContin for some time now. Got a lock on the local market. Alejandro's heroin, though, it's gotta be siphonin' off some of the Dragons' customers and vice versa. Some people will tell you that heroin and Oxy and horse be exactly the same, 'ceptin' for the way it's ingested."

"'Hillbilly Heroin' is what some call it, call Oxy," Herzog said.

"Average Oxy user, he's spendin' $70 to $140 per day for his pills," Chopper said.

"About the same for heroin," I said.

"So, Alejandro and the Dragons are chasin' the same dollar, and the Dragons, I speak from experience when I say they don't like competition."

"We should start a good old-fashioned gang war. Is that what you're suggesting?"

"War already be waging, McKenzie. I'm just sayin' it might be fun to let both sides know the face of its enemy."

I like it, my inner voice said.

"Except it won't get my friend clear," I said aloud. "It might even have the opposite effect. Reyes would need resources to fight a war. It could force him to tighten his grip on Salsa Girl."

"I feel ya, man, but now that I got it in my head—I don't mind seein' some blood on the streets if it don't belong t' me or someone I care about," Chopper said. " 'Specially if it's Red Dragon blood. Once you take care of your friend, I might drop a name here and there kinda incognito like. See if that don't spark a confrontation."

"Feel free. In the meantime, knowing about the Dragons is another argument in my favor."

"We're back to that?" Herzy said.

I opened the gym bag and pulled the soft sides down so he could get a good look at the money inside.

"Ten thousand for you," I said. "Another five each for as many people as you think we might need, up to half a dozen."

Herzog stared at the money for a few beats, closed his eyes for a few beats more, and opened them.

"Who's runnin' the show?" he asked.

"You are," I said.

"Got a location in mind?"

"You decide."

"How much time we got?"

"As much as you need."

"You makin' it hard for a boy to say no."

"Oh, Herzy, neither me nor anyone I know is dumb enough to call you boy."

Herzog turned toward Chopper.

"How'd you git to be friends wit' this asshole, anyway?" he asked.

"Fuck if I know," Chopper said. "I'm still wonderin' where he's gonna take us to dinner."

Dinner had to wait for a more convenient date, because once he made up his mind, Herzog moved quickly. It wasn't that he didn't want to take some time to think about what he was doing; he didn't want to give Reyes time to think. He went to his phone, his back to me; it made a helluva buffer so I couldn't hear what was said or to whom. Chopper made small talk. Billy Joel was coming to Target Field, and he was sure that he'd make the score of the year scalping his tickets. I wasn't sure if the man was a big enough draw to make scalping his tickets worth the effort.

"Man's old," I said. "I mean, I love him, but he's been singing the same songs for decades."

"Pretty good songs, though," Chopper said.

"Do you think the millennials are going to line up to hear him? Think the man can sell out a forty-four-thousand-seat stadium?"

"Yeah, I do. Easily. And you know, millennials aren't the only ones going to outdoor concerts. Plenty of ol' farts like you, McKenzie, wanna relive their childhoods."

Herzog finished with his phone and turned toward me.

"You parked somewhere your car won't be towed?" he asked.

"Yes, in the surface lot down the street."

" 'Kay. You ride with me, then. And, ah"—he waved a finger at the gym bag—"bring the money."

"Should I contact Alejandro?"

"Not till I tell you."

If you look it up on a map, you'll see that the City of West St. Paul is actually located due south of the City of St. Paul, albeit on the west side of the Mississippi River. I suppose they could have called it "South" St. Paul, except the name was already taken by the City of South St. Paul, which was more or less east of the capital city.

Garlough Park is located in the bottom half of West St. Paul; I have no idea who it was named after or why. I did know that it had a nine-hole disc golf course with a B+ rating. I'd never once played the game, so I didn't know if that was good or bad.

Herzog and I were sitting in his SUV on Marie Avenue bordering the park. It was nearly six forty-five with a bright, cloudless sky; the sun wouldn't set for another seventy-five minutes, yet I was unable to see inside the park because of the trees. Traffic drove past us, but there wasn't much of it. We hadn't spoken while he drove me there from Minneapolis, but my curiosity wouldn't allow me to remain silent any longer.

"I notice this isn't much of a public place," I said.

"Nope."

"What are we doing here?" I asked.

"Waiting."

"Uh-huh. After we're done waiting, will we then be going to a public place, you know, with lots and lots of people?"

"We're where we're supposed to be."

"I don't want to tell you your business ..."

"Then don't."

"Humor me."

"West St. Paul has a solid Hispanic and Latino population; this is where most of the Cinco de Mayo events are held. 'Kay? So the man's gonna feel more comfortable; less like he's rollin' into an ambush."

"Yes, but why here, exactly?"

"I know the ground. McKenzie, did you think I didn't?"

"You've done something like this before, is what you're saying. I thought you were out of the life."

"You ain't the only friend tryin' to drag me back in."

"Now I feel bad."

"You should feel bad corruptin' a brother what's tryin' to become an upstandin' citizen."

A few seconds later a second SUV rolled to a stop behind us.

"They're here. Stay until I call," Herzog told me.

I stayed.

Herzog left our vehicle and moved to the driver's side window of the second vehicle. I angled the sideview mirror to watch him. A few moments later, he returned.

"Get out," he said. "Bring the money."

I opened the door and stepped out of the SUV. The gym bag was on the floor. I scooped it up by the handle and moved to the back of the car. Herzog was now standing there with three other African Americans. All of them were bigger than I was. None of them looked young.

"Gentlemen," I said.

Herzog spoke before I could say anything more.

"Open the bag," he said.

I opened the bag. The men glanced inside. None of them seemed surprised by what they found there.

"This is the money," Herzog said. Only he wasn't speaking about the cash. He was speaking about me. "Nothing bad happens to the money. We clear?"

The men nodded.

" 'Kay. You know what to do."

The men moved to the back of their SUV, popped the trunk, and removed three gun cases. They carried the gun cases into the park.

"You ready to call Reyes?" Herzog asked.

"Sure."

He told me what to say.

"He's not going to like it." I waved at the park. "Hell, I don't like it."

"I don't care what he likes."

Or you either, my inner voice said.

After making the call, I locked the gym bag inside the SUV along with the sling—there was no reason to let Reyes know I was hurting. Herzog and I entered the park. We followed a narrow footpath until we emerged from the woods into a clearing. At the top of the clearing was a hill.

"Up there," Herzog said.

I followed his lead to the top of the hill, where I discovered that it wasn't a clearing after all, but rather a fairway of the disc golf course; the fifth hole, to be exact. At the top of the hill the fairway sloped dramatically downward toward a metal basket target. I found two green benches angled toward each other. They were surrounded on three sides by thick brush and trees. Herzog's people could have been ten feet away and I wouldn't have seen them. 'Course, the same could be said of Reyes's people.

It was not an unusual setting in the Twin Cities. There were dozens of these miniature forests, some surrounding parks, some surrounding lakes, some of them just there—giving people a refuge from the asphalt and concrete, allowing them the feeling that they were "up north" even though there was a Taco Bell three minutes away. But instead of solitude, I was feeling isolated; I was feeling like a target.

"Are you sure about this?" I asked.

"Don't look for my crew," Herzog said. "They can see us fine."

"That doesn't answer my question."

"What time is it?"

I glanced at my multipurpose watch—7:22 P.M. We had told Reyes to be there at seven thirty exactly because at seven thirty-one we'd be gone.

"He won't have time to position his people, make sure it's safe," Herzog said. "Instead, he'll come with an army; try to intimidate us with sheer numbers."

"You say that like it's a good thing."

"You'll be doin' all the talkin' when the man gits 'ere. I won't be sayin' a word. Just gonna stand 'ere lookin' bored. 'Kay? If I do talk, though, man, you best you do what I say."

I nodded in agreement.

"Nervous, Dyson?" Herzog said the name as if he were making fun of it.

"Who?" I said. "Me?"

By using the name Dyson, Herzog told me that it was time to get into character. Despite what could be described as an occasional bout of moral ambivalence, McKenzie was more or less a nice guy. Dyson, on the other hand, was a sonuvabitch with no moral code at all. With him, it was all about self-preservation. To become him, I told myself how lousy life was, how unfair. I listed in my head all the crimes that had been committed against me going back to my childhood. The teacher who accused me of cheating even though I hadn't. The criminals I arrested who went free because of some county attorney's incompetence or the brain-dead stupidity of a jury. I thought of my mother who died of cancer when I was twelve and my father who died when I was thirty-six. I thought of the cops who refused to talk to me because I accepted the reward on the embezzler to give my father a cushy retirement before he died. I thought of the men who had tried to kill me over the years and the ones that I had killed. I thought of those friends I'd helped and those I failed to help. By the time Reyes showed, I was pretty angry.

He and his people emerged from the forest at the bottom of the fairway near the disc target. He started climbing the hill toward us. I counted seven gunmen with him.

I'm supposed to be impressed? my inner Dyson said. *Fuck that.*

I reached behind me and adjusted the Taurus, making sure I could reach it in a hurry.

As they climbed the hill, Reyes's men spread out until they were approaching in a skirmish line. I noticed they were all dressed as if they were going to a ball game. No gang colors, no flags. When they came closer I also noticed—no tats. Chopper was right. They knew how to maintain a low profile.

Reyes—I assumed it was Reyes—was in the center of the line. When he got into shouting distance I called to him.

"You're late."

Reyes didn't reply until he was near enough to where I sat that he could speak without raising his voice. His voice was relaxed, nearly as relaxed as Salsa Girl's, but not quite.

"Did you bring my goods?" he asked.

"No. Did you expect that I would?"

Reyes motioned with both hands. His men closed in a tight semicircle. I wondered if they started shooting how many of them I would get before they got me. Not enough, I decided. I glanced at Herzog. He stood behind me and to my left. He was dressed in black. His weapon was hidden under his jacket—if he had a weapon. Truth was, I hadn't even bothered to ask. His hands were folded over his belt buckle. As promised, he looked as bored as death.

"If you don't return my product, I'll kill you," Reyes said.

"I figured you might take that attitude."

Reyes smirked. He nodded at the man next to him. The man

slipped a Hi-Point .45 out from the waistband of his pants. A cheap handgun, I thought. He's planning to use it and then dump it.

At the same instant, three red dots of light from three different laser sights mounted on three different rifles centered on Reyes's chest. His first thought was to brush them away with his hand. His second—*"Para, hombre!"*

The hombre stopped moving.

I glanced at Herzog. He hadn't budged an inch. I would have smiled at him but I knew he wouldn't like it. I gestured at the semicircle.

"They might kill me, Alejandro," I said. "But you won't. Do you understand my meaning?"

Reyes regained his balance.

"What's your play?" he said.

"Are we done posing for each other?"

"It's your meeting."

I noticed that his accent was very slight, and I wondered, Where is he from, anyway? Instead of asking, I said, "Tell your crew to put its guns away and keep their hands in plain sight. You." I pointed at the hombre next to the Reyes. "Drop the Hi-Point on the ground."

He did, but only after Reyes gave him a nudge in the ribs with his elbow.

Reyes sat down on the bench across from me. The red dots disappeared.

"Talk to me, what?" he said.

"First, you gotta know I'm not interested in your business."

"I didn't think so, a professional heist artist like you."

"Ahh, you looked me up. I'm flattered."

"What do you want?"

"I'm here to have a conversation and that's it. You listen while I say what I was hired to say and everybody goes home."

"What about my product?"

"We'll get to that."

"Better get to it quick," the hombre said.

"Be quiet," I said. "Adults are talking here."

The hombre bent at the waist and reached for his Hi-Point. The three dots returned to Reyes's chest. He spoke so quickly that my high school Spanish wasn't good enough to translate. The hombre must have understood his meaning, though, because he froze, his fingers scant inches from the butt of the .45. Slowly he stood up and folded his arms across his chest.

Herzog still hadn't moved.

"What I'm trying to say, Alejandro," I said. "May I call you Alejandro? What I'm trying to say is that I'm not your problem here. I'm just the guy who's trying to explain your problem."

"What's my problem?"

"Your problem is that you made a deal with that dipshit Randy Bignell-Sax. I mean, why would you want to work with some rich dick doesn't know which end is up, some thirty-year-old who's still got snot coming out of his nose, pretending he's a gangster? You had to know that sooner or later he was going to fuck up. It was as inevitable as the sun rising in the east. Instead of taking the loss in stride—every business has its ups and downs, am I right? Instead of dealing with it, though, what did you do? You cut him, man. What? Did you think that would scare him? Well, it did. Scared him to death. Only when rich assholes like Randy get scared, they go running to Mommy and Daddy. And what did they do when they discovered that their baby had been led astray by a bunch of immigrants? They started making phone calls.

"It ain't white privilege, pal. It's all about green privilege. You got a lot of green, you got a lot of friends who are happy to do your biddin'. Randy's folks, they know people who know people who know people like me who'll take care of their issues for a price. They want this one, meaning you, to go away with a minimum amount of muss and fuss."

"*Pendejo habla demasiado,*" the hombre said.

I pointed at him but spoke to Reyes.

"Did he really just call me an asshole?" I said. "Did he really say I talk too much?" I turned my eyes back on the hombre. "Fuck you, pal."

"Nicholas," Reyes said. "We have business to discuss."

I liked it that Reyes used Dyson's first name. It meant he was attempting to defuse the situation. But Dyson wouldn't let it go.

"I don't like you, asshole," he said. "I might decide to have words with you."

The hombre took a fleeting look down at the Hi-Point in the grass at his feet. The other members of Reyes's crew glanced nervously at each other and shifted their weight. Herzog remained still.

"Nicholas," Reyes said.

"Yeah, yeah. Where was I? Oh, yeah. I'm here to say you're done with Randy. You're done with Salsa Girl. You're gonna have t' find a different way to bring your product across the border because you won't be using the Salsa Girl trucks."

"That would be very inconvenient."

"Nobody gives a shit, Alejandro. I'm just telling you—this ain't me, remember. I'm just delivering the message. The message is move on."

"Move on? Just like that?" Reyes pounded his chest. "What am I supposed to do now? How am I supposed to meet the demands of my customers?"

"You could go into a different line of work."

"Listen to him," Reyes told his hombre. To me he said, "You're not solving my problem."

"Solving your problem isn't our line," I said.

"We deal in lead, friend," Herzog said.

Both Reyes and I looked up at him. Herzog shrugged imperceptibly.

"Isn't that a line from a movie?" Reyes said.

Steve McQueen to Eli Wallach in The Magnificent Seven, *the original film, not the remake,* my inner voice said. *Damn, Herzy.*

"I don't care what you do," I said aloud. "But just so you know, the next phone call Randy's mommy and daddy make, they won't be making it to me. It'll be to Assistant U.S. Attorney James R. Finnegan. The man's a prick, believe me. I've had dealings with him. Worse, he's a prick with political ambitions. With the Bignells financing his run, you don't think he'd love to get his name out there by launching a joint task force to take down the illegal Mexicans bringing drugs, bringing crime, into the country? C'mon, you read the news. This is pure gold for a right-wing nut-job politician—prove he's tough on crime. Finnegan will come after you with the biggest army and the most noise he can possibly muster. Randy's name—I promise you, it'll never even be mentioned. And his partner, fuck, she still doesn't know what's going on.

"In the meantime, you've also got the Red Dragons to deal with. I heard they're lookin' to have a conversation with you, too, because you've been cuttin' into their OxyContin trade. What do you think they're gonna say when they find you?"

"I have no issues with the Dragons."

"Yeah, that's probably gonna change if you don't listen to reason. Look, Alejandro. I'm not threatening you. Maybe you're afraid of the Feds and the Dragons; maybe you're not. Maybe you think you can push back at Randy and his family, threaten to hang a drug rap on the kid or somethin' if they don't give up, give out, give in. 'Course, sooner or later the partner will be dragged into it, and who knows, she might be opposed to lettin' you use her business to mule your shit. Hell, she might even be an honest woman. In any case, you gotta admit, if you don't back off, pretty soon doing business in the Twin Cities—man, it's gonna become such a bitch. And this after years of having it nice and easy, too. Personally, I'd take the easy way out. But that's just me. All right? That's all I have to say, all I was asked to say. You do what you think is best. Now, let's part friends. You go your way and I'll go mine, and good luck to you."

"What about my product?"

"Your four keys of heroin. I forgot about that for a sec. Here's the thing, my instructions are to hang on to it until everyone's satisfied that you're playing nice with all the other children. Call it an incentive. 'Course, you might decide to call the bluff and keep trying to use Salsa Girl, in which case your other shipments will be disappearing, too. I have no use for your product, so I'll probably unload it somewhere. Maybe the Dragons'll take it off my hands. So there's that."

"Patrón," the hombre said, "I do not believe him. I do not trust him." He spoke English because he wanted me to know what he was saying.

I stood up and stepped near enough to smell his breath.

"Believe what you like. I don't care." I held my closed fist out at my side and opened it as if mimicking a mic drop. "I'm out."

"Hijo de mil putas," the hombre said. "This is not over, yet."

McKenzie probably would have smiled and walked away; certainly he would not have shown much anger at being called the son of a thousand whores. Hell, he might even have laughed at the silliness of it all. Dyson, though, was never one to let an insult go unchallenged. I smiled benignly, slowly reached down for the hombre's Hi-Point, and came up quickly, smashing him in the jaw with the butt.

"How 'bout now?" I said.

I hit him again.

And again.

"Is it over now?"

And again.

"How 'bout now?"

Reyes jumped to his feet and yelled something in Spanish. Three red dots centered on his chest.

The men standing in the semicircle reached for their weapons.

I hit the hombre yet again, knocking him to the ground. I took the business end of the .45 and shoved it into his ruined mouth. He gagged on the barrel. Blood flowed down his cheeks and puddled on the ground. His eyes were wide with fear. He brought his hands up to pull the gun from his mouth. I gripped his throat with my free hand and pressed a knee against his chest. Instead of slowing me down, the stabbing pain in my shoulder just spurred me on.

"Is it over now?" I said.

A lot of men were shouting. I heard only one voice clearly.

"Dyson." It was Herzog calling my name, Dyson's name. I looked up at him. "We done here?"

I released the hombre's throat, lifted my knee from his chest, and pulled the gun out of his mouth. He rolled onto his side and began coughing and spitting blood.

What the hell is wrong with you? my inner voice asked.

I stepped away from the hombre. The other six Mexican bandits were pointing their weapons at me. I turned to Reyes. The dots were still centered on his chest.

I dropped the Hi-Point at my feet and raised my hands high enough so that everyone could see that they were empty.

"Can't we all just get along?" I said.

Reyes spread his hands wide as if he were wondering the same thing.

The sun had set and the air had turned chilly by the time Herzog and I returned to the SUVs. His men were already there and speaking quietly. They stopped talking when we approached. I paid them and thanked them for their time. They drove off. I gave Herzog his ten thousand. He dropped it into his trunk as if it were something he didn't want to embrace for too long. I put the sling back on and slipped my arm through it; my shoulder hurt almost as much as when I had first injured it. I took my time climbing into the passenger seat of Herzog's SUV. He drove us back to Minneapolis.

"That worked out pretty well considerin' you nearly got us killed," Herzog said.

I sat back against the seat. The gym bag, now $25,000 lighter, was on my lap; the Taurus, Dyson's IDs, and Randy's flip-phone were tucked inside it. My eyes were closed. I made a point of breathing through my nose.

"It wasn't me," I said. "It was Dyson."

"Crazy fucker, you ask me."

"He does have his moments."

"You know, there's somethin' the whaddaya-call psychologist told me once when I was inside that I've been thinkin' on ever since. He said, *We are what we pretend to be, so we must be careful about what we pretend to be.*"

"Kurt Vonnegut."

"Who?"

"Kurt Vonnegut. He said it first."

"Whatever, man. It's good advice."

Herzog was right, only I didn't say. I didn't speak another word.

Herzog drove to the surface lot near Chopper's building where I had parked my Mustang. I thanked him for his help and told him that dinner was still a thing we would do as soon as his, Chopper's, and my schedules could be reconciled. He told me about a joint in Fridley called Crooners that he wanted to give a try; said it was supposed to have good music. I told him that would work as I slipped out of his SUV. He said something then that kind of threw me—"I worry about you, McKenzie."

If a man like Herzy is concerned about the things you do, maybe it's time for you to start reassessing your life's choices, my inner voice said.

"I'm good," I said aloud.

"If you say so."

Herzog drove away, leaving me standing alone next to my car, the gym bag gripped in my hand, my arm pressed against my side to help alleviate the ache in my shoulder. The lights of Target Field illuminated the downtown Minneapolis skyline, but mostly the harsh light flowed upward and didn't reach the lot where I was standing. Still, I was close enough to the baseball stadium that I could hear the crowd cheer for, well, I hoped it was for a member of the Twins organization doing something right for a change and not the Red Sox. I hated the Red Sox, at least for the duration of the home stand. In a few days I'd start hating the Toronto Blue Jays.

A glance at my watch told me that the Twins were probably playing the fifth, possibly sixth inning by now. I wondered if Salsa Girl and Ian were enjoying themselves.

You need to talk to her, my inner voice reminded me. *The sooner the better.*

Tomorrow, I told myself. I didn't want to intrude on Erin's date.

I opened the Mustang, tossed the gym bag on the passenger seat, climbed in, and drove off.

I didn't learn about the Acura that was following me until later.

The call came five minutes after I entered the condominium. I almost didn't go home, debating with myself whether it would be better to drive to Rickie's instead, have a drink or two or three while listening to some tunes. The emotional residue of my visit with Alejandro Reyes and his hombre was still clinging to me, though, and I didn't want it to rub off on anyone else, especially Nina.

I answered the phone. Jones—or was it Smith?—said, "Mc-Kenzie, you'll want to come down and take a look at this."

A few minutes later, I was standing in front of the security desk. Both Smith and Jones were seated behind it, their chairs facing the TV monitors.

"When did you two start working nights?" I asked.

"We're working a double shift so we can get tomorrow off for the ball game," Smith said. "Come around here and take a look."

I circled the desk until I was standing behind their chairs and looking at the TV screens. My first thought—Coyle and his blue Camry had returned.

Smith hit a button, and the center screen was filled with my Mustang.

"This is you a few minutes ago," Smith said. "Now watch."

I did, watching myself driving down the street, signaling for a right turn, entering the driveway leading to the opening of the underground parking garage, and disappearing inside.

So what? my inner voice asked.

Smith's hand came up and he pointed at an image of a black Acura following behind my Mustang, slowing as it passed the driveway, speeding up until it reached the intersection, hanging a U-turn, coming back, and parking across the street at a meter with an unobstructed view of the garage doors.

Oh.

"It gets better," Jones said.

He hit a few more buttons, and I was treated to the sight of my Mustang doing the exact same thing as before, only this time it was in broad daylight.

"This was you arriving at about—well, exactly four sixteen P.M. today," Jones said.

You were coming home after finding the heroin in the Salsa Girl prep room, my inner voice reminded me.

"Okay," I said aloud.

"Now, this is you leaving again ten minutes later."

Jones tapped a few more buttons, and I saw myself driving away from the garage, also in daylight, and proceeding to the intersection, where I executed a rolling stop before making a right turn.

On your way to Chopper's place.

"Here," Smith said. He was pointing at the Acura again as it pulled out of its parking space and began trailing me.

"Dammit."

"Someone is following you," Jones said.

"I can see that."

"We probably wouldn't have noticed ourselves except that we've been paying close attention ever since you asked us to keep an eye out for the Toyota the other day," Smith said.

"I appreciate this," I said.

"We ran the footage back ever further, and we discovered that the Acura first arrived at the building at exactly two seventeen P.M. today," Smith said. "We figure the surveillance didn't start until then. The Acura parked where he parked and didn't move an inch until you left at"—he glanced at his timetable—"four twenty-eight."

I reviewed my movements in my head: I left for Salsa Girl Salsa at approximately eight that morning, stayed there until about one thirty, came home, received Alice Pfeifer's phone call a short time later, drove to her apartment, went back to Salsa Girl to remove the heroin at about three thirty, and came back here. That's when the Acura picked me up. It knew nothing about my movements before I drove to Chopper's.

Could he have followed you to West St. Paul? my inner voice asked.

I didn't think so. Herzog and I had been pretty careful; we

would have known if we were being tailed. Besides, we didn't take the Mustang. Instead, we left in Herzog's SUV; it had been parked behind Chopper's building in an employees-only lot. If the Acura was sitting on the Mustang, the driver wouldn't have seen us leave. So whoever was following me knew only that I drove to Chopper's building, went inside, and later returned to the parking lot. 'Course, he would have seen Herzog dropping me off; probably the driver would have been pissed that I had managed to slip away without him knowing. Just as probably he would have taken down Herzy's license plate number.

He's not going to like it when you tell him, my inner voice said.

"About that," I said aloud.

"What?" Smith said.

"Did you get the Acura's license plate number?"

"Of course."

"You realize that we're not supposed to run it, though," Jones said. "The Department of Public Safety has been clamping down ever since it lost a million-dollar settlement to that woman who sued after she learned that over a hundred guys had accessed her info at one time or another for no better reason than to learn her name and marital status."

"She was a babe," Smith said.

"It's okay," I said. "I know a guy who owes me one."

"So do we," Jones said. "We're just messing with you, McKenzie. Fishing for another big tip."

"What do you have?"

"Not much, I'm afraid. The Acura is a rental. It's assigned to an agency near the airport. We gave them a call, but the rental agency refused to put a driver in the car for us."

"Something about privacy rights and court orders," Smith said. "Silly stuff like that."

So now what? my inner voice asked.

I was pretty sure it wasn't Alejandro Reyes. He hadn't even

known that I existed until I called him at about six forty-five, and anyway, he knew me as Dyson. And Dyson didn't live in a high-rise condominium in downtown Minneapolis with his beautiful girlfriend.

That left Greg Schroeder and his minions, except—Greg wasn't following me, he was following Salsa Girl.

Which brings us back to the original question—what now?

I could confront the Acura's driver the way I had braced Darren Coyle, only the way the day was going, I didn't want to press my luck. Besides, my shoulder was killing me.

"Gentlemen," I said, "what would you normally do under these circumstances—you see someone spying on one of your tenants, whom you've been sworn to protect?"

"Actually, we're paid to protect the building," Jones said.

"Whatever."

"Why, McKenzie," Smith said, "we'd call the police."

While we waited for one of Minneapolis's finest, I went upstairs, popped the top off three bottles of Summit Ale, and brought them back to the security desk. We sipped the beer while we watched the officer at work.

He pulled his squad behind the Acura, the squad's bright lights illuminating the inside of the car. He approached the vehicle cautiously, just as he had been trained. The driver unrolled his window; I noticed that he kept both hands on the steering wheel while he spoke to the officer.

He's done this before, my inner voice said.

The officer asked for the driver's ID and insurance information. It was given freely. The officer returned to his vehicle and called it in. The driver remained in the Acura and watched the officer through his rearview mirror. Minutes passed. The officer returned to the driver and restored the driver's possessions. More words were exchanged. The officer returned to his cruiser.

The driver started his Acura, signaled, and pulled away from the parking space into the street. We watched him on the TV monitor as he turned left onto Washington Avenue and disappeared into the traffic.

"He may come back," I said, "but not in the Acura. Probably he'll also try to find a perch outside the range of your cameras."

"We'll pass word to the other shifts to watch for him," Jones said.

A moment later, the Minneapolis police officer entered the building's foyer. Smith was quick to take our beers and place them out of sight.

"Good evening," Jones said.

"Good evening," the officer replied.

"What's his story?" Smith asked.

The officer spoke freely even though I was standing behind the desk; no doubt I looked like an authority figure to him, with my arm folded across my sling.

"Asshole's from Chicago," he said. "His name is Levi Chandler. That mean anything to you?"

We all shook our heads.

"I checked and he's not in the system, so I don't know. He claimed he was lost and that he was waiting for a friend to call and tell him where to go."

"I'd like to tell him where to go," Jones said.

"It's bullshit," the officer said. "No law against that, though. I shooed him away, but that don't mean he's going to stay away."

"We were thinking the same thing," Smith said.

"Keep an eye out. What else can I say?"

"We will," said Jones. "Thanks, Officer."

"Have a beer on me."

Smith took a Summit out from behind the desk and saluted the officer with it. Jones and I did the same as the officer left the building and returned to his vehicle. We watched him drive away through the big windows.

Now what? my inner voice asked yet again.

If I see Chandler again, I'll attempt to have a conversation with him, I told myself. Hopefully, it will be as uneventful as the one he had with the officer. In the meantime ...

"I appreciate everything you've done for me, guys," I said.

"We appreciate the beer," Smith said.

"If I find anything lying around in the corridor, I'll be sure to bring it to the lost and found."

"You know," Jones said, "Billy Joel is coming to town."

"As it turns out, I know a guy."

I left them after that and took the elevator to my condominium. On the way my inner voice asked, *Who did you piss off in Chicago?*

ELEVEN

My aching shoulder woke me enough times during the night that I was reconsidering my position on the pain pills. I finally slid out of bed when the clock read 7:25. In my philosophy, 7:25 on a Saturday morning is like the crack of dawn—emphasis on crack. I crept from the bedroom into a huge walk-in closet complete with shelves and drawers and carefully closed the door behind me. The closet led to a bathroom with double sinks and a glass-enclosed shower big enough for two people to play tag in. Beyond that there was a storage area with enough room to park a car.

I showered, dressed, and put my arm into the sling without benefit of the radio. It was my habit to listen to NPR in the morning to learn if the world was still spinning on its axis—to learn if it was worth getting out of bed—only I wanted to avoid waking Nina. Instead, after closing the bedroom door, moving into the living room area, and sitting on the sofa, I turned on CNN, keeping the volume low. As expected, the world was still spinning, but if you believed the pundits, it had picked up a serious wobble. When I was a child, I was devoted to a weekly TV program called *Horror Incorporated* that introduced classic horror, science fiction, and cult movies, even though it scared the beejesus out of me. These guys were worse.

Or maybe it was just my poor mood. Not only was I in pain, I discovered that it was snowing. The middle of April and it was snowing. Granted, most of the flakes were melting as they hit the ground. Still ...

I found refuge in the NHL Channel. Forget the Twins, at least for now. My Minnesota Wild, which was projected to go deep into the Stanley Cup playoffs, were down two games to nothing in a best-of-seven series with the St. Louis Blues that began—last Wednesday? How did I miss that? Oh, yeah—I was being blown up at the time.

I grabbed my smartphone with the intention of calling Salsa Girl but changed my mind when I noted the time. Eight fifteen was way too early to call someone with anything but bad news. Besides, there was a chance that she and Ian Gotz were canoodling after their date, and I was never one to get in the way of a good canoodle.

After getting my fill of hockey, I switched to the MLB Channel and discovered that the Twins had lost to the Red Sox in eleven innings. I remember leaning back against the sofa and sighing. The next thing I remember is the sound of someone rummaging in the kitchen area. I turned to find Nina pouring herself a healthy glass of orange juice. She was wearing her silver nightgown and nothing else that I could see.

"How long have you been up?" she asked.

I glanced at my watch—9:55.

"Hours," I said.

Nina moved to the sofa and sat with her legs tucked beneath her. God, she looked good, even with bed hair.

"How's your shoulder?" she asked.

"Fine."

Nina reached out and gave it a nudge. I winced at the contact.

"I thought it was getting better," she said.

I explained why it wasn't, carefully downplaying Dyson's near-suicidal blowup.

"Do you want me to kiss it and make it all better?" Nina asked.

"You're welcome to try."

She nudged me again. I winced some more.

"Pity," she said.

"I'm sure there's a medically sound procedure that we can—wait."

Nina had left the sofa and was headed for the bedroom. She spoke to me over her shoulder. "I need to get dressed."

"Why?"

She didn't answer.

Dammit!

I grabbed my smartphone and called Erin Peterson. My thinking was selfish at best: If I couldn't canoodle because of her, why should she? Only she didn't answer. Instead, I was kicked to voice mail.

I identified myself and said, "Call me. Your life has become more complicated, I'm afraid."

Or not. Despite the pain it caused me, I believed my altercation with Alejandro Reyes and his hombre had the desired outcome. They had to realize that attempting to use Salsa Girl Salsa to move their dope was no longer a viable option. Which meant Erin was off the hook with them. But what about the man from Chicago?

I left the sofa and moved to the glass door that led onto the balcony. The snow had stopped while I was asleep, yet there was a thin white glaze over everything that wasn't made of asphalt. I slid open the door and was immediately assaulted by a gush of cold fresh air. Most people would have found it exhilarating. I found it frightening. See, I suffer from acrophobia, an irrational fear of heights. Usually when I stepped onto the balcony, which wasn't often, I stayed close to the glass wall and as far from the railing as possible. I rarely looked down but instead nearly always looked out. This time, though, I forced myself to move to the railing and gaze over the edge, which was hard to do. For one thing, I had to balance my weight so I could do it without actually leaning on the railing, because my phobia convinced me that it would break off at the slightest provocation and I would tumble to my doom. Looking down didn't do me any good anyway. There were plenty of black cars parked on the streets around the building, but there was no way I could identify any of them as an Acura.

I went back inside the condominium, closing the glass door behind me. I found my smartphone. I had called Herzog the previous evening, but he hadn't picked up. I was convinced he swiped left because he didn't want to talk to me. I couldn't say I blamed him. I left a message, but he didn't text or return my call to tell me that he had heard it.

I called him again.

"What?" Herzog said.

"I'm sorry. I didn't wake you, did I?"

"Whaddya want, McKenzie?"

"I called last night—"

"Yeah."

"Left you a message."

"Black Acura."

"Uh-huh."

Herzog recited the license plate number.

"Okay, you got the message," I said. "I was afraid—"

"You know who this dude is?"

I said that I didn't, but that I was sure the Acura driver wasn't connected to our meeting with Alejandro Reyes and explained why.

"For what it's worth, I don't believe he's law enforcement either," I said.

"You're assumin' the po-lice officer told you the truth last night."

"I am."

"Why would you do that?"

"Why wouldn't I?"

"The po-lice, they ain't got no reason to lie, do they?" Herzog said.

"If they do, I don't know what it is."

"How you stay alive this long as trusting as you are? McKenzie, I expect you to figure this out."

"I will."

"Cuz I'm on parole like I said. I can't walk up to the man, shove a piece in his ear, and start askin' questions, you know?"

"You shouldn't do that even when you're not on parole."

"I can't go all Nick Dyson on his ass—"

Is that going to be a thing now? my inner voice asked.

"—cuz he just might be law enforcement no matter what you say," Herzog said.

"I understand."

" 'Kay. I'll watch for 'im, but McKenzie, there ain't never just one, you know that right?"

I hadn't actually considered that there would be more than one person following me. I said, "Right," anyway because there probably was more than one person following me.

"Call when you got it figured out," Herzog said.

"I will."

Herzog hung up without saying good-bye.

I stared at the cell phone for a few beats.

What the hell are you going to do? I asked myself.

My inner voice answered with a question. *Why do you follow someone?*

To find out where they're going and who they meet when they get there.

They know where you live; they knew from the beginning.

So?

So it's not necessarily about you.

Who, then?

How many possibilities are there?

I called Erin Peterson again. She didn't answer her phone, and I declined to leave a message. Instead, I called Ian Gotz. He answered on the third ring.

"McKenzie." His voice suggested that he was annoyed.

"Hey, Ian. How's it going?"

"What do you want, McKenzie?"

"I don't want to make a big deal out of this, but do you know where Salsa Girl is?"

"I told you, she doesn't like it when you call her that."

"Ian, please, this is important."

"Yes, I know exactly where Erin is. Hang on."

I heard him speaking, but his voice sounded far away as if he had lowered the phone.

"McKenzie wants to talk to you," he said.

"Tell him I'll call him back," Erin said.

"McKenzie? Erin said—"

"You think this is a goddamn game?" I said. "Put her on the fucking phone."

Ian's voice became distant again.

"McKenzie's a lot like you," he said. "He hardly ever yells. You should talk to him."

I heard a muffling sound followed by Erin's cheerful voice.

"Good morning, McKenzie," she said.

"I've been trying to reach you."

"I know. I received your message."

"Then why didn't you return my call? I've been worried."

"That's kind of you, being worried about me. But there's no need."

"Erin, I don't think you appreciate what's happening."

"I spoke to Alice Pfeifer late yesterday afternoon. She told me about Randy and his drug-smuggling activities, so yes, I do appreciate what's happening."

"I knew Alice wouldn't be able to keep a secret like this."

"She was very upset about betraying me. Of course, I had to punish her."

"Erin, you didn't fire her?"

"No. What kind of person do you think I am?"

"I haven't decided yet."

"Alice has to buy donuts for the coming week. McKenzie, this drug business—what have you done about it?"

"What makes you think I've done anything?"

I heard the smile in her voice when she answered. "Because you're you and a girl can never have a better friend."

"Yeah, well …"

"And because when you drove off, Alice said she was reminded of Daniel Day-Lewis in *The Last of the Mohicans*. You know that scene where he tells Madeleine Stowe to stay alive no matter what occurs, where he says he will find her no matter how long it takes?"

"She couldn't think of a more modern movie? God, I am so old."

"No, you're not. Tell me what you did."

I gave her an abbreviated version of my day, starting with removing the heroin from her premises and ending with my belief that Alejandro Reyes would no longer be a problem.

"I don't know how to thank you," Erin said.

"Unfortunately, I don't believe that's the end of it." I explained why.

"The driver of the Acura, Levi Chandler, you say he's from Chicago?" Erin said.

"That's what the police officer said."

Erin's voice remained relaxed and calm, as usual, yet coming from her the word sounded like an explosion: "Fuck."

"Does that have some significance to you, Chicago?" I asked.

"Not necessarily. I was just wondering who we know who has a presence in that city."

The name came to me without my having to think about it very hard. "The Bignells. Isn't that where Brian Sax flew off to just the other day?"

Erin sighed as if it were exactly the answer she wanted to hear. "I wonder what Randy told his family about the gash on his cheek," she added.

"Why don't I ask them?"

"I'm going back to bed."

"Aren't you at Ian's—never mind."

"I'll be home later this afternoon. Please call me."

"Have fun," I said.

"That is my intention."

I spent fifteen minutes taking advantage of the one-way streets in and around downtown Minneapolis to make sure I wasn't being followed before jumping on the freeway that took me to Highway 65. Forty minutes later I was in Cambridge. I stopped on the shoulder near the private road leading to the Bignell estate and waited. Nothing happened.

Huh, my inner voice said. *That was easy.*

I steered the Mustang down the lane and parked in the driveway near the immense garage. I followed the sidewalk to the house, making sure my leather jacket was zipped to my throat. After climbing the steps to the portico, I crossed to the front door and rang the bell. Randy Bignell-Sax answered.

"Shit," he said.

"Good to see you, too."

"What are you doing here, McKenzie?"

His hand flew to the bandage on the side of his face as if that provided part of the answer.

"I'd like to speak to your mother," I said.

"No."

"Relax, kid. You probably don't know it or believe it, but I might have saved your ass yesterday."

"I want you to leave."

"After I speak to Marilyn."

"Get out."

"Do you want me to raise my voice? Do you want me to make a scene? Forget your mother. Let me speak to your grandfather instead."

"Every time things start going my way, someone messes it up."

"Things are going your way?"

"Why are you doing this to me?"

"It may come as a shock, but not everything is about you, Randy."

"What's not about Randy?"

I looked over his shoulder to see Marilyn moving toward us. She was wearing tight jeans and a baggy sweater with the sleeves pushed up. Her sneakers squeaked on the hardwood floor the way they do when you play basketball. For a moment I was reminded of a teacher I had a crush on when I was a freshman in high school. I shook the thought away quickly, though; the teacher gave me such a poor grade in algebra that I nearly wasn't allowed to play JV hockey.

"Mrs. Bignell-Sax," I said.

"Ms. Bignell is fine," she said.

"I take it from the new moniker that you dropped the hammer on Brian."

"That's what the hammer was for."

"I don't need to listen to this," Randy said.

"Wait," Marilyn said. "Randy ..."

Only Randy wasn't listening. He turned and retreated into the bowels of the enormous house. I don't know what kind of shoes he was wearing, but they didn't make a sound. Marilyn watched him go.

"The way he's behaving, you'd think I was divorcing him," she said.

"I don't suppose it matters how old you are; if your parents divorce, it has to hurt."

Marilyn grabbed a coat hanging on a rack near the door and stepped out of the house onto the portico, closing the door behind her. She pulled on the coat, pressed a hand against my shoulder, and nudged me along the porch.

"Twenty people live in this house," she said. "Privacy is an illusion."

We found some rattan furniture and sat on two chairs that were facing each other. The view was very nice if you like huge, open fields.

"Do you believe this weather?" Marilyn asked. "It shouldn't be this cold in April, should it?"

"Minnesota," I said. "What are you going to do?"

"How's your shoulder?"

I lied and told Marilyn it was feeling much better.

"I heard my father and Randy screaming at each other after we left Salsa Girl Thursday afternoon," she said. "I know it was Randy who planted the bomb in Erin's truck."

"Yes."

"I'm so sorry."

"It wasn't your fault."

"I know, but—you're not going to ..."

"Shoot Randy?"

"Call the authorities."

"Probably not to either thought, and believe me, I've had both."

"It's because of her, isn't it—Erin Peterson? That's why he hasn't been arrested."

"Yes."

"I don't know if I should be grateful to her or not."

"I'd pick grateful, but that's just me."

"Why have you come here, McKenzie?"

"I have questions."

"About Randy?"

"What did he say happened to his face?"

"He claimed he was injured while trying to protect a woman from her abusive boyfriend—a woman named Alice Pfeifer who works for Salsa Girl Salsa. Of course he was lying. I love my son, McKenzie, but he would never put himself at risk to help someone else. Part of that is because of how he was raised—this house, the people who live in it. We should never have raised him in this house. We should have ... There's a lot of things I should have done for that boy that we didn't. I don't even know who he is anymore. I'm not sure that I ever did. What kind of mother does that make me?"

I didn't answer. Marilyn hadn't expected me to.

"Do you know how Randy really was hurt?" she asked.

"Yes."

"Will you tell me?"

"His story sounds better."

"His grandfather certainly likes it. So does Brian."

"Where is Brian?"

"He was told to stay in Chicago."

"By whom?"

"My father. For the record, when I told him about Brian's affair, my father blamed me. He said that Brian would never have committed such a grievous sin against God and man if I had been a better wife to him. Do you know what I mean by a better wife?"

"I can guess."

"My father has called an emergency meeting of his executive staff to decide how best to deal with the Brian Problem. That's what he calls it—the Brian Problem. He wants to oust him from the company with the minimum impact on business. He's also meeting with a divorce attorney."

"*He's* meeting with a divorce attorney."

"Apparently he doesn't believe that I'm capable of dealing with such a delicate matter as my own divorce. Besides, he said there's Bignell property and Bignell money involved. Before he left for Minneapolis this morning, he also made it official. He was so impressed by Randy's tale of selfless courage, coupled with the initiative he took in trying to take over Erin's company, that with Brian gone, Randy now becomes his heir apparent."

"I wonder what the Carlson School of Management would say to that."

"Randy draws a salary from Minnesota Foods starting Monday."

"Not what you planned at all," I said.

"We'll see. Time is on my side, not my father's. You haven't answered my question, though—why are you here?"

"I wanted to ask, are you still having Erin followed?"

"No, why would I?"

"Are you having me followed?"

"Again no, why would I? Mr. Schroeder and his investigators have already given me everything that I needed."

"When did you tell Brian that you knew that he was sleeping with another man?"

"Thursday evening. Why does it matter to you?"

Thursday, my inner voice told me. *And the talent from Chicago began following you the next day. That works.*

"What did Brian say when you told him that you had proof that he violated the infidelity clause in your prenuptial agreement?" I asked aloud.

"He said the clause works both ways. But McKenzie, I've

never cheated on my husband. Not once in thirty-two years, and believe me, I've had plenty of opportunities."

"Brian saw us speaking the night of the party. It's possible that he's having me followed because he hopes that we're having an affair, that he can use it against you."

Marilyn stared silently at me long enough for it to become uncomfortable.

"About Randy," I said.

"McKenzie, are you married?"

"No, but—"

"Give me your cell phone."

"Marilyn ..."

"Please."

I drew a diagram of a home plate to unlock the phone and handed it to her. Marilyn tapped the face about fifteen times and paused. I heard the cell phone that she carried in her pocket ring. She tapped the face again, and the ringing stopped. She handed back the phone.

"If you're interested, call me in a couple of months," she said.

I didn't say if I would or wouldn't, just nodded my head and slipped the phone into my own pocket.

"What about Randy?" Marilyn asked.

"Nothing."

"The people who hurt him—how much trouble is he in?"

"He's not in trouble anymore. At least I don't think so."

"Did you help him?"

"In a manner of speaking."

"You helped her, Salsa Girl. By helping her, you inadvertently helped Randy, too. That must have been what happened. You wouldn't have bothered otherwise, would you?"

I slipped a hand beneath the sling and caressed my bandage.

"No, probably not. But Marilyn, keep an eye on him. If you notice him freaking out for some reason, if he's hurt again, give me a call."

"Thank you. I will."

I took my leave after that. Marilyn walked me to my car yet didn't say a word until we reached the Mustang.

"About Salsa Girl," she said. "Tell her ... tell her that I am grateful. Tell her that I'll remember."

"I will."

"By the way, did you ever find out who she really is?"

"I told you. She's my friend."

I drove the Mustang down the long, narrow private road until it intersected a county thoroughfare that led me around the city of Cambridge. That's when I picked him up in my rearview mirror—the black Acura.

"So that's where you were," I said aloud. "Staking out Marilyn."

His sudden presence so close to the Bignell estate more or less convinced me that I had guessed right, that Brian Sax had hired him. I thought of stopping the Mustang, letting the driver come up on my bumper, and asking him about it. But where was the fun in that? I wondered. Besides, what if I was mistaken?

I led the Acura to Highway 65 and drove south. The driver stayed a quarter mile behind me and on my right. Very professional.

As much as I hated to use my cell phone when I was driving, I put in a call to Herzog.

"What now?" he said.

"I'm being followed."

"The black Acura or someone else?"

"It's the Acura again."

"You got a plan?"

"Yeah, I have a plan, but you're not going like it."

"Is this plan anything like what we did yesterday?"

"Pretty close."

" 'Kay, but here's the thing. It's gonna cost you 'nother five grand and you're gonna do all the heavy lifting."

"That works for me."

"I don't wanna see no fuckin' Dyson this time, neither."

"Amen to that."

Exactly thirty minutes later I drove into the same parking lot near Chopper's building as the evening before. Herzog had picked the spot because he figured it would make the driver less anxious than being led out of the city to some isolated location and because he already knew there were no cameras anywhere nearby; that was the kind of thing Herzog paid attention to. There were plenty of high-rise condos and apartment buildings, of course, but we were far enough away from them that anyone who bothered to look outside their windows would only see a couple of indistinguishable figures in the distance.

Herzog was already parked in the lot. I drove past his SUV and stopped my Mustang about thirty spaces away and at a right angle to him. The black Acura slowed and came to a halt on the street. I don't know if he had ID'd Herzog's vehicle or not. I removed the sling for the same reason that I had when I met with Reyes the day before and slipped out of the Mustang. I leaned against it while giving the Acura what Victoria Dunston called a microwave, holding my gloved hand still while slightly wagging my fingers.

I half expected the car to drive away. Instead, it pulled in to the lot and slowly proceeded to a spot about three car lengths away from where I was standing. The car stopped again, its driver's side door was opened, and a man slid out; I noticed that he kept the motor running.

It was the first time I got a good look at the man who had been identified as Levi Chandler. He was about my age and dressed in a wool overcoat that made him look like he worked in one of the tall buildings that made up the Minneapolis skyline. He threw a glance over his shoulder to where Herzog's SUV was parked.

"Is your friend going to join us?" he asked.

"Let's hope it doesn't come to that."

Chandler closed the door and circled the Acura. I folded my arms over my chest as he approached even though it caused my shoulder to throb.

"You've been following me," I said. "Why? Were you too shy to just walk up and say hello?"

"My boss wanted to know everything about you before we talked."

"Who's your boss?"

"Carson Brazill."

Not Brian Sax, my inner voice said. *Although it could be his lover, I suppose.*

"I don't know him," I said aloud.

"He knows you."

"What does he know?"

"He knows where you live. He knows some of your friends. He knows about your woman and the club she owns in St. Paul. It's a nice club. I've been there."

"Do you know which way is east?"

"East? What?"

"Do you know which direction is east from where you're standing?"

Chandler glanced around as if looking for a sign. He found the sun over his left shoulder and pointed to the right.

"Turn that way," I said.

He looked at me as if he were unsure whether I was pranking him or not. I gestured with my chin. He turned to his right. I flicked my hand at Herzog's SUV, and a red dot of light from a laser sight centered on Chandler's chest. He brought his hand up as if he wanted to brush the dot away, just as Reyes had done, but then let it drop. He actually straightened up, his hands at his side, as if bravely facing a firing squad.

"Is this supposed to frighten me?" he asked.

"It frightens me, and I'm not the one who's going to be shot."

"What do you want?"

"You're the guy who's been following me around. You're the guy who's threatening the people I care about."

"I didn't threaten—"

"What do you want, Levi?" I deliberately used Chandler's first name. It's an old cop trick designed to make the suspect feel inferior.

"My boss wants to speak with you, Rushmore."

So he knows the tricks of the trade, too, my inner voice said.

"Fine," I said aloud. "Get him on the phone."

"He wants to meet with you in person."

"Oh? Somewhere we can have each other shot with high-powered rifles?"

"Somewhere public. Somewhere where we can all feel safe. How about Rickie's?"

I took a step toward him and raised my left hand. I made sure Chandler saw me do it.

"If you go anywhere near that place again I'll kill you," I said. "Do you understand?"

He stared at my hand as if I were the one holding the rifle.

"Do you understand?" I repeated.

"Yes."

"Say it."

"I won't go anywhere near Rickie's again," Chandler said.

"You claim you know all about me. Then you know I'm not fucking with you. Not about this."

"This doesn't need to be a thing."

"Then don't make it one."

I stepped backward and slowly lowered my arm until my hand was resting against my thigh. I didn't feel the pain the gesture had caused my shoulder until I heard Chandler sigh.

"Look, McKenzie," he said. "It really doesn't need to be a thing. Talk to the man. He's not going away until you do, and then afterward we can all go home."

My inner voice repeated what it had said the evening before. *Who did you piss off in Chicago?*

"Mall of America," I said aloud. "Are you familiar?"

"Near the airport. What about it?"

"Third floor, south food court, across from Panda Express. Have Brazill meet me there in thirty minutes. In thirty-one minutes, I'll be gone."

"Panda Express? Are you kidding me?"

"You don't need to eat it. Now get out of here."

Chandler moved cautiously to the driver's side of his Acura. The fact that the red dot stayed with him each step of the way made him nervous. Eventually he drove off. I went to the back of the Mustang and popped the trunk. Inside the trunk were the gym bag still filled with the $15,000, the Taurus nine-millimeter, Nick Dyson's IDs, and Randy's flip-phone. I took out $5,000 and closed the bag and the trunk. By then Herzog had driven up. He unrolled the window, and I handed him the cash. He handed it to whoever was sitting behind him. I didn't bother to look for a face.

"So, what?" Herzog asked.

I told him.

"Mall of America," Herzog said. "Want me to go with you?"

"I'd like that very much, but you know those people. Black man like you—security would be watching every step you took from the moment you entered the mall until you left. I want to be safe, but I also want to move about unnoticed."

"They have metal detectors everywhere, McKenzie. You'll never get a piece inside the building."

"Neither will Brazill and his people."

"Yeah, I gitcha. 'Kay. Give me a call later. Let me know if I should be worried."

I said I would.

The Mall of America, just south of the Twin Cities in Bloomington, might have been the most secure building in Minnesota. It had its own on-site police precinct, K-9 units including bomb-sniffing dogs, 150 security guards, many in plainclothes, bicycle patrols around the perimeter, holding cells in the basement, and a dispatch center that monitored God knew how many cameras in the mall itself plus its various parking ramps. It wasn't only that it wanted to protect its 520 stores, 50 restaurants, half-dozen museums and theme parks, 12,000 employees, and 35 million-plus yearly visitors. Apparently it also feared African Americans, Hispanics, anyone who looked Somali or Muslim, shoppers who wore apparel that was likely to cause a disturbance, whatever that meant, and teenagers. Teenagers were forbidden to enter the MOA after 4:00 P.M. unless accompanied by an adult.

I had only been in the place a half-dozen times in the past twenty-five years and never as a result of my own free will. I remembered the Panda Express from the last visit, though; don't ask me why. I was seated at a small round table in the food court opposite the fast food joint, my leather coat draped over the back of the chair, and sipping a root beer from the A&W. I had the distinct impression that I was being watched, although I couldn't tell with any certainty who was doing the watching. I attempted to observe the people around me without being obvious about it. There were many dozens. They all seemed suspicious to me.

I once dated the woman who created the MOA's original theme line—*There's a place for fun in your life ... Mall of*

America. Only I couldn't imagine anyone having fun in what was ostensibly a colossal shopping center. At least I didn't.

My all-purpose watch told me that Brazill was tardy. I was tempted to blow him off, see how much he liked it, when I saw Chandler approaching with a deliberate gait. There was a man walking with him, only not as fast; Chandler needed to slow down so he could catch up. I placed him at about sixty, with white hair and a three-piece Tom Ford suit. He looked like a guy whose idea of fast food was a four-course meal at the Commodore, a bar and restaurant where F. Scott Fitzgerald once hung out.

When they reached my table, Chandler said, "Mr. Brazill, this is—"

"McKenzie," Brazill said.

He made no attempt to shake my hand, so I didn't try to shake his. Instead, I sucked the rest of the root beer through the straw until I hit the bottom of my paper cup and started making a loud slurping sound.

"You're late," I said.

Chandler rolled his eyes as if he couldn't believe I was behaving like such a putz.

Clearly he doesn't know you as well as he thinks he does, my inner voice said.

Brazill glared at me as if he were trying to melt my face with his X-ray vision. I made a production out of looking at my watch.

"So, you want to talk, what?" I said.

Chandler grabbed a plastic chair and held it for Brazill. Brazill glared at him, too, as he sat at the table. Neither of them removed his winter coat.

"I don't like being followed," I said. "It makes me uneasy."

"I don't care," Brazill said. "I have some questions to ask, and you're going to answer them. Make no mistake about that, McKenzie. You're going to answer them. We can do it the easy way or we can do it the hard way, but you're going to tell me what I want to know."

"Wow, that was impressive."

It really was, my inner voice said.

"I might have been frightened, too," I said aloud. "If I knew who you were."

"If you were from Chicago, you would know Mr. Brazill," Chandler said.

"Yeah, well, this isn't Chicago. Fellas, there's a thing we call Minnesota Nice. It's all about being polite and courteous even to people we dislike intensely, like minorities. If you act nice to me, I'll be nice to you. Or not. You never know. Give it a try, see what happens."

Chandler rolled his eyes some more. Brazill leaned in close to me.

"Where's Christine Olson?" he said.

I tried hard not to react to the name. Apparently I didn't do a very good job of it, because Chandler said, "What?" I leaned back in my chair and regarded Brazill carefully before glancing up at him.

"Christine Olson, the woman who went missing in Chicago fifteen years ago?" I said. "That Christine Olson?"

"You do know who she is," Brazill said.

"I don't. I really don't. I came across her name while I was searching for someone else."

"Don't lie to me, McKenzie."

I wagged my finger at Brazill.

"I'd be offended by that suggestion," I told him, "except I have no idea what you're talking about. How would you know what research I'm doing? Why would you care?"

"I've been searching for this woman for fifteen years. You're going to tell me where she is."

"I don't know. Who is this woman, anyway? Who is she to you? A relative? A friend?"

"She has something that belongs to me, and I want it back. Now, where is she?"

The food court grew quiet; heads turned toward us.

"Hey, pal," I said. "This is the Mall of America. You're not allowed to raise your voice here."

Brazill glared some more but said nothing.

"McKenzie," Chandler said, "you told us that you came across Christine's name while searching for someone else. Who?"

"I saw Christine's photos on the missing persons website. It's not the same woman."

Chandler and Brazill exchanged glances as if I had told them something important. This time I was the one who asked, "What?"

"Who were you looking for?" Chandler asked.

"I told you, it's not the same person."

Brazill slapped the tabletop. "Who?"

Brazill's outburst caused more silence and more head-turning. A security guard with a white shirt, gold badge, and blue patch on his shoulder approached from the right. A plain-clothes guard moved on us from the left. Two other men, both wearing suits, rose from their tables. They didn't look like they worked for the MOA, though. They looked like they worked for Brazill.

"Now see what you've done," I said.

The plainclothes man was the first to reach us. He showed a gold badge, flashing it with pride just the way I used to when I was with the cops.

"Is there a problem here, gentlemen?" he asked.

"It's none of your goddamned business," Brazill said.

"Sir, you will lower your voice."

"Fuck you."

Brazill's two henchmen closed on the table. Counting Chandler, he now had three associates surrounding the two fifteen-dollar-an-hour security guards who were flanking him and me.

The security guard remained calm, probably because he knew reinforcements were on the way. "What is your business in the mall?" he asked.

Brazill glared at him.

I had a terrible feeling that this was about to become a Dyson moment, so I stood slowly. I smiled, making sure everyone could see the smile, while I slipped my jacket off the back of the chair.

"I ask you," I said. "If a man can't have a quiet root beer in the Mall of America, where can he? This is all going on my Yelp review."

Brazill glared some more.

I made my way to the corridor, slowing only long enough to deposit my paper cup in the waste bin and put on my coat. By then more security guards were descending on the food court. I wondered if Brazill was dumb enough to pick a fight with them. I hoped he would. In any case, I didn't bother to look back.

TWELVE

Erin Peterson lived in a Minneapolis neighborhood called Prospect Park that had somehow managed to find its way onto the National Register of Historic Places. The houses were built very close together, mostly in the Queen Anne and Colonial Revival styles along narrow, winding streets barely wide enough for two cars to pass. It was easy to get lost, which I did, turning right when I should have turned left. Yet I was able to correct myself by using the Prospect Park Water Tower, often called the Witch's Hat because of its fanciful green ceramic roof, for reference. Some say it was the inspiration for the Bob Dylan song "All Along the Watchtower" because it was clearly visible from Dylan's former home in Dinkytown on the north side of the University of Minnesota campus.

Parking was an issue, as it nearly always was, especially on a Saturday afternoon, and the closest empty spot I could find was six houses past Erin's on the opposite side of the street. There were plenty of people moving through the neighborhood, some riding bikes, some walking dogs, and some walking children. Erin's 1920s house was perched on a low hill. I climbed the concrete steps to her tiny porch and rang the bell. There was a spyhole built into the front door, and a shadow passed over it before the door was yanked open.

Erin appeared. She was wearing tight jeans and a soft green sweater that contrasted nicely with her hair.

"What are you doing here?" she asked. "I thought you were going to call."

"We need to talk."

Erin held the door open so I could pass through it into her house. There were hardwood floors, arched entryways, beamed ceilings, a brick fireplace, vintage lamps, and furniture that looked like it was made the same year as the house. Nina had loved the place when we were last there about two years ago.

I unzipped my leather jacket but didn't take it off.

"Coffee?" Erin said. "Beer?"

"I'm good."

"I hope you don't mind if I have something," she said.

Erin passed into her kitchen with me following behind. Unlike the rest of the house, the kitchen looked like it had been built yesterday as a showplace for a design company. It made for an interesting dichotomy.

There was a delicate-looking cup and saucer already on the granite counter. Erin filled the cup from a French press and took a sip while holding the saucer beneath it. For some reason I thought this was odd, but then I grew up in decidedly blue-collar Merriam Park and drank from a mug emblazoned with an image of the *Millennium Falcon*.

"Are you sure I can't offer you anything?" she asked.

"Carson Brazill."

"Yes, I was afraid it might be him when you mentioned that you had been followed by someone from Chicago."

"He said he's looking for Christine Olson."

"I'm sure he is. It's more comfortable in the living room."

Erin moved past me. I followed her again. She found a spot on a mohair-upholstered chair with carved wooden arms and feet, balancing the saucer with one hand and drinking from the cup with the other.

"Tell me you weren't followed," she said.

"I wasn't followed."

"Are you sure?"

"Very sure. Who's Carson Brazill? Who's Christine Olson?"

"Christine is a figment of my imagination. I wish I could say the same of Carson. How did he look, by the way? Did you see him?"

"He looked like a congressman who dreams of one day becoming a lobbyist for the coal industry. Erin—"

"What did you tell him?"

"About Christine? I told him I never met the woman, that I had no idea who she was."

"He didn't believe you, though, did he?"

"No."

"I wouldn't think so."

Erin set the cup on the saucer and held both in front of her as she leaned her head against the back of the chair and closed her eyes. She was speaking to herself, yet I heard her just the same.

"So close, so close," she said. "I can't lose now."

"Salsa Girl?"

Erin's eyes snapped open and she looked up at me.

"How can I help you?" I asked.

"You might not want to after you've heard my story."

"Have you murdered someone?"

"Of course not."

"Then tell me what I can do for you."

"Really? Not being a murderer is where you set the bar when deciding whether or not to help someone? That's awfully broadminded."

"It helps that we're friends."

"I could use a friend." Erin turned her head and stared out

of her living room window at the sidewalk and street beyond. "I'm not sure, though, that—oh." Erin's eyes grew wide and she sighed deeply, dramatically. "Not followed, huh?"

I rushed to the window and looked out. Four men, all dressed in suits, stood in the center of the street three houses down. I recognized them all—Brazill, Chandler, and their two minions. They were looking at the houses around them as if they were unsure which direction to turn.

"How did they …" I smacked my forehead with my left hand; I figured I deserved the stab of pain the gesture brought to my shoulder. "Dammit, Erin. This is on me. They must have tagged my Mustang while it was in the parking lot last night. That's how they found me in Cambridge this morning, only I was too dumb to catch on at the time."

"You were in Cambridge?"

I turned around. Erin had left the comfort of her chair and was standing behind me, balancing the saucer in one hand and the coffee cup in the other. She seemed perfectly calm.

"We have much to talk about," I told her.

"Where are you parked?" Erin asked.

"A block down from here and across the street."

"That means they have no way of knowing which house we're in."

"Judging by the way Brazill and Chandler are wandering up and down the street—no. Maybe they think we'll step outside and wave, invite them in for French press coffee."

Erin sipped what was left of the brew and set both the cup and saucer on an antique table.

"What would you do if you were them?" she asked.

"They can't loiter much longer, not in this neighborhood. Someone is bound to become suspicious and call the police. What I would do, I'd go back to my car and pretend to be inconspicuous. But first, I'd take down the address of every house in the immediate vicinity. While I was sitting in the car, I'd use my smartphone to run the addresses one at a time through the Hennepin County property tax website. Among other things, that would provide me with the name of each homeowner, as well as whoever is paying taxes on the property—this is all public record, you see. If that didn't tell me what I wanted to know, I'd Google each of the names, using the addresses to narrow the search. Between Facebook, LinkedIn, Whitepages, and all the other sites that are available and the images that are posted on them, it shouldn't be too hard to decide which door to knock on."

"How long do you think that would take?"

"Twenty minutes."

"Plenty of time."

"To do what?"

"Make good my escape."

"Erin, you can always call the cops yourself."

"No, I don't think so. Besides, what could they do for me besides delay the inevitable? These people have been chasing Christine Olson for fifteen years. They're not going to stop now."

"Who exactly are these people?"

"The Outfit."

"The Outfit? The organized crime family based in Chicago that was started by Johnny Torrio and Al Capone—that Outfit?"

"Yes."

"Oh, oh, oh, oh, oh ..."

"You seem concerned."

"Wait. The Outfit doesn't have a presence in Minneapolis. The Cities have been pretty much free of organized crime ever since they put Isadore 'Kid Cann' Blumenfeld away for violating the Mann Act and jury tampering in the early sixties."

"I know. That's why I originally moved here."

"I was right before—we really do have a lot to talk about."

"There's no reason for you to continue involving yourself in my troubles."

"You mean besides the fact that I'm responsible for leading a squad of career criminals to the street where you live?"

Erin made the sign of the cross in the air in front of me.

"I absolve you of all your sins," she said.

"What? No penance?"

I stared out the bay window at the street. The four gangsters had split up and were now moving independently up and down the adjacent streets, peering at houses as if they could see inside them.

"I need to get to my car," I said.

"Your car has been tagged, remember. They probably attached a tracking device to your bumper and used a sat nav system to determine your location."

"Let me rephrase—I need to get something out of my car?"

"What?"

"A gym bag filled with $10,000 in cash, a burn phone, fake IDs, and a nine-millimeter handgun."

"Always prepared; I knew you were a Boy Scout. But McKenzie, we don't need those things."

"Fifteen years you say you've been running from these guys? Do you want to keep running? For how long? The rest of your life? Think of what you've built here. Think of what you'll be giving up."

"I have been. I've been thinking about it very hard, believe me."

"Well, then."

"Don't tell me you already have a plan."

I tapped my temple with two fingers.

"The wheels are spinning," I said. "But I'm going to need to get to my car."

"In that case, I have an idea."

Erin told me what it was.

"I have to say, Salsa Girl—I'm astonished by how calmly you're taking all of this."

"I assure you, McKenzie, I am anything but calm. And don't call me Salsa Girl."

I escaped Erin's house through her back door, crossing her tiny yard, hopping a fence—which caused my shoulder to ache some more—cutting through the yard of the neighbor directly behind her, and moving in a straight line, crossing two streets and four more yards until I reached the base of the small park where the Witch's Hat was located. I hung a left, walked nearly a quarter mile, hung another left until I hit Erin's street, and started walking back toward her house and my Mustang. I saw one of Brazill's henchmen a couple of blocks directly in front of me, only he was on the other side of my car and facing the opposite direction.

My leather jacket was unzipped, and when I lowered my head it looked as if I were speaking to my inside pocket.

"I'm nearly there," I said.

I kept walking; it was all I could do to keep from breaking into a run. The only reason I didn't run was I was afraid of bringing undue attention to myself.

"Thirty seconds," I said.

Up ahead, the henchman stopped and watched while a BMW backed quickly out of Erin Peterson's garage and down her short driveway. 'Course, he didn't know whose garage and driveway it was. The car backed into the street. For some inexplicable reason, the henchman glanced over his shoulder. And saw me.

"It's him." He pointed in my direction. "There, there, there."

I didn't see who he was yelling to, and I didn't bother to look. Instead, I sprinted the rest of the way to the Mustang. I popped the trunk with the button on my key fob and grabbed the gym bag. The henchman was nearly on me. But Erin had been quicker. She screeched the BMW to a halt next to the Mustang.

I stepped into the street, opened the passenger door, and slid inside. Erin drove off as I was closing the door. I glanced behind me. The henchman held a gun. He raised it with two hands and sighted on us. Before he could shoot, though, Chandler appeared at his side. He placed his own hand on the henchman's gun and pushed downward until the muzzle was pointed at the ground.

Meanwhile, the black Acura pulled out of its parking space and motored down the street behind us. It stopped only long enough for Chandler and the henchman to climb aboard. Erin turned, and I lost sight of it.

"I should drive," I said. I pulled my cell phone from my pocket and tapped the END CALL icon; that was how Erin had heard me talking to her.

"Because?" Erin said.

"Police academy." I slipped the cell back into my pocket. "I was trained to do this."

"I thought you were going to say it was because you're a manly man who does manly things in a manly way."

"Excuse me. What?"

"Something I heard you say once when you were asked why you still play hockey at your advanced age."

"Advanced age? How old do you think I am?"

Erin was glancing at her rearview mirror when she said, "Put on your seat belt, please."

I glanced through the rear window. The Acura was on our tail and coming fast. I was relieved to see that Chandler and his pals weren't leaning out the windows of their vehicle and spraying Prospect Park with bullets like they do in the movies.

Professionals, my inner voice said.

I put on the seat belt.

Erin accelerated hard while threading her way through the narrow streets. She let the Beemer drift to the left side of the street as she approached an intersection, braking gradually at first and then more heavily before swinging the steering wheel hard to the right, making sure her tires were as close as possible to the inside edge of the corner as she turned. Once clear she stomped on the accelerator again, and the BMW leapt forward.

The most important thing to remember in a high-speed chase, or so I had been instructed, was not to crash, because even if you survived the accident you were going to be a sitting duck. That's why high speeds were not recommended. By keeping your speedometer under sixty miles per hour, you'd have greater control of your vehicle and evasive maneuvers would be easier to accomplish. Erin seemed to understand this; Brazill and his minions not so much. I didn't see it because Erin had maneuvered the BMW through another tight right turn, but I was sure I heard the distinct crunch of metal against metal behind us. Erin made two lefts and one more right that brought us to University Avenue heading for St. Paul, where she slowed to the speed limit. I could no longer see the Acura.

"Ms. Peterson?" I said.

"Mr. McKenzie?"

"You can drive."

She thought that was awfully funny.

We didn't remain on University for long, only a couple of blocks, before Erin turned off. My first thought was that she was heading for her place of business; not a good idea. I would have told her so except that a couple more turns brought us to the service road that ran alongside I-94. At the end of the service road was a sprawling, three-story storage facility. I decided it wasn't a coincidence that the facility was located almost midway between where Erin lived and where she worked.

She halted the BMW at the gate leading to the storehouse,

slipped out of the car, and walked quickly to an electronic control unit mounted on a steel pole. She inputted a code from memory, and the gate began to slide open. Once back in the car, she waited until the gate was opened fully and drove through it, following the concrete driveway to a metal garage door large enough for furniture trucks. She paused until the gate behind us closed. When it did, the garage door opened automatically, and Erin drove inside.

The building reminded me of a parking ramp, except instead of spaces, there were car-sized storage units lining the walls on both sides of the wide driveway. We followed it, passing a bank of huge elevators where people could unload their belongings onto dollies and lift them to the smaller storage units on the second and third floors. Finally Erin halted the BMW. She turned off the car, got out, and made her way to a garage door. There was a lock that she opened with a key. The door was on rollers, and it was easy for her to push it open. Inside the storage unit was a car, its hood up, its battery connected to a charger that was plugged into a wall socket.

She disconnected the charger, closed the hood, negotiated the narrow space between the garage wall and the car, and opened the driver's side door. She slipped inside. The car started with little effort. Erin drove it out of the garage onto the storage facility's wide driveway. I recognized it as a two-door Toyota Solara coupe, a car they stopped manufacturing in 2008. It was light brown, Desert Sand I think they called it, the least noticeable color for a car. Erin turned it off and got out. She threw me the keys. I caught them with my left hand and winced.

"Where's your sling?" Erin asked.

"I left it in the Mustang."

"Was that a good idea?"

"No."

"Put the Beemer inside."

I did as she asked. After parking the BMW, I carried my gym bag out of the garage. Erin had removed both her coat and her green sweater and was now standing with her naked back to me. I considered briefly how smooth her skin looked—*C'mon, McKenzie,* my inner voice said, *focus*—and then shook the thought from my head.

The trunk of the Solara was open. Erin reached inside and pulled out a light blue pullover that matched the color of her bra and put it on. I moved to the trunk and looked at the contents. There were two suitcases. One was opened. Along with clothes, it contained a number of burn phones and a handful of prepaid credit cards bound with a rubber band. I picked up the credit cards.

"Prepaid credit cards can be purchased without a credit check." Erin used a hair tie to pull her golden hair into a ponytail. "They aren't connected to your bank account, and because the money is front-loaded, your transactions are never reported to credit agencies." She flipped the ponytail over the top of her head and secured it in place with a wig cap.

"How much is here?" I asked.

Erin carefully fit a medium-length red wig over the cap.

"About fifty thousand," she said. "There's cash, too."

I dropped the credit cards back into the suitcase and tossed the gym bag next to it.

"Pretty elaborate go-bag," I said. "Obviously you've been planning this for some time."

Erin used a handheld mirror to make sure her wig fit properly.

"I've been tinkering with it every few months for over ten years," she said. "It's like maintaining a storm shelter in your backyard. You never actually want to use it. How do I look?"

I examined the red wig.

"Good," I said. "Although I prefer you as a blonde."

"That's because it's what you're used to. Here."

Erin gave me a Minnesota Twins baseball hat. I put it on while she slipped on a black fleece jacket.

"Keys," she said.

I returned them to her. Erin slammed the trunk lid shut and moved back to the garage door. She pulled it down and locked it.

"Is your shoulder okay?" she asked. "Are you good to drive?'

"Yes."

She tossed the keys to me as she started back to the Solara. I climbed into the driver's side while Erin made herself comfortable in the passenger seat.

"Straight at the door," she said. "Not too fast."

I drove slowly toward the huge garage door at the end of the driveway. It opened when I was close enough to trip an electronic eye. I drove out of the storage facility toward yet another gate. This one also opened without our having to input a code. We soon found ourselves on a city street.

"Where to?" I asked.

"You decide."

"I have property up north."

"Then we should go in the opposite direction. Give me your phone."

I passed my cell over and maneuvered the Solara onto I-94 and headed east. Erin opened my phone, removed the battery, and gave both back to me. I slipped them into my pocket.

"Nice car," I said. "I'm surprised Toyota stopped making them."

"They didn't sell as well as the Camry. This is a first-generation model, built in 1999. You'll notice it has no computer, no GPS."

"I did notice. I assume that's why you dismantled my cell phone, to deactivate the GPS."

"Better safe than sorry."

Soon we were crossing the Lafayette Bridge and driving south on Highway 52.

"Who goes first?" I asked.

"What do you mean?"

"Should I tell you my story, or would you prefer to tell me yours?"

"How badly did Randy hurt me?"

I explained, starting with Alice Pfeifer's phone call yesterday afternoon and ending with my meeting with Carson Brazill at the Mall of America that morning.

"Randy Bignell-Sax." Erin spoke as if they were the saddest words she had ever heard. "Can you believe anyone is that stupid? Now they're going to put him in charge of Bignell Bakeries and Minnesota Foods. That's a corporate catastrophe waiting to happen. I never thought I'd feel sorry for Marilyn."

"Yeah, well, that's what's happening on the north side of the Cities. On the south side we have two people fleeing the Outfit in a nineteen-year-old Solara."

"Nothing of what you said Randy did explains how Carson found me."

"I'm still not entirely sure who this Carson is. Or who you are, either, for that matter."

Erin spent a lot of time staring out the side window. She didn't speak until we were approaching Hastings.

"Once upon a time, there was a young woman," she said. "No, not a woman. A girl who was nowhere near as smart as she thought she was ..."

She was sure everyone was looking at her and wondering what kind of woman she must be to expose herself like that—sprawled out on a beach lounge in the skimpiest bikini she had ever seen much less worn. She had a white cardigan cover-up, but her boyfriend wouldn't allow her to put it on. Averill

*Naylor had worked hard over the years to make himself rich,
and he wanted everyone to know it. He was almost desperate
to flaunt his wealth and the things that it could buy, like his
Brioni suits, gold Patek Philippe watch, Jaguar XJ sports car,
and beautiful blond girlfriend who was literally fifty years
younger than he was, so no, he wouldn't let her conceal her
body even if the Jamaican sun was sautéing her pale skin. Nor
would he let her cover her bare shoulders with a chiffon shawl
when she entered the dining room in the strapless sequined
gown he had bought for her, or even wear her sunglasses in public. He wanted her to be seen, all of her, he said. That's why he
brought her to the resort. So people could see her. So they could
see him with her.*

*She knew all that, of course; she understood perfectly that
she was little more than an ornament to him. It embarrassed
her anyway. She worked hard not to show it, though. Averill
would become upset if she appeared uncomfortable when they
went out together. Once he caught her tugging on the bodice of
her evening gown because she was afraid it would slip down
and bare her breasts. He slapped her hands and hissed, "Don't
do that." Later, he apologized. He wasn't a bad man, she told
herself. Most of the time he was very pleasant company, kind
and generous, even sweet. But the slap reminded her why she
had agreed to let him escort her to Jamaica and Las Vegas and
to all those parties and openings and charity galas in Chicago.
She did it for the money.*

*It wasn't the career path she had originally chosen for herself.
She had studied economics at Northwestern University, but
her bachelor's degree had left her with over $100,000 of debt.
She had job offers, mostly from banks and insurance companies.
To pay her bills, she took a position at a credit bureau even
though she knew it was a dead-end job. As it was, after subtract-
ing the barest living expenses, she discovered that her salary
scarcely allowed her to pay the interest on her student loans,*

much less whack away at the principal. Nor did she have family she could lean on, parents she could live with while she dug herself out of the financial hole that college had dropped her in.

"I told you the truth when I said I was an orphan, McKenzie," Erin said. "My father really did die when I was a child. My mother passed just two months after I started school. My inheritance paid for my first two years' tuition."

"You lied when you said you went to the University of Wisconsin."

"I lied about a lot of things."

"When you said—"

"Do you want me to tell you the story or not?"

"Go 'head."

She attended a party with many of her former classmates, some of whom were in the same position as she was, including an ex-boyfriend who had attended DePaul University. Alcohol was consumed and stories were exchanged. Late in the evening a woman pulled her aside, an art history major, who told her that she knew how a girl who was both smart and pretty could make some easy money if she was willing. The art major was very beautiful, and the young woman was jealous of her.

"Startling blue eyes and short black hair," Erin said. "She looked a little like Nina."

"Yeah, okay," I said.

Still, she was outraged. Was the art major suggesting prostitution? Turning tricks in some hot-sheet motel for $100 a client?

Acting in adult films perhaps, making $1,000 to $1,800 per sex scene? The art major was upset that the economics major would think so little of her. I was trying to do you a favor, she said. What favor? I know people I can introduce you to. What people? Never mind. No, tell me. Older men. What about them? They'll pay you to be seen with them. Prostitution. No. What do you call it? An economics professor at the University of Chicago says it's like renting a trophy wife by the hour. That's where the smart part of it comes in, the art major said. According to her, these men wanted young and attractive women that they could have an intelligent conversation with, women they could introduce to their friends and associates without being embarrassed. Who's smarter than you are? the art major asked. Who's prettier?

The economics major appreciated the art major's compliments, yet said thanks-but-no-thanks just the same. That's when the art major mentioned that she had made $6,000 for twelve hours of work the previous week and hadn't slept with anyone she didn't want to. The economics major did the math quickly—at $500 an hour for twelve hours a week, she could pay off her student loans in a little over four months. Quicker, if she logged more hours.

She reminded herself that she wasn't a virgin saving herself for marriage; she had had a healthy sex life at Northwestern, mostly with college boys who had no idea what they were doing. What difference would it make if she hooked up with older men for a change, she asked herself? She wouldn't be like a real prostitute. Real prostitutes worked the streets because they were being forced to by some guy, or because they needed money for drugs, or whatever. It was a bad situation, but it wouldn't be her situation. She'd be a partner in her exploitation. No, not a partner. She'd be the sole proprietor of a service business that was ostensibly no different than accounting or banking.

She hadn't entirely talked herself into it, though. Even economics majors have some sense of morality. Yet she had agreed to accompany the art major to a gathering on Sheridan Road. It was surreal—so many older men and a few older women mingling with so many younger women and a few younger men with no age group in between, as if the world had somehow skipped an entire generation. What surprised her even more, though, was how much she enjoyed herself. The conversations were about art, history, politics, the theater, even economics. No one spoke about sports or work or the latest Marvel superhero movie.

Averill Naylor approached her while she was examining a quirky painting by Chagall. The small canvas caught her eye while she was returning from the restroom. She looked closely to see if it was real or a print. Of course, it was real. Averill asked if she was an admirer. The economics major said that she didn't particularly care for the modernists but that one had to admire Chagall's use of color. He asked what kind of art she favored. She said that it might seem like a contradiction, but she admired the realists like Courbet and Daumier as well as the Pre-Raphaelites like Rossetti and Waterhouse.

Averill smiled at the young woman as if he were proud of her and introduced himself. She said her name was Christine Olson . . .

"So that is your real name," I said.

"No, it's not," Erin said. "Pay attention, McKenzie."

Averill Naylor was a handsome man for his age, tall and thin with a shock of white hair, and looking at him, the economics major knew that if he asked her out she would accept. Yet something tugged at her. Maybe it was her sense of propriety; she didn't know. She did know that if she agreed to enter Averill's world, it would be only for a short time; she would take what she needed, and afterward she would never look back. At the same time, she wanted to be sure the life wouldn't follow her. So she invented her new identity on the spot, and Averill accepted it without question. Not once during the time they were together did he ever ask to see her ID.

"Eventually I would create a false identity to go with the name Christine Olson," Erin said. "We'll get to that later."

For their first date, Averill escorted her to the Art Institute of Chicago. He was very attentive and very knowledgeable, and they held hands like lovers as they maneuvered from one exhibit to another. Christine noticed people watching them, the old man holding the young woman's hand. Averill enjoyed the attention. Christine felt awkward and uncomfortable, yet she never once removed her hand from his. After he drove her to her apartment, he gave her an envelope. She hesitated before taking it, and when she did, she pushed it down into her purse without opening it. He seemed to like that, too.

Averill asked if she would spend more time with him. Christine agreed. She said something then that surprised them both, mostly because it was so obviously true—she couldn't remember the last time she had enjoyed herself so much in a man's company. Averill kissed her cheek.

Later, alone in her apartment, Christine opened the envelope. It contained $2,000.

They didn't sleep together until her earnings topped $25,000, and then it was she who made the first move, literally taking Averill's hand and leading him to the bedroom. Christine didn't do it for the money. She did it because over the weeks she had come to genuinely care for him. Averill had been as surprised *by the turn of events as Christine was. Yet he never stopped giving her envelopes, and she never stopped accepting them.*

They had reached $64,500 when Averill died of a heart attack in his condominium overlooking Millennium Park. Christine had stepped out of the bathroom wearing only her panties and discovered him lying naked on his bed, his hands clasped behind his head as if he had been contemplating something pleasant.

She could have gotten dressed and walked out; there was no foul play involved, nothing for the police to investigate once someone discovered Averill's body. Yet she couldn't leave him like that for some cleaning woman to find. Instead, Christine called 911 and told the operator that her friend had died— because she was his friend.

Averill's death had affected Christine more than she could have imagined. She spent the next three days in bed, calling in sick to work, leaving her apartment only to attend his funeral. She remained in the back of the chapel, keeping to herself. Yet the whispers floated around her. Somehow the mourners had learned that she was "that woman."

Averill had scrupulously kept her away from his family. Now they came at her—sons and daughters, brothers and sisters, nieces and nephews. They said that Averill had merely been going through a difficult phase, a bad patch, and that she had taken advantage of him; it was as if they believed he had been suffering a midlife crisis at age seventy-one. They told her if she was expecting more money, if she thought that somehow she had weaseled herself into Averill's will, to forget it. They had friends in City Hall. They would crush her. Christine listened to it all, suffering their slings and arrows without comment even when they called her a whore and a prostitute. She wasn't entirely sure they were wrong.

Finally, as Christine was leaving, a woman her age— Averill's granddaughter, as it turned out—intercepted her at the door. She said that Averill had been deeply unhappy for many years after his wife had died, except for those months at the end when he had been involved with Christine. She hugged Christine and said thank you, told her she was a good person, and wished her a happy life.

Christine ran to her car, hoping to get inside before she broke down in tears. She nearly made it . . .

"I can't tell you how much that small act of kindness meant to me, McKenzie," Erin said. "It changed my life. Not then, though. No, it was much, much later. I had to hit rock bottom first."

THIRTEEN

We had left Highway 52 and were now on Highway 61, still heading south. The city of Red Wing was receding in the rear-view mirror. On our right was a cyclone fence that was both long and high, with the top curved inward to deter people from climbing over it. On the other side of the fence was a series of Romanesque buildings that reminded me of the kind of English boarding school that you only see in the movies.

"What is this place?" Erin asked.

"Minnesota Correctional Facility, mostly for juveniles and a few adults the system still believes it can save."

"Maybe we should stop and I could check in, save everyone a lot of trouble."

"You're determined to be a pessimist, aren't you?"

"I was still heavily in debt, McKenzie ..."

Averill had paid Christine nearly $65,000, but she hadn't used it all to pay down her student loans as she had originally planned. Instead, she bought a car and upgraded her wardrobe and moved to a better apartment. As a result, she still owed well over $50,000, and because of the apartment and car, she also had a higher overhead than when she started. After a few weeks, she decided to return to the house on Sheridan Road. She was welcomed there; Averill had sung her praises to his friends. Dates were arranged. Christine didn't enjoy them nearly as much as she had enjoyed her time with Averill, though. Most of the men were more sexually aggressive than he had been. One in particular—his name was Len Grollman—had all but raped her. Afterward, he told Christine how much fun he had and said he hoped that they could do it again some-time. The contents of the envelope he gave her did little to as-suage her anger. Or her despondency. The evening with Grollman made it clear to her what she had become.

The rational part of Christine's mind told her to quit, told her that a lot of people had student loans and got by just fine. It told her to concentrate on her daytime job, make more of an effort, work herself up into a management position. But the dark side that she had tapped into when she returned to Sher-idan Road after Averill's death wouldn't allow it. It was as if she were trying to punish herself. How else could she explain why she had subjected herself to a second date with Grollman, one that had left her both physically bruised and emotionally shaken? It might have been role-playing for him, yet it was real enough to Christine.

That's when Carson Brazill approached her.

He was older than Christine by about fifteen years, which made him young compared to the men she had been seeing. Plus, he had an easy charm; there was nothing desperate about him, which was something else that was new to her. He asked if she had ever considered a life of luxury and deceit. It was an old Rodney Dangerfield line, something from one of his movies, and there was a time when it would have made her laugh. Only now she didn't think it was particularly funny and told him so. Brazill said that was the response he was looking *for. He said he knew about her relationship with Averill Naylor and with the other men she met on Sheridan Road; he said he knew everything about her, which Christine discovered weeks later to be untrue. He didn't know her real name, for example. Christine asked him what he wanted. He said he needed a partner. Five hundred dollars an hour, she said. Not that kind of partner, he said. What, then?*

"Lenny Grollman—we're going to fuck him up."

Christine liked that idea very much and asked him what he had in mind. Brazill told her she merely had to endure one more rendezvous with Grollman, only this time there would be audio, there would be video. Blackmail, she guessed. In a manner of speaking, he said. What was in it for her? Ten thousand dollars. Again her rational mind tried to warn her, telling Christine that ignoring whatever else she had been doing up till then, this was a real crime; she would be a real criminal. Looking back later, she was shocked by how quickly she said, "Okay."

The last time Christine saw Grollman in person was when he was leaving a hotel room with a tourist's view of Grant Park. He was upset that Christine wouldn't stop weeping after he took her and said he didn't think this relationship would work out; she didn't have the proper attitude. She would, however, see Grollman's photograph in the newspapers and his image on TV in the coming weeks as an alleged sex scandal forced him from his position on the Cook County Board of Commissioners— Christine hadn't even known he was a commissioner. The sex scandal was "alleged" because it was something that anonymous sources whispered to the media; no details and no names were reported except for the name of the hotel on Michigan Avenue where Grollman's assignations were supposed to have occurred. Certainly Grollman didn't explain his abrupt resignation except to say that he wanted to spend more time with his family.

A short time later, the Board of Commissioners approved a real estate development along the North Shore by a head count of nine to eight. Grollman's replacement had cast the deciding vote. On a previous ballot, Grollman had voted against the development.

Shortly after that, Brazill approached Christine again, this time with a small bag filled with the promised $10,000 in cash and a job offer.

"Have you ever heard of Murder Incorporated, McKenzie?" Erin asked.

"Yes."

"Then you know that it was an enforcement arm for organized crime in the thirties and forties. How it worked—if a boss needed someone killed in, say, St. Louis, he would contact the Commission in New York. If the Commission approved, Murder Incorporated would be given the contract. It would send a hit team to St. Louis to execute the contract while making sure that there was little or no collateral damage to both civilians and the local police. The killers were paid a regular salary as well as an average fee of $1,000 to $5,000 per killing. Their families also received monetary benefits. If the killers were caught, the mob would hire the best lawyers for their defense. Murder Incorporated killed a couple of thousand people before it was finally exposed.

"I learned during my meeting with Carson that he was a dues-paying member of the Outfit and that the Outfit had been so delighted with how well he had handled the Grollman situation that they agreed to let Carson assemble and manage Blackmail Incorporated—that's what I called it. I don't think it had a real name. Instead of killing their opponents, the Outfit tasked the group with finding nonlethal methods to compro-

mise them—to get them to see things their way, if you know
what I mean. Either that or frame them for some misdeed or
another that would render them powerless to oppose the Outfit's plans, whatever they might be. Carson wanted me to join
his team. At the time, I was also so pleased with what had happened to Grollman that I said yes."

*Christine was surprised at how much fun it was, especially in
the beginning. Typically the marks they targeted were smart—
politicians, prosecutors, police officers, businessmen and women,
journalists, even clergymen. Many of them also had people
around who were looking out for their interests. That meant,
for the most part, they were not susceptible to something simple
like the badger game; they were not going to allow themselves
to be lured into a motel-room tryst and then extorted. Only
the long con would do, and that required preparation and
research—something that Christine had always excelled at,
one of the reasons she had become an economist. Blackmail Incorporated would scrutinize their targets with great intensity
to learn their weaknesses, and then she and Brazill would create a character to exploit them that Christine would invari-
ably play.*

"I doubt Meryl Streep or Cate Blanchett ever prepared for a role
as meticulously as I did," Erin said.

*Each role Christine performed was different because each mark
was different. Yet they were all based on real people. If the
character needed to be well versed in anthropology to appeal
to the mark, Blackmail Incorporated would scour the alumni*

records of various colleges and universities until they found a woman with a degree in anthropology who fit Christine's general age and appearance, and Christine would then claim that identity for her own. If a mark or one of his people checked with the school, the school would say yes, of course, Ms. So-and-So graduated on a certain date with a bachelor's and/or master's degree in such-and-such. More often than not, that was as far as the background searches would go, the marks deciding if one thing was true, then all of Christine's story must be true. If they did look further, at her job or family history, for example, Blackmail Incorporated would have salted the internet with enough social media evidence to cover that as well.

For the duration of the con, Christine would become a different person—a New England Brahmin, Southern Belle, Midwest Farmer's Daughter, California Golden Girl, soft or hard, flirtatious or shy, pious maiden or promiscuous minx. It distracted her from what she had become so drearily, a woman without illusions.

"Should I tell you the secret, McKenzie?" Erin asked. "The secret is that you never, ever approach the mark. You make the mark approach you. You make it seem as if it's all his or her idea. That's how I justified myself. If the marks had kept their distance, if they had just said no, nothing bad would have happened to them. I told myself they had brought the misery on themselves—like I had."

"You said you hit rock bottom."

"I didn't have an epiphany, if that's what you mean. There wasn't a specific moment when I saw myself for what I was and vowed to change my life. It was more like a general ache, a kind of throbbing pain that filled all of my days when I wasn't working, when I wasn't pretending to be someone else. I kept replaying the scene where Averill's granddaughter thanked me for bringing happiness into his life. I hadn't brought a moment of joy to anyone else since, not even to myself, and it was eating me alive. McKenzie, I lived in the gutter for so long …

"Finally, one morning, I got into my car, my rental car—we were working a mark in Raleigh, North Carolina, of all places. I got into the car and drove away. I didn't tell anyone; I left no notes. Carson must have thought the mark had made me and took steps to protect himself. That gave me some extra time. I knew Carson would come after me when he discovered the truth."

"He said you have something that belongs to him."

"I'm sure he sees it that way, but the thing is—we were skimming, McKenzie. The Outfit would ask us to compromise a mark in order to convince him to appoint a certain person to a certain commission or support a specific candidate for sheriff or drop charges against one of its people or, I don't know, plant a story in the *Chicago Sun-Times*; something like that. But we also took money. The Outfit didn't know about that, though, the money. We had kept it all to ourselves. When I left, I took half of the cash we had collected, $680,000 and change. If I had known Carson was going to be such a prick about it, I would have taken it all."

I pulled the cell phone and battery from my pocket and gave them to Erin.

"Put that back together," I said.

"McKenzie …"

"You can make sure the GPS is turned off, but I need the phone."

"Why?"

"Because I can never remember anyone's number, that's why."

Erin did what I asked. I took the phone, unlocked it with

my thumb, and scrolled to my phone contact information. I tapped the icon for her business because Nina often leaves her cell in her bag when she was working. A woman's voice said, "Rickie's, how may I help you?" I recognized the voice.

"Jenness," I said, "this is McKenzie. Let me speak to the boss."

Half a minute later, Nina said, "Are you all right? I've been trying to reach you, but your phone keeps sending me to voice mail."

"I'm fine. Why have you been trying to reach me?"

"You have that sound in your voice."

"What sound?"

"That serious sound you get when you think I might be in trouble."

"Why were you trying to reach me?" I repeated.

"You told me this morning that you were being followed, remember? Well, there's a man sitting at the bar nursing a Heineken. All he's been doing for the past thirty minutes is watching the door—and me."

"Describe him."

She did. It was the wool coat that clinched it.

"Yeah, that's what I was afraid of. Don't go near him, and don't leave the club."

"Are you coming over?"

"No. I'm too far away and heading in the opposite direction. I'll send somebody else."

"Who?"

"You'll know him when you see him."

"McKenzie, should I be afraid?"

"No. The man in the wool coat is there to frighten me."

After saying good-bye, I ended the call and used my thumb to find another contact on my phone list. I tapped his icon. He answered after two rings.

"McKenzie, what?" Herzog said.

"Nina's at Rickie's. So is Levi Chandler."

" 'Kay."

"Herzy?" I said.

He was already gone. I returned the cell to Erin, who promptly took the battery out.

"We could go back," she said.

"We will go back, just not right now."

"If they're threatening Nina—I don't want anyone hurt because of me."

My inner voice knew the truth. *If it comes down to a choice between Nina and Erin, that's a trade we'll make in a heart-beat. Let's just hope it doesn't come to that.*

"Finish your story," I said aloud.

Christine went on the run. It wasn't a particularly difficult thing to do if you knew how. After all, there's a reason why the FBI's Ten Most Wanted Fugitives list hardly ever changes.

Christine knew you never tried to fake your own death. They had a name for that—pseudocide—and it brought out cops and volunteers and dogs and news crews and helicopters and questions about your remains. Faking sent up emergency flares.

She knew that you never tried to create a false identity, either. It might work for the short term, the length of a long con, for example. Yet it would never fool the cops, FBI, or customs agents. And if you shelled out the bucks for a black-market spe-cial complete with Social Security number, you might find yourself buying someone else's bad debts and arrest record. Not to mention that the black-marketer probably sold the same ID to a dozen other people as well.

Instead, Christine knew that to disappear successfully, you needed to diminish the shadow you cast. You kept your iden-tity, but you hid your location. You melted into the crowd— no sports leagues, no social clubs or networks, no Facebook or

LinkedIn accounts, nothing that said, "Look at me." You never
snuck home to try to reclaim some of what you left behind. You
never Googled yourself to learn what people were saying about
you. You never visited the sites where information about miss-
ing persons was stored, because cops and skip tracers could be
waiting to capture your IP address and trace your location . . .

"Oops," I said.

"What?"

"That's how Brazill must have found me. I looked up Christine Olson on the missing persons page of the Illinois State
Police website."

"I asked you not to research me, didn't I?"

"Yes."

"But you did it anyway. You just can't help yourself, can
you?"

"Now I feel bad."

"I hope you do."

"I'm sorry."

"Damn, McKenzie . . ."

"The pics that were posted on the website—they weren't of
you."

"Carson must have provided them. He doesn't want anyone
to find me but him."

Christine had a plan. It involved leaving bread crumbs for
Brazill to follow. She would make a phone call from Nashville,
six months later send an email from Oklahoma City, and six
months after that accidentally bump into a member of the
Outfit she knew in Dallas. Slowly, meticulously, she led Brazill
across the country. Finally she made it known that Christine

Olson was working in a restaurant in Sierra Vista, New Mexico.

"Best salsa I ever had," Erin said. "The owners of the restaurant made it themselves. I stole the recipe."
    "Of course you did," I said.

By the time Brazill and his people arrived in Sierra Vista, however—poof—Chrstine had disappeared, leaving evidence that she had managed to cross the border into Mexico. That's where the trail went cold until some self-important kibitzer decided to play detective.

"I said I was sorry. Besides, if you hadn't used the name when you went to visit John Ripley from Central Valley International, I wouldn't have even thought of Googling Christine Olson."
    "Nonetheless ..."

Erin Peterson moved to Minnesota because the Outfit had no presence there; it was highly unlikely that she would ever encounter someone who knew her from her previous life. It was difficult at first because she had lived so long under the name Christine Olson that sometimes she didn't respond to her own.

"Erin Peterson is your real name?" I said.
    "Yes. I was born and raised in Naperville, Illinois. You can look it up. I was able to use my own birth certificate, my own Social Security number, and my own passport again. But just

to be sure I was safe, I adopted the identity of a woman who majored in horticulture at the University of Wisconsin. She left after her junior year, so I had to as well."

"She went back and finished her degree."

"Good for her. But you see why I manipulated the facts the way I did. I had to salt my personal story with enough information that if anyone had checked, they would think I was her. It's also the reason I invented Salsa Girl. This way the real Erin Peterson could hide in plain sight."

So far, so good. Except it would be difficult for Erin Peterson who had a degree in economics from Northwestern to get a job while pretending to be Erin Peterson who had an incomplete degree in horticulture from Wisconsin. Fortunately, Erin Peterson had a plan fueled by her ability to create fact from fiction, a recipe for the best salsa she had ever eaten, and well over half a million dollars in cash.

Using the skills she had mastered as Christine Olson, she made herself familiar at the clubs and social meccas where Minnesota's elite gathered. Eventually she identified the perfect mark—Randy Bignell-Sax. He thought he was smart but wasn't, thought he was irresistible to women, which was also untrue, and was needy because his family had turned off the money tap.

"I lucked out with him," Erin said. "At least I thought I did. Randy was a ditz, but he had an important name, one that nobody would question. He was also easy to manipulate. I pretended to give him the money that he pretended to loan me, and I used it to create the first production plant that made my salsa. I put his name on the building so his parents would be proud. When my salsa started selling, I pretended to pay off the loan.

In exchange for his assistance, I gave Randy ten percent of the net profits. That guaranteed he would keep my secret; the man needed the money. Plus there was the fear of being arrested for aiding and abetting money laundering and tax evasion. The fact that he was able to help me gain access to Minnesota Foods was a bonus."

"You were convinced that you had control of him, but Randy thought, because he knew some of your secrets, that he had control of you."

"I realize that now. It's what convinced the soulless prick that he could use my business to move his heroin, which impelled me to seek help from you, which brought me to this sorry state. Damn. So close to the finish line. But McKenzie, you need to know, everything that I did—this was all before I met Ian. He doesn't know anything about it. I don't want you to think that he was somehow involved. You can't let him be involved."

Me? my inner voice said.

"You told a convincing story about selling your salsa at farmers markets," I said aloud. "Everyone believed it, including Ian."

"Remember what I said about branding? What's funny, I'll meet people today who will tell me that they remember buying jars of my product on the Nicollet Mall. One woman told me that as much as she liked my salsa now, she claimed it tasted better when I was selling it in Madison. She said it was because I was using Wisconsin tomatoes back then instead of tomatoes grown in Minnesota.

"McKenzie, I don't want to give all this up. I love being Salsa Girl. I love ... from the day I said good-bye to Christine Olson until now, I have tried to live a life that would make up for the life I lived before. I don't mean just giving money to charity. I mean trying to be kind, trying to be—I don't know how to say it. The statute of limitations ran out a long time ago on all of my past crimes, my sins. I was hoping that meant now I could be the person I've always wanted to be, the person my parents raised me to be. If you can help me, please help me. If you can't—I have everything I need to disappear again in my trunk. I can drop you off and ... before, I was running toward something, though. I didn't know what exactly, but I know now. I was trying to reclaim my humanity. But if I take off again I wouldn't be running toward anything. I'd just be running from, with nowhere to go."

"Is that what you think we're doing?" I asked. "Running away?"

"What are we doing?"

"Position analysis. It's a chess term. Right now we're studying the board. We're comparing our material to theirs, noting the position of the kings and the activity of the pieces, determining who controls the diagonals and the center, clarifying how much space we have to move in, who has the stronger pawn structure—all of which goes into determining not only what's the best play for us but also for our competitors."

Erin stared at me for a few beats as if I were speaking gibberish, which, let's face it, I mostly was.

"You're having fun, aren't you?" she said. "This is some sort of game you're playing."

"Erin ..."

"You like this. You like danger. It's what you do instead of drugs."

"If that's what you think, you misjudge me."

"What should I think?"

"You should be thinking about what our next move is going to be."

Erin stared some more.

"Please tell me that you play chess better than you play poker," she said.

The Anderson House in Wabasha, Minnesota, was built in 1850, so of course it was supposed to be haunted. Its most famous spirit was named Sarah. It was said that she committed suicide in the hotel because of her despair when she was told that her husband had been killed in a steamboat accident on the Mississippi River—which turned out not to be true, by the way. Apparently she didn't hold that mistake against the living, though. The proprietor of the hotel says that she has remained quite friendly over the decades, often leaving the staff dime tips to express her appreciation for how well the hotel is being run.

I stopped the Solara on West Main Street in front of the hotel.

"Do you have something in mind?" Erin asked.

"Our opening move."

"Is this going to be a thing—you talking in chess terms?"

"Come along, Mrs. Dyson."

"Do you want me to get the suitcases?"

"Just the gym bag."

"I'm going to need more than that."

"No, Erin. We're not staying."

"We're not?"

"Hell, no. The place is crawling with ghosts."

I used my fake ID to register. The woman at the desk put us in the Queen Suite, which gave us a nice view of the river as well as the Wabasha-Nelson Bridge that spanned it, connecting Minnesota with Wisconsin. I sat on the bed. Erin removed her black fleece jacket, sat in a rocking chair, and watched me.

"Who's Nick Dyson?" she asked.

"A real jerk."

"So I'm married to a jerk, then?"

I retrieved my cell and its battery from my pocket and put them together again. Erin didn't say a word when I made a production out of activating the GPS function. I called Nina.

"Hey, you," she said.

"Are you all right?"

"Of course."

"What's going on?"

"Herzy's here. We've been talking about old movies."

"Ask him if he's seen *The Magnificent Seven*."

"Herzy, McKenzie wants to know if you've seen *The Magnificent Seven*."

Nina must have raised her phone to catch his voice, because Herzog sounded a long way off.

"Fuck 'im," he said.

"Did you catch that?" Nina asked.

"I did. What about Levi Chandler?"

"He left a long time ago. Actually, he took off a minute after Herzy walked through the door. I watched him drive away."

"Good."

"You have that sound in your voice again."

"Yeah, about that. I don't want you going anywhere near the condo tonight. Stay with Bobby and Shelby instead."

"All right."

"And don't leave Rickie's until Greg Schroeder and his people get there."

"It is serious, isn't it?"

"We'll see."

"All right."

"Nina, you're amazing. How can you just say 'all right'? How can you not ask me where I am or what's going on?"

"Herzy has already told me some of it. I believe if you had the time, you would tell me the rest. This isn't—what is it you guys like to say? This isn't my first rodeo."

"I'll explain it all the first chance I get."

"I'll be waiting. Tell me one thing, though. Is Salsa Girl with you?"

"Yes."

Nina hesitated before she said, "Be careful. Both of you."

I ended the call and pressed the icon for another number. While it rang, I said, "Nina wants us to be careful."

Erin chuckled.

"She didn't mean it that way," I added.

"Then she truly is amazing. McKenzie, you can't put her in danger because of me."

"Oh, I won't."

Erin looked as if she believed me.

Shelby Dunston answered the phone.

"Hi, sweetie," I said. "Is Bobby around?"

"What? You can't talk to me?"

"I'm sending Nina to stay with you tonight. She'll be accompanied by a battalion of armed guards."

"See? Was that so hard? Hang on a sec."

A moment later, Bobby Dunston was on the phone. Unlike Nina, he asked, "What's going on?"

I gave him a much-abbreviated version of the story.

"What do you want me to do?" he asked.

"Nothing yet, but with a little luck I'm going to help you cure your heroin epidemic."

"I'll believe it when I see it. Be careful."

"I will."

"Is Erin Peterson with you?"

"Yes."

"Tell her to be careful, too."

I ended the call and started another.

"Bobby also wants us to be careful," I said.

Erin nodded.

The cell rang three times before it was answered.

"Greg Schroeder," a voice said.

"This is McKenzie. I'm sorry to bother you at home."

"What do you need?"

I would never take on a bodyguard gig, I told myself. It required that you set aside the idea that your life was more important than someone else's; that you made yourself willing to get hurt, perhaps even killed, to protect a client. I could see myself doing it for Nina without hesitation. And Erica. And Victoria and Katie and Shelby Dunston. I would even do it for Bobby, although it would piss him off immensely. But no one else. Greg Schroeder, on the other hand, was the consummate professional. He would do it on principle alone.

I told Greg what I wanted. I told him why. He asked me where Nina was. I told him.

"I'll take care of her," he said.

"Greg—"

"Nothing will happen to her that doesn't happen to me first."

"I like the way you think, but that's not what I was going to say. I was going to say that Herzog is watching over her now."

"The bruiser that hangs with Chopper Coleman? Thanks for the heads-up. I'll have my people approach him with caution."

"Thank you, Greg. I appreciate this."

"Yeah, well, wait until you get my bill."

I ended the call, turned off the phone, and removed the battery yet again. I put both in my pocket. Erin was still watching me from the rocking chair.

"You realize, of course, that Carson Brazill is not a stupid man," she said. "You could argue that he taught me everything I know. What's more, he has multiple resources at his disposal."

"Meaning?"

"Meaning he and his people should be here in roughly ninety minutes."

"What time is it now?"

Erin answered without looking at her watch. "Nearly four."

"Plenty of time."

"For what?"

"To grab something to eat and do a little shopping." I gestured at my clothes. "This is all I have."

"And then what?"

"In chess, they call this a silent move, a move that has a dramatic tactical effect but doesn't actually attack or capture an enemy piece."

"God help me."

Erin closed her eyes and began rocking more aggressively in her chair.

"This is all on me," she said. "I suppose I need to take whatever happens."

"It'll be fine," I said.

"If you say so. McKenzie, ever since giving up Christine Olson I've worked very hard at trying to be a good person. I try not to lose my temper. I try not to swear. I try not to raise my voice, even. Only after everything that's happened today . . ."

"Go 'head."

"Goddamn motherfuck sonuvabitch!"

I waited for more, but that was all Erin gave me.

"Feeling better?" I asked.

"Not really, no."

Wabasha had been the setting for the film *Grumpy Old Men*, starring Jack Lemmon and Walter Matthau. Several scenes took place in Slippery's near the river. Except when we entered the place, we discovered that while the movie retained its name, actually filming took place in the Half Time Rec, a bar in St. Paul. Oh, well. Slippery's served a decent walleye sandwich, anyway.

It was while we were eating that I explained my strategy.

"I'd argue with you," Erin said, "but at the moment I don't have a viable alternative."

"All we need to do is convince them that they're smarter than we are."

"That shouldn't be too difficult."

"Actually, we need them to think that they're smarter than

I am. They already know you would never make a mistake like the one I made, using a GPS-activated cell phone to make a call from what they probably already know is a hotel in Wabasha. They'll think I'm the weak link. That'll be important later."

"Why do we need to let them chase us around, though? And I'm begging you, McKenzie, don't answer in a chess term."

"We're working a short con here. That's more your business than mine; at least it was your business. Erin, what was the most important thing you looked for in a victim?"

"The men who were easiest to con were those whose emotional needs were closest to the surface, the ones who weren't afraid to tell you how much they loved their wives and kids and grandkids and"—she was looking at me now—"their girlfriends. Those men weren't thinking about whether or not they were being scammed. They were thinking, Here's a fix for my problems."

"Why men?"

"Despite what you might have heard, men are more emotional than women. They're grandiose and full of ego. Most are driven by insecurity and a general feeling of inferiority."

"And if I was frightened as well? If I had just escaped the bad men by the proverbial skin of my teeth?"

"Carson would think that you'll be easy to crush or kill—those are the terms con men use for closing the deal, by the way. Although in this case, they could be literal."

"So Brazill needs to see me being frightened."

"I get it, McKenzie. I just don't like it. I'm hoping we're not making a blunder."

"Ahh, good one."

"What?"

"Blunder—in chess, that's what they call a very bad move."

At five thirty we were sitting in the Solara parked on the opposite side of West Main Street and facing the Anderson House.

The sun was still high in the sky but did not reach us where we sat beneath the Wabasha-Nelson Bridge. It was cold, yet I didn't start the car or its heater. Salsa Girl moved restlessly against the passenger seat, clinging to herself in an effort to keep warm. Either that or she was nervous. I leaned against the door and stared straight ahead.

Unnecessary complexity as well as inattention to detail has ruined many a good plan. So I was careful to keep mine both simple and straightforward. First, I slowly drove the downtown Wabasha streets, taking note of high-traffic areas, pedestrians, the location of stoplights and how they were timed. I was particularly intrigued by the bridge that connected Wabasha, Minnesota, with Nelson, Wisconsin. It did not end at the river's shore as expected but instead continued for several blocks, spanning the downtown area until it finally reached 4th Grant Boulevard and the sports fields beyond. What's more, its entrance and exit ramps were flanked by high concrete walls, so it was not only impossible to view traffic on the bridge unless you were actually crossing it, you couldn't see beyond the bridge while you were driving next to it. If I could lure Brazill and his boys onto the bridge, they wouldn't be able to stop or turn around. They'd be trapped until they reached the far bank.

Highway 61 was on the other side of the sports fields. It was easy to see cars heading in that direction. If they didn't see me, if they were sure I wasn't headed that way, they might assume I was trying to escape to Wisconsin. Meanwhile, I could continue to follow 4th Grant to Allegheny Avenue, hang a left, and head back toward downtown. Allegheny was more like an alley than a street. A quick right, though, would put me in an actual alley that ended at the back of a Catholic church complete with steeple. There were plenty of places to hide a car back there.

If that didn't work—Plan B. A couple of quick turns would put me on Hiawatha Drive that led directly to City Hall and the Wabasha Police Department. I figured if the boys were reluctant to shoot at us in Prospect Park, they'd be even less inclined to resort to violence in a cop-shop parking lot.

And then what? my inner voice asked.

Geezus, do I have to think of everything?

Finally, a black Nissan Maxima pulled to a stop directly in front of the hotel. I gave Erin a nudge, but she had already spotted it.

"You were right," she said. "They must have plowed the Acura into another car when they were chasing us in Prospect Park, or they wouldn't be driving something else now."

Brazill and Chandler emerged through the front doors of the Maxima, and the two henchmen slipped out of the back doors. Brazill stretched. Chandler examined the street. There were plenty of cars parked there but none that interested him, including ours. He gestured at one of the henchmen to watch the hotel doors. Afterward, he, Brazill, and the second henchman entered the hotel.

"They'll go to the front desk," I said. "They'll ask for my room. The woman will say that no one by the name of Rushmore McKenzie has checked in. They'll try Christine Olson. No, the clerk will say, not her, either. How about Erin Peterson? By now the clerk will become anxious. She'll start wondering who these guys are. She'll ask them what they want. The boys might give her a convincing answer, but I doubt it. More likely they'll resort to describing us, describing me and an attractive blonde who's five-six and weighs about a hundred and thirty pounds ..."

"One-twenty," Erin said.

"Forgive me. There's a small chance that the clerk might give us up—that she might say something about a man and woman checking in earlier, except that the woman had red hair instead of blond. I doubt it, though. Instead, she'll probably point out that the hotel guarantees privacy to its guests and ask Brazill and the boys to leave. They'll think about going over the desk, grabbing the clerk, grabbing the registration information off the computer. But Chandler has already proven himself to be a cool customer. He'll thank the clerk for her courtesy and make the others back off, thinking he can stake out the hotel and wait for us to appear. They'll leave the hotel—wait. Here they come. Get down."

Erin slipped off the seat and sat on the floor of the Solara, her head well below the windows. I started the car and drove down the street. I slowed when I reached the hotel, an expression of astonishment on my face. Brazill was the first one to see me. He pointed.

Astonishment gave way to an expression of fear; at least I hoped it did. I dropped the transmission into first gear and stomped on the accelerator. Tires spun as I launched the Solara down West Main Street. I tried to make them squeal as I turned the corner onto Bridge Avenue.

I shot down the street, driving the two long blocks until I reached 4th Grant. I forced myself to slow down so that the Nissan had time to fall in behind me. I needed the driver to see me turning left onto the boulevard. I punched it again, driving another two long blocks past the bridge entrance ramp to Allegheny Avenue. I hung another left and then a right into the alley that led to the church.

I was sure that the passengers in the Maxima could not have seen me. I was equally sure that they would see the empty streets around the sports fields, realize that I was not heading toward the highway, and decide that there was no smart place for me to go except onto the bridge.

I stopped in the alley behind a large white garage and turned off the engine. From where we were parked, we could see two side streets. Nothing moved on them for five minutes. Wabasha was a small town; I was convinced that if the Maxima were still in it I would have known by now.

I started the car, pulled out of the alley, and headed for

Highway 61. Erin crawled back onto the passenger seat and buckled her seat belt.

"Where are we going now?" she asked.

"Pipestone."

"Isn't Pipestone way on the other side of the state?"

"Southwestern corner."

"Okay, next question—why Pipestone?"

"Because it is on the other side of the state and because there's a place called Lange's Café that bakes the best pie I've ever eaten."

Lange's Café was one of the few places still open when we reached Pipestone four and a half hours later. Not that it was busy; only one booth was occupied when Erin and I rolled in. The place prided itself on never once locking its door in nearly sixty years. It also prided itself on its sour cream raisin pie, which had been featured on NPR's *The Splendid Table,* among other places. Unfortunately, they were all out by the time we arrived, so I had to settle for Dutch apple. Erin inhaled a pecan pie à la mode, and I asked her if she was sure she weighed only 120 pounds. She gave me a look that suggested my life was in jeopardy, so I let it slide.

A half hour later, we drove to the Calumet Inn, one of the other few places open in Pipestone at 10:30 P.M., and checked in under the names Nick and Nora Dyson, using my fake IDs and credit cards. If things went sideways, I knew that Erin would need hers.

Like the Anderson House, the Calumet Inn was built in the nineteenth century and was supposed to be haunted. Each of the rooms had an evocative name like Sherwood Forest and Eden, except for 308. That's where Charlie, the most celebrated of the resident ghosts, was supposed to reside. We were registered to Summertime. It featured a lot of Victorian furniture including a single queen-sized bed. Neither of us remarked on it while we unpacked.

Afterward, we retired to the Calumet Lounge on the hotel's ground floor. The décor was pretty grand if you viewed it from a distance—ornate wooden bar, large windows, tin ceiling, brick walls. Up close it seemed middle-aged, like most of its customers, with no new work done for years, only maintenance. It was doing good business. There were plenty of Saturday night carousers, men and women, many divorced, not so much attempting to relive their youth as escape what they did with it.

We sat at a table next to a window with a good view of the Pipestone County Museum and shared a paper boat of free popcorn. I had ale. Salsa Girl drank bourbon. I told her that I'd never seen her drink anything but bourbon.

"I was never a white wine kind of girl," she said. "What does Nina drink?"

"When she drinks, she'll have something sweet like a Bailey's or the adult milkshakes they serve at Ward 6 in St. Paul. She's developed a deep fondness for the hard ciders that she discovered when we were in England, but they're tough to get here in the U.S."

We didn't have much to say to each other after that. I had no idea what Erin was thinking. I was thinking about Sunday.

We finished our drinks and returned to the room. After locking the door, I propped a wooden desk chair against its handle. I moved another chair, this one with deep mohair upholstery and soft arms, so that it was facing the door. I pulled the nine-millimeter Taurus out of the gym bag and checked the load.

"You take the bed," I said.

Erin stared at the gun in my hand.

"Are you sure?" she said.

"I'm sure."

We took turns using the bathroom to get ready. Finally the lights were extinguished. Erin settled under the sheets of the bed, and I made myself comfortable in the chair. Ten minutes passed before she spoke.

"Your shoulder must be killing you."

"It's not too bad."

"McKenzie, you're welcome to join me."

"Who would like that less, I wonder, Nina or Ian?"

"Just because we're in the same bed doesn't mean something has to happen."

"Yea, though I walk through the valley of the shadow of death, I will fear no evil: for thou art with me."

"What now?"

"Something the Reverend Billy Graham used to say."

"I don't get it."

"I'll quote Bobby Dunston, then—be careful."

Erin chuckled at that. A few minutes later, she spoke again.

"Are you ever afraid?"

"Frequently."

"I was never afraid. Not even when I was letting Carson chase me across the country. Yet I am now."

"That's because you have so much more to lose."

"Ian—I love him more than I have words to say."

"Is that why you've never told him, because you didn't have the words?"

"How could I tell him one thing without telling him all the rest?"

I didn't have an answer to that, so I said, "Good night, Erin."

"Good night, McKenzie. Thank you for being my friend."

FOURTEEN

The Calumet Inn served a pretty good Sunday brunch in its dining room. I was working hard at a Belgian waffle and some strawberries; Erin just picked at her eggs Benedict.

"Did you make your phone calls?" she asked.

"While you were in the shower. You take long showers, by the way."

"I almost didn't get out at all. How much time do we have?"

I glanced at my all-purpose watch.

"Three hours if they're hurrying," I said. "They're not hurrying, though. Not like they did in Wabasha. They'll make sure they get it right this time."

"What'll we do while we wait?"

Although it was located in the heart of Yankton Sioux territory, the quarries that later became the Pipestone National Monument, located about ten minutes north of the city, were considered neutral ground by most Native American tribes. It was their only resource for catlinite, or "pipestone," the red stone that was used to make the ceremonial pipes that were vitally important to traditional Plains Indian religious practices, so it was agreed that, regardless of their differences, the tribes would have unfettered access at all times. Even today, only people of Native American ancestry are allowed to quarry the pipestone. Nothing bad was ever supposed to happen there.

At least that's what I told Salsa Girl as we strolled along the Circle Trail that was squeezed along the quartzite cliff walls. Still, we were both on high alert, more interested in the people that approached us than we were in the historical markers, tallgrass prairie, and the quarries themselves. When a man said, "Excuse me," we both flinched.

He was old and accompanied by a woman who claimed that her walker was only temporary while she recovered from some unnamed surgery. He asked if we would take their photograph against the walls of the cliff—without the walker—and we did. The woman was very friendly. She told Erin, "You have red hair; you must be from Ohio"—don't ask me why—and asked, "Are you a college student?"

Erin said she wasn't but thanked the woman for saying so just the same. As they passed us on the trail, the woman told me, "Your wife is very beautiful."

"I think so, too," I said.

Erin watched them move up the trail and then turned her gaze out at the park.

"Like Dr. Samuel Johnson, I set a high value on spontaneous kindness," she said. "I want to be like that woman."

I glanced at my watch again; I had been doing so every ten minutes since we arrived. I told her, "As another wise man once said—ain't nothing to it but to do it."

Erin dropped me off at the Pipestone County Courthouse. It was built in 1901 in the neoclassical style with the same reddish quartzite stone that was found near the pipestone quarries and featured a Renaissance dome on top of a high clock tower. A bronze statue of Lady Justice stood on top of the dome. I found it comforting, but just barely.

As I started to slide out of the Solara, Erin grabbed my arm. I turned to look at her looking at me. Her face seemed to be filled with words, but the only ones she spoke were "I'll see you soon."

I gave her a nod.

After I got out of the car and shut the door, she drove off. I didn't watch her. Instead, I walked the two blocks back to the Calumet Inn. I walked slowly.

Sunday in the historic part of Pipestone was very quiet; that was one of the reasons why I picked it. I saw no pedestrians on the street and no one sitting in a parked car. Nor was there anyone loitering in the hotel lobby. I made my way to the third floor and moved toward the room designated Summertime.

I unlocked the door, opened it, and started to step inside. I stopped when I saw Carson Brazill lying on the queen-sized bed, both pillows stacked behind his head. Levi Chandler was sitting in the stuffed chair and reading something on his phone. A strong hand fell on my left shoulder and shoved hard; I tried not to react to the pain it caused. I stumbled into the room, nearly falling. The door was closed and locked behind me.

"The girl?" Brazill asked.

"Just him," said the henchman who pushed me. "Frankie went down to the lobby to watch for her."

Play it cool, my inner voice said.

"Hotel management is going to be very annoyed when it finds out you guys—"

I didn't finish the sentence because the henchman hit me hard in the mouth, driving me to the floor.

That hurt.

While I was on the floor, the henchman searched me thoroughly to make sure I wasn't armed or wearing a wire. When he finished he said, "Clean."

"Pick him up," Brazill said.

The henchman grabbed me by the shoulders and hoisted me onto my feet.

"Where is she?" Brazill asked.

"Who?"

The henchman hit me again, and again I ended up with a face full of carpet.

That hurt, too. Clearly cool isn't working for you.

"Do I have to ask you again, McKenzie?" Brazill said. "I don't mind, but Carl's hand is probably getting sore."

"No, it's okay," Carl said. "I could do this all day."

"Did you hear that, McKenzie?"

"Yeah."

Carl pulled me to my feet and tossed me into the straight-back desk chair that I had propped against the door handle the night before. It was made of carved wood and wasn't very comfortable. I fought the urge to bring my hand up and caress my shoulder, which hurt just a tad more than my face.

"Where ... is ... she?" Brazill asked.

"I ... don't ... know."

Brazill shook his head. Carl cocked his fist as if that were a signal to punch me again. I brought my arm up to fend him off. I spoke quickly.

"I don't know," I said. "I really don't. She dropped me off and drove away. I don't know where. We thought it would be safer if I didn't know."

Brazill rolled off the bed and found a corner to sit on. He glanced at Chandler, who had turned off his phone and stuffed it into his pocket.

"He thinks he's clever," Brazill said.

Chandler shrugged in reply.

"Did Christine tell you why I'm looking for her?" Brazill said.

"Something about $680,000."

"To be precise, $683,240."

"She only gave me a round number."

Carl smacked the back of my head with the flat of his hand.

"C'mon," I said.

"Speak respectfully," Carl said.

"The money is only part of it," Brazill said. "There's a lot more to it than that."

"What?"

"Didn't Christine tell you?"

I tried to look confused. It wasn't hard; confusion was my natural state of mind.

"She said—she said she'd be willing to pay the money back," I said. "With interest. She doesn't want to run anymore. She said she's tired of running."

"Too bad for her."

"Brazill—"

Carl slapped me again.

"That's *Mr.* Brazill to you."

"Mr. Brazill, what do you want?"

"What do I want? After fifteen years? I want her head"—I waited for him to say "on a plate"; instead he finished with the words "in my lap. You know, I never touched her while we were working together. Not once. It would have been unprofessional. But after what she did—the contract in North Carolina that I made with the Outfit went unfulfilled because she left. My superiors were very annoyed. I lost several other contracts after that because I couldn't find a woman with the proper skill set to take Christine's place. The Outfit shut me down. I went from a top earner to middle management just like that."

You know what? my inner voice said. *This is going to work.*

"All good things must come to an end," I said aloud.

Instead of using the flat of his hand, Carl used his fist, this time connecting just below my ear. It shook me off the chair onto my knees. I didn't need to pretend that they were beating me into submission.

"Do you want those to be your last words?" Brazill said. "Is that what you want carved on your tombstone?"

Carl used my collar to drag me back onto the chair.

"The money," I said. "We can make a deal."

"Deal? You think I drove all the way to this bodunk town to make a deal with you? I might make a deal with her, but not with you, McKenzie. With you I'm offering a trade. Christine Olson for Nina Truhler."

My heart skipped several beats. I sounded out of breath when I asked, "You have Nina?"

Brazill laughed.

"No," he said. "That would be kidnapping. A federal crime, and me with no desire whatsoever to get involved with the Feds. I know where she lives, though, when she's not staying with your cop friend and his wife and daughters. I know where she works. I even know where her daughter's apartment is in New Orleans. The Outfit has people down there. It would be an easy matter to reach out to them. But let's concentrate on Nina, for now. You have good people watching over her, McKenzie. How long is that going to last, though, hmm? How long can you afford to guard her day and night? How long will she let you? I've spent fifteen years chasing Christine. Do you have that kind of patience?"

I made a show of anger. Brazill would expect anger, I told myself.

"If you touch her—"

"What? Are you threatening me? Well, are you?"

I glanced up at Carl, who was sneering, and at Chandler, who looked like he was waiting for a bus. I altered my expression from anger to fear.

"No," I said.

"You're not as dumb as you look. McKenzie, you're trying to be a gentleman; I can see that. It fits your reputation. Yes, I know who you are. But do you know who Christine is? Did she tell you about the archbishop she seduced in St. Louis? How about the woman who ran a homeless shelter in Philadelphia who just wouldn't be a sport and move a lousy two blocks? Christine is not a good person, McKenzie. She's not deserving of your loyalty. Even if she was, are you willing to trade Nina Truhler for her?"

"I don't know."

"You don't know? McKenzie, this should be an easy choice to make. Or did she turn you just like she did all those other marks, make you her bitch? I notice there's only one bed in this room."

"It's not like that."

"What's it like?"

"You don't understand. I was just trying to do Christine a favor. Someone was sabotaging her business, Salsa Girl Salsa."

"We know all about that now. What she did with her life after she ran out on me. Erin Peterson—what a name."

"It turned out to be her partner who was messing with her. He was using Christine's business to mule heroin up from Mexico. It was sold on the streets of St. Paul, well, throughout the Twin Cities, I guess, by a man named Alejandro Reyes."

"How much heroin?" Chandler asked.

Brazill looked at him as if he were speaking out of turn yet said nothing

"At least four keys a week," I said. "Probably Reyes could have sold a great deal more, but he was trying to maintain a low-profile operation. His competitors are the Red Dragons, and they have a corner on the OxyContin market. Reyes doesn't have the numbers to go up against them."

"What's the grade?"

"Pure white."

"So we're talking approximately seventy G's a week; about three-point-six million a year."

"Closer to four million, I think."

"You're saying that Christine didn't know anything about this, the heroin?" Brazill said.

"No, it was all her business partner."

"Business partner," he repeated slowly.

"Junior partner. Punk named Randy Bignell-Sax. Erin was using him as a front. She didn't want any part of his side job. She made much more than that selling salsa."

"How much more?" Chandler asked.

"I heard the number six million."

"Hmm."

"Hmm, what?" Brazill said.

"Just wondering if there's a way to make a profit from all of this."

"I was wondering the same thing."

"What profit?" I said. "I shut down the pipeline, told Reyes he'd have to find another way to ship his H. Besides, the Outfit doesn't have a presence in the Twin Cities or anywhere else in Minnesota. Not since they put Kid Cann away something like, what, sixty years ago?"

Chandler leaned close to his employer's ear, although I could hear his whisper anyway.

"Mr. Brazill," he said. "If you should reopen the pipeline, think how happy the bosses would be to get a foothold in the Twin Cities again."

"No," I said. "Erin won't have anything to do with that."

"But Christine might," Chandler said. "Especially if it squares things with you."

"She'll have to do more than that to square things with me," Brazill said.

"I'll be happy to watch the door while you take what you want."

"No," I said.

I jumped to my feet. Carl knocked me down.

"Tell me where Christine is," Brazill said.

"I don't know. How many times do I have to say it?"

Brazill slid off the bed onto his knees. He grabbed me by the hair and yanked upward. His face was one huge snarl as he spoke.

"I'll be happy to take Nina Truhler behind closed doors instead. Or her daughter. Would you like that better?"

"Please ..."

"Where is she?"

"I told you, we separated. She took off without telling me where in case you didn't take the deal. She has a go-bag filled with fake IDs and credit cards, even a passport. I don't know what names they're under. I only know she's been preparing to run for something like ten years."

Brazill yanked my hair some more out of pure antagonism; pain rippled through my core.

"McKenzie," Chandler said. "McKenzie, if we had agreed to the deal she offered, how would you have contacted Christine to let her know?"

"I wouldn't have. I can't. Instead, she's supposed to call me. I have a burn phone in my bag. Here, I'll get it."

I tried to rise, but Carl put his shoe against my spine and pushed me down. Chandler crossed the room to the bureau where my gym bag was resting. He opened it. "Would you look at this?" He pulled out a packet of cash and a wallet filled with fake IDs. "Oh, tsk, tsk, tsk." He found the nine-millimeter Taurus and held it up for everyone to see.

"You disappoint me, McKenzie," Brazill said.

Carl put the point of his shoe in my ribs as if that were what he always did when Brazill was disappointed.

I sat in the straight-back chair and waited. I waited for a long time, all the while pretending that my shoulder and my ribs and my face weren't throbbing. Brazill was waiting, too, only he was doing it in the queen-sized bed. A couple of times, he dozed off.

You had to admire the man's patience. Most criminal masterminds on TV and in the movies are portrayed as volatile lunatics, just as apt to take out their frustrations on their own people as they were on their enemies. I always wondered why anyone would ever work for them. But Brazill was calm and quiet. Like Salsa Girl.

Chandler not so much. He sat in the comfy chair and played with his phone, making comments, mostly unfavorable, on whatever he was reading without explaining what he was reading. When he became bored with that he watched some TV, flipping between the NBA and NHL playoffs and a baseball game, again tossing in a lot of derogatory remarks, until he shut off the TV and dropped the remote on the table. He left the room, came back, watched more TV, left the room again, and came back again. I wondered if he was wandering down to the lounge for a bump or just stretching his legs.

Meanwhile, Carl and Frankie had worked out a schedule, taking turns at the door. Half hour on, half hour off. I had no idea what they did during their downtime.

"You had better be right about this," Chandler said. He said it at least half a dozen times as the afternoon dragged on.

Brazill didn't say much of anything.

Finally my burn phone rang. Even though we were waiting for it, the sound made us all recoil.

"Put it on speaker," Chandler said. "Don't forget what we talked about."

He showed me his gun just in case I did.

I answered the cell. "Erin."

"Are you all right?"

We could all hear the sound of wind blowing through a window; clearly she was driving somewhere fast.

"I've been better," I said.

"Did they rough you up?"

"Of course. They had to prove to me that they were in charge."

"I'm sorry, McKenzie."

"It's okay."

"Did they accept my offer?"

"Brazill wants one million dollars."

Carl was miffed that I left off the "Mr." and clenched his fists, but didn't do anything with them.

"A nice round number," Erin said.

"Do you have it?"

"I can get it."

Brazill grinned at Erin's response.

"What else?" she asked.

"He wants to be partners again."

"In what? The salsa business?"

"Heroin."

"He knows about Reyes?"

"I'm afraid so." I didn't tell her how he knew; I figured Erin could guess. "He wants you to let Reyes use Salsa Girl Salsa to mule his heroin into the Cities. He's going to try to make a deal with Reyes to take over part of his operation."

"And eventually take over all of it. I get it. What else?"

I didn't say.

"McKenzie," Erin said, "what else?"

"He wants to hurt you."

Brazill's grin became a smile.

"Yeah, I figured," Erin said.

"Do you know what I mean by hurt you?"

"I know."

"Fuck these guys, Erin. Just keep driving. You have nothing to come back to."

Brazill slid off the bed and hovered above me. Chandler raised his gun.

"Ten years ago I would have agreed with you."

"Erin ..."

"All those marks we hustled over all those years, do you know why they nearly always did exactly what we told them? It's because they were like me. They didn't have anywhere else to go."

"Erin, please. What the bastard has planned for you ..."

"Yeah, well, maybe I have it coming. Let me think about it. I'll get back to you. Probably tomorrow."

Erin turned off her phone.

I turned off mine.

Brazill smiled down at me.

"A hero to the end, aren't you, McKenzie."

He nodded at Carl. Carl's fist drove me back to the floor.

The Pizza Ranch was next door to the Calumet Inn, and Brazill sent Frankie over for a couple of large pies. I would have preferred Dars about a mile away, but it's not like they gave me a vote.

The pies arrived along with bottled beers that Carl scrounged. It was hard to eat; my teeth felt loose, and my mouth and jaw were sore. Dinner conversation centered on where the best pizza could be found. Chandler said he had grown very fond of the thin-crust sausage pizza at the Side Street Saloon near St. Alphonsus in Lake View, which I guessed was a neighborhood in Chicago. Brazill favored the deep-crust pie you can get at Lou Malnati's.

"Which location?" Chandler asked.

"The one on Rush and State Street in the Gold Coast."

I suggested that the best pizza I ever had was at an Italian joint called La Trattoria on Rue de la Convention in Paris.

"Who asked you?" Brazill said.

"Shut the fuck up, McKenzie," Chandler said. "They don't have pizza in France."

Yeah, okay.

Night came without any message from Salsa Girl. The boys tied me up and left me on the floor. I asked for a pillow, which they thought was pretty funny. I didn't think there was anything funny about it unless you count the fact that I was paying for the room and I had yet to use the bed.

What seemed like a short time later, someone opened the window blind. A harsh sun found my face on the floor. I opened my eyes into a glaring light. The way my mind worked, my first thought was of the old Harry Belafonte song—*Day-o, day-ay-ay-o, daylight come and me wan' go home* ...

My burn phone rang while the boys were discussing breakfast plans. I was quickly untied, but not quickly enough. The phone stopped ringing before I could answer it.

"The bitch had better call back," Brazill said.

She did, ten minutes later. I answered, putting the cell on speaker as ordered.

"McKenzie, are you all right?" Erin asked.

"Yeah. I'm sorry I didn't answer the first time you called. I was tied up."

"They're listening, aren't they? We're on speakerphone like we were the first time I called, right?"

"Yeah."

"Good morning, Carson."

"Hello, Chris," Brazill said. "It's been a long time."

"Yes, it has. Are you doing well?"

"Not as well as I was doing before you ran out on me."

"How angry are you, exactly?"

"Pretty angry."

"Angry enough that you would let it obstruct a lucrative business arrangement?"

"That depends on the deal."

"First the money. You'll get it, but not in a lump sum. Not unless you want the Treasury Department to knock on the door and ask what I'm doing with all that cash."

"You have thirty days," Brazill said.

"I need six months."

"Are you trying to negotiate with me, you fucking whore?"

Erin responded in her typically serene voice. "Don't call me names. Do you want your million dollars or don't you?"

"You're going to give me a lot more than that."

"First things first. Do you want—"

"All right, six months. You better not try to screw me."

"Perish the thought. About the heroin—what the hell, Carson? Do you think you're going to sell it in open-air markets like they do on the West Side? People lined up in their cars like it's a drive-through? This is the Twin Cities, not Chicago."

"Reyes is moving four keys a week in your squeaky clean Minnesota. I can do better."

"If the Red Dragons let you."

"What do you know about them?"

"I pay attention."

"You haven't changed at all, have you? You're still the same girl who used to fuck old men for money and stock tips."

"Four keys, you say." Erin paused as if she were impressed by the number. "If I do this for you ..."

"If you do this for me, you get to keep breathing. Take it or leave it."

"Carson—"

"You hurt me, Chris. Taking off like you did without even saying good-bye, that hurt a lot. After all we've been through—I thought we were friends. Worse, what you did embarrassed me with the Outfit. It nearly ruined my career. So you're going to do what I tell you to do. Otherwise, I will find you and I'll do what I've been promising myself I'd do for the past fifteen years."

"I'll let you use my business—"

"Damn right you will."

"But you will not interfere with my business. You will

keep your operation separate. I don't want to know anything about it."

"That's because you're such a sweet and innocent little girl."

"I know exactly what I am, Carson."

"What you are is my bitch. From now on, whenever I say jump you're going to say how fucking high."

"Don't do it, Erin," I said. "Keep running."

Carl hit me in the back of the head and drove me to the floor once again; he hit me hard enough to knock me unconscious. Only I wasn't unconscious. I was pretending.

"McKenzie," Erin said. "McKenzie?"

"He's fine," Brazill said. "But he won't be if you try to fuck with me."

"McKenzie has nothing to do with our arrangement. Let him go."

"I'll let him go when you and I have a face-to-face."

Erin paused again.

"All right," she said. "Tonight at Salsa Girl Salsa. Make it seven thirty, after everyone's left."

Erin silenced her cell phone. Chandler closed mine.

"Do you trust her?" he asked.

"Of course not," Brazill said. "She'll try to find a way to protect herself, if she hasn't already."

"Cops?"

"I don't think so. That'll bring too much scrutiny. Someone might ask her if Erin Peterson was her real name. They might ask how she got the money to start Salsa Girl. No, no cops. What you have to remember, Levi, is that when Chris and I worked together, the first thing we always did when sizing a mark was to ask, What does he want? What can't he live without? In Christine's case, it's her business. She won't do anything that'll jeopardize it. She loves it too much. Which is why I'm going to take it away from her. After I take her body. After I take her pride."

"What's our play?"

"Get McKenzie up."

Carl and Chandler dragged me to my feet and wrested me into the straight-back chair. They held both of my arms while Brazill tossed a glass of water into my face. I sputtered and opened my eyes.

"Still with us, McKenzie?" Brazill asked.

"What happened? What did Erin say?"

"It looks like we're going to do business after all. Now I have something for you to do."

"I want no part of your shit."

Carl raised his hand to hit me again, but Brazill stopped him.

"No need for that," he said. "McKenzie's going to cooperate. Aren't you, McKenzie?"

I didn't say if I would or wouldn't.

"I have a few tasks for you to perform," Brazill said. "You do those for me, you'll get to go home—go home to Nina Truhler and her daughter and live happily ever after."

"I don't trust you."

"I'm a businessman, McKenzie. First and foremost. I only hurt people to get what I want and only if they won't cooperate otherwise. If you had cooperated from the beginning, no one would have laid a finger on you, no one would have threatened your woman. We can get past all that, though. Please, just do what I ask."

"What do you want?"

"I need you to make a couple of phone calls."

"To who?"

"To whom. First, Christine's business partner, what's his name?"

"Randy Bignell-Sax," Chandler said.

"Yes. First we'll call Randy. Then I want you to contact this Reyes punk."

"Reyes doesn't know me as McKenzie," I said. "He thinks my name is Dyson."

"Same as the name on the fake IDs in his bag," Chandler said.

"I don't care what name you use just as long as you convince him to meet with me."

"Where?"

"At Salsa Girl Salsa. Make it eight o'clock tonight."

"He doesn't know us," Chandler said.

"Yeah, I know. He'll need an incentive."

I hesitated as if I had to think about what I was going to say before I said it. "I have $80,000 worth of his heroin."

"My, my, my, McKenzie, aren't you full of surprises," Brazill said. "Tell me—what were you going to do with all that dope?"

"Flush it down the toilet."

"You have no vision. That's your problem. All right, after Reyes, the Red Dragons. Tell me you know someone connected to the Red Dragons?"

"Why talk to them?" Chandler asked.

Brazill waved his finger at his lieutenant.

"She's getting careless in her old age," he said. "Either that or she's out of practice. The old Christine would never have mentioned the Dragons."

"I don't understand."

"That's who Christine is going to use against us. She probably already has them itching to take us out when we get to Salsa Girl. Don't forget, I know how that bitch's mind works. By the way, what makes you think we're going to talk to them? Hmm? I want you to call Chicago. We're going to need a couple more soldiers. We're going to need them right away."

"Yes, sir."

"McKenzie, I asked you a question. Do you know someone connected to the Dragons?"

"As a matter of fact, I do," I said.

FIFTEEN

The sun wasn't supposed to set for another half hour, but the western sky was filled with gray clouds, so it was pretty dark at seven thirty when we arrived at the offices of Salsa Girl Salsa. We had taken two vehicles. I was on the floor of the van. The jostling I took during the long drive from Pipestone did nothing to alleviate the pain in my shoulder or my ribs, which, I was now convinced, were fractured. My face was swollen and beginning to show signs of serious bruising. All in all, I was in lousy shape, yet I felt both excited and happy.

You are one screwed-up individual, my inner voice told me.

Who was I to argue?

The boys took their own sweet time driving around the industrial park in search of an ambush, although Brazill didn't expect one.

"The Red Dragons are probably running for the hills by now," he said, whatever that meant.

Still, they dropped a couple of soldiers at key intersections to keep watch while the rest of us drove into the parking lot. We parked in front of the door. Carl and Frankie dragged me out of the van and pushed me forward; my hands were tied behind my back. Brazill stopped us before we entered the building.

"Where did you say you hid the H?" he asked.

"It's in a box behind the front tire of the bombed-out truck in back. Do you want me to go get it?"

Brazill smiled at the suggestion. He nodded at his lieutenant. Chandler began to circle the building at a nice clip. Frankie moved to the front door and opened it. Brazill stepped inside. Carl shoved me in after him.

Erin Peterson was inside the foyer, leaning her backside against the edge of the reception desk. She was wearing a clingy sweater dress, her arms folded across her chest, just as she had been when I met her—was it really just a week ago? It seemed longer.

"Hello, Carson," she said.

Brazill had an odd expression on his face. It was as if he were happy to see Christine in spite of himself. He walked across the foyer as if he meant to hug her. Instead, he slapped her hard enough that she staggered several feet. She quickly regained her balance and gently rubbed the spot where his blow had landed.

"Now that we have that out of the way," she said. "McKenzie, you look terrible."

"I feel terrible."

Erin moved past Brazill to my side, turned me around, and began untying the rope that bound my hands. The expressions on Carl and Frankie's faces when they looked at each other suggested that they didn't know if they should stop her or not. Their eyes fell on Brazill. He was watching Erin as if he were both impressed and incensed at her audacity and didn't know which emotion to grab hold of.

After she finished, Erin took the rope and tossed it on the reception desk. I massaged my wrists where the rope had chafed them nearly raw. She winked at me—an astonishing thing to do, I thought, considering the circumstances.

She turned toward Brazill.

"Why are you doing this to us?" Erin asked. Her usually calm voice was loud and filled with both fear and uncertainty.

"Are you trying to be funny?" Brazill asked.

Clever girl, my inner voice said.

Chandler stepped through the door.

"Look what I found," he said.

I thought he was referring to the box of vegetables he carried, four plastic bags filled with heroin resting on top for everyone to see. But Randy Bignell-Sax entered right behind him, so . . .

"Randy," Erin said. "Randy, what have you done?" She crossed the foyer in a hurry and slammed both of her fists against Randy's chest as if he were a door and she wanted it to open. Randy fell backward. She kept pounding. "You brought drugs into my place? You brought drugs into my business?" Randy grabbed both of her wrists to keep from being pummeled. At the same time, Frankie circled Erin's waist with his arm and pulled her backward. Randy released Erin's wrists. Frankie swung her around until she was facing Brazill. Erin kept shouting at Randy.

"You were my friend," she said. "I trusted you."

Brazill laughed.

"We all make mistakes," he said.

"I'm sorry, Erin," Randy said. "I didn't know who these people were when I first got involved with them. I thought I was just buying vegetables."

"You should have said something. You should have told me."

"I guess."

Brazill laughed some more. Chandler smirked. I gestured with my bruised face at the box he carried.

"So that's what heroin looks like," I said.

"Sometimes it's black; sometimes it's brown," he said. "I never use the shit myself."

Which was exactly the kind of response I was hoping for.

Erin wiggled out of Frankie's grasp. The effort made her slide to the floor. She looked up at Brazill.

"I won't have anything to do with this," she said.

Brazill squatted down in front of her.

"You're in the drug business now, bitch," he said. "Get used to it."

Brazill slapped Erin again. She rolled to her side on the floor. Randy said, "Hey." I stepped forward as if moving to her defense. Frankie set a hand on my chest and shoved to keep me in my place.

Chandler's cell phone rang. He handed the box of vegetables and heroin to Randy.

Perfect, my inner voice said.

Chandler answered his phone. He listened for a few beats. "Make sure they're clean," he said. He ended the call and turned to face Brazill. "They're here."

"It's going to get pretty crowded," Brazill said.

"This way," I said.

I moved toward the employee lounge, hoping everyone would follow. I didn't want them to go into the production plant. There was no audio in the production plant. Along the way, I helped Erin to her feet.

"What's happening?" Erin's voice crackled with emotion. "Why are they doing this to me?"

"You picked the wrong friends."

Brazill chuckled at my remark.

"Now you know how it feels," he said.

I moved Erin to a chair that was far enough away from the door that no one would be suspicious, but with an unobstructed path if we needed to make a run for it. Brazill took charge of a table facing the door, sitting behind it, using it as a desk. Chandler took a position next to him, standing with his hands folded over his belt. Randy stood in the center of the room, still carrying the box. He seemed befuddled.

Alejandro Reyes stepped inside the foyer. He hesitated for a moment and then started walking toward the employee lounge; Brazill's people were behind him. I watched them through the door. I'd thought he might bring his entire crew— at least those I saw at Garlough Park in West St. Paul. Instead, Reyes brought the hombre only. His face looked worse than mine. He saw me standing next to Salsa Girl's chair. He walked straight up and grabbed my chin. He squeezed hard. I let him.

"*Para, hombre,*" Reyes said. "We're not here for that."

The hombre pushed my face away.

"*Hablaremos más tarde,*" he said, which my high school Spanish translated to mean "We'll talk later."

Not if I can help it, my inner voice said.

The hombre stepped next to Reyes. Reyes was staring at me when he spoke. "You have something for me?"

Chandler moved to where Randy was standing and relieved him of the carton. He placed it on a table next to Reyes.

"Compliments of Mr. Brazill." Chandler returned to Brazill's side.

"I understand this was stolen from you by Mr. Dyson," Brazill said.

Thank God he didn't say McKenzie, my inner voice said.

"What do you want for it?" Reyes asked.

"Nothing."

"Then we'll say *gracias,* take our property, and leave."

Reyes nodded toward the hombre. The hombre moved toward the box. He stopped when Brazill spoke.

"That might not be wise," he said.

"*¿Por qué no?*" Reyes said.

"First, let me explain why I am here. I represent a group of serious businessmen based in Chicago."

The hombre leaned close to Reyes and whispered in English loud enough for everyone to hear, "Mob."

"These businessmen would like to do business with you," Brazill said.

"I have no need for partners," Reyes said.

"That might not be entirely true. In any case, allow me to explain. The way I understand it, your distribution network has been compromised. I'm in a position not only to restore it but to expand it."

"No," Erin said.

Reyes was staring at her when he said, *"¿Puedes controlar a la puta?"*

"What did he say?" Brazill said.

"Can you control the whore?" I said.

Erin glanced up at me.

"Just trying to move the conversation along," I told her.

"Yes, I control the whore," Brazill said. "Don't worry about that."

"If you want," Randy said, "I can keep acting as your go-between—for the same price as before."

"See," Brazill said. "Business as usual."

"What do you want in return?" Reyes asked.

"Thirty-five percent."

The hombre snorted.

"Vamos a salir de aquí," he said.

Reyes held up his hand. "Wait," he said.

"¿Por qué?"

"Tiene más que decir. You do have more to say, don't you, Mr. Brazill?"

"I am in a position to help you expand your business."

"How?"

"By eliminating your competition. In fact, I have already taken the liberty."

"I don't understand."

"I ordered a hit on the Red Dragons." Brazill made a production out of looking at his watch. "About an hour ago, two vans with sliding side doors pulled up in front of a restaurant in West St. Paul where I am reliably informed that the Dragons enjoy having their dinner. Inside the vans were two .50 caliber machine guns."

"Oh, no," Erin said.

"They fire 324 rounds each without reloading. 'Course, the Dragons didn't know it was me that opened up on them. They think it was you."

"No, no, no ..."

The hombre's face became red with anger. Reyes was pale.

"Now, we can go back to Chicago and let you deal with the fallout," Brazill said. "Or we can join forces to take complete control of not only the heroin trade in Minnesota but OxyContin, too. Once we've eliminated the Dragons, that is."

"We do not deal in opioids," Reyes said.

"We do now."

Reyes spoke softly. "I will need to discuss this matter with my associates in Mexico."

"Certainly," Brazill said. "For my part, I recommend that next week we increase the shipment by fifty percent. Yes, six keys of heroin will do nicely, for now. It's a new world, Alejandro."

"*Sí.*"

Brazill stood, crossed the room, and shook Reyes's hand.

"*Sí,*" he said again.

The hombre picked up the carton, and together he and Reyes moved back down the corridor to the front door. Carl and Frankie followed them out.

Brazill turned toward Chandler.

"And that's how it's done," he said.

"How long before we take everything?"

"We might not. As of now the Mexicans are supplying the dope. Reyes has the runners. To replace both would increase our overhead. It might be more profitable to let them do all the heavy lifting and simply collect a percentage."

Brazill moved to where Erin was sitting. He grabbed a fist-ful of her blond hair and pulled hard. Her face was angled toward his. I thought he was going to force her into a kiss, but he didn't. At least not yet.

"Sorry about your friends," he said.

"My friends?"

"The Dragons. It seems they're not coming to your rescue after all."

"I don't know what you're talking about. I don't even know who they are."

Brazill yanked Erin's hair some more. She cried out.

"Leave her alone," Randy said. "There's no need to hurt Erin. I can take care of the drugs. I'm the one who brought them in here in the first place."

God bless you, Randy, my inner voice said.

Brazill kept yanking on Erin's hair. She kept moaning in pain.

"Leave her alone," I said. Randy crossed the room and laid his hand on Brazill's shoulder. Brazill shook it off. Chandler grabbed Randy and spun him around. He punched Randy very hard in the stomach. Randy folded and dropped to the floor. I knew how he felt.

"You're going to need to learn your place, boy," Brazill said.

"My family ..."

"What's he talking about? His family?"

Down the corridor just inside the front entrance, Carl ap-peared. He had his gun in his hand, pointing it low. He stared through the glass as if he were looking at something that amazed him.

"Cops," he said. He started running down the corridor toward us. "Cops. They're all over the place."

"Cops?" Brazill sounded like he had never heard the word before, had no idea what it meant. He released Erin's hair and stood straight. "Cops? They shouldn't be here."

I grabbed Erin's hand, pulled her to her feet, and started

running for the door of the employee lounge, dragging her along. We reached the door just as Carl did.

"Stop them."

Carl seemed confused as we approached. It was as if his brain were asking "Did he mean these two?"

I released Erin's hand, lowered my undamaged shoulder, came up with an elbow, and hit him just under the chin with the best illegal check I had ever made in a lifetime of playing hockey. He flew up and back against the wall. The force of the blow caused him to drop his piece. It didn't occur to me to stop and pick it up. I kept running.

Erin had managed to take the lead. She was two strides in front of me when we reached the foyer. She turned toward the front door and stopped. I nearly ran into her. Frankie stood on the other side of the door. He didn't seem confused at all as he raised his gun and pointed it at us.

I pushed Erin toward the left.

A shot rang out. Only it wasn't Frankie. Chandler was shooting at us from the entrance to the employee lounge. Darting to the left probably saved my life, because a bullet smashed into the wall on my right where we had been standing.

There was more shooting, but the bullets sounded far away.

The shots are coming from outside, my inner voice said.

This time, Erin took the lead, grabbing my hand and leading us to the door that led to the staging area and production plant beyond. Another shot was fired; the bullet smacked into the door above my head. I didn't look to see if it was Chandler, Carl, or Frankie who had fired it. I lowered my head and dashed inside the room behind Erin.

She shouted, "Do you think shooting us will help you now?"

No one answered.

I yanked the door shut behind me.

It wasn't completely dark; there was light coming through

the windows on the far side of the production plant. But my eyes hadn't adjusted yet, so everything appeared black to me. Erin seemed to know exactly where she was going, though. She pulled my hand, and I followed without resistance. We moved slowly, but that didn't keep me from tripping on the low trough that held the foot bath.

She led us into the production plant; light glinted off her stainless steel mixing tanks, yet it was still difficult to see. She moved us away from the light toward another door that I didn't see until she opened it. We were passing through it just as the door leading to the reception area was flung open behind us. Light streamed in.

"Christine," Brazill said, "we can still make a deal."

Erin carefully closed the door. I didn't know if Brazill or whoever else was chasing us in the dark noticed, but I assumed they did.

"You know what kind of deal he wants to make, don't you?" Erin said.

We were now standing in the corridor between Erin's production plant and the outside loading dock.

"We need to find somewhere to fight," I said.

"You are such a guy. What we need is to find someplace to hide."

"Here."

I moved to the metal cage that contained all of Erin's chemicals. I opened the cage and pulled out a tall plastic bottle. I opened the bottle and took a whiff. It smelled awful.

"What are you going to do?" Erin said.

"Throw it in his face when he comes through the door."

"McKenzie, do you think we use dangerous chemicals to clean machinery that makes food?"

I found a plastic bucket and poured the liquid into it. Behind the door I could hear voices and more shooting. I moved to the door and prepared to throw the liquid on Brazill or any of his henchmen when they came through. Afterward, I planned to attack them and get their guns.

"Run," I said. "Find someplace to hide."

Erin folded her arms across her chest again and sighed as if she had never heard anything so silly.

"I've had enough of that," she said.

I took a deep breath. As if on cue, the door opened quickly. I splashed the liquid on the first shadow I saw.

"Damn," someone said.

I dropped the bucket and leapt forward, catching the attacker in the chest and pushing him against the doorframe. We both fell to the floor. I wrestled with him, groping for his gun.

"Damn," he said again.

I recognized the voice and stopped wrestling.

"Harry?" I said.

Lights were turned on. I saw him lying on his back.

"Harry."

He held up his ID like a soccer referee giving me a yellow card.

"FBI," he said.

"I'll be damned."

"Probably, yeah."

I helped Harry to his feet. There were several special agents behind us. They were taking Brazill and Chandler into custody.

Harry gestured at the liquid that covered his face and clothes.

"What the hell is this?" he said.

Erin quickly closed the distance between them and wrapped her arms around his waist. She squeezed tight, her face pressed against his chest.

"Soap," she said. "Harry, it's soap."

It took us about twenty minutes to move from the corridor to Salsa Girl's office. She pulled out her bourbon and filled a trio of glasses.

I had asked before and he had already said yes, but I asked again anyway. "Did you get it?"

"Crystal-clear audio and video," Harry said. "Even when it was dark and Chandler went to the truck to get the carton filled with heroin. I must say, Marshall Lantry does very nice work."

"It's legal, right? It's all admissible?"

"That's my understanding."

Erin downed her bourbon and poured another. "You guys want some of this?"

I sure did. Harry hesitated, though. Finally he picked up a glass and took a sip.

"You're not seeing this," he said.

There was a great deal of movement outside Erin's window, and lots of lights. The area became even brighter when the TV vans showed up. Someone had drawn a chalk outline around Frankie's body as well as the hombre's, but other than that, no one did anything about them. Brazill, Chandler, Carl, Alejandro, and Randy were all cuffed and stuffed into separate vehicles and driven away.

"Where's Bobby?" I asked.

"West St. Paul coordinating with the Westies."

"Sonuvabitch. Brazill really did hit the Red Dragons."

"Four dead, six wounded is what I heard. You seem surprised. It was all part of your strategy, wasn't it?"

"I was hoping when Brazill heard where the Dragons hung out, he'd try to negotiate with them."

"C'mon, McKenzie. Who are you kidding?"

Only yourself, my inner voice said.

Erin was listening to every word we said but didn't comment on any of it. She sat in her chair and leaned back, her eyes closed. Harry circled the desk and gazed down at her.

"I must say, you played your parts perfectly," Harry said. "Especially you."

Erin opened her eyes and looked up at him.

"All the world is going to see the distressed damsel standing up to the bad-hombre drug dealers," he said. "You're a hero."

"I'm sorry I'm not that woman, Harry. I wish I were."

Harry leaned down and kissed her forehead.

"Close enough," he said.

The way her eyes welled up, you'd think she had just received a Top Ten Rating from *Consumer Reports*. She didn't allow the tears to fall, though. Instead, she brushed them away with her thumb.

We sipped bourbon for a while.

Erin had nearly finished her second glass when she announced, "We need to help Randy."

"Why?" I said.

"Because he doesn't deserve what's going to happen to him."

"Sure he does," I said. I reached across the desk anyway. "My cell."

"Oh, yeah." Erin opened her desk drawer and removed my smartphone. I had given it to her right before she left Pipestone because I didn't want it falling into Brazill's hands. I found a number and tapped on it. I listened until the phone was answered.

"Marilyn," I said, "this is McKenzie. Your son needs you."

After I finished my conversation, a special agent I didn't know poked his head into the office.

"We're ready," he said.

Harry extended his hand toward Erin.

"Let's go," he said.

She took it, and he helped her out of the chair onto her feet. He continued to hold her hand as we made our way into the corridor and headed for the foyer.

"Should I call my lawyer?" Erin asked.

"Why? Did you do something illegal?"

"It doesn't matter. I'll take whatever's coming to me."

"You'll be all right," I said.

"Just tell the truth when you give your statement," Harry said. "The truth and nothing but the truth. The statute of limitations will protect you."

Erin nodded, but I don't think she believed him.

"Don't forget," I said, "the assistant U.S. attorney will need your testimony to put these guys away. You hold all the cards."

"What do you know about holding cards?" Harry said. "You are the worst poker player in the world."

"People keep saying that."

"That's because it's true."

Erin said, "Yes, but—where did you learn to play chess?"

"Didn't McKenzie tell you?" Harry said. "He was in the chess club in high school. Played when he was in college, too."

"Really?" Erin sounded surprised. "A jock like you? How did that happen?"

"Well," I said. "There was this girl ..."

JUST SO YOU KNOW

As it turned out, Assistant United States Attorney James Richard Finnegan really did have political aspirations. Who knew?

You could tell by the way he handled the media. Half of the statements released by his office sounded like the opening paragraph of a campaign flyer: The man who smashed an international drug cartel that was bringing heroin into the Twin Cities. The Top Cop who thwarted the plans of an organized crime syndicate that was attempting to expand into Minnesota. The leader of a joint task force consisting of special agents of the Federal Bureau of Investigation and members of the St. Paul Police Department Major Crimes Unit that squashed a gang war that had already taken the lives of four young men of Hispanic descent.

Bobby wanted to throw him off the Robert Street Bridge to see if he sank or floated in the river below. Harry was ready to elect him president. And as happy as Chopper was that I had helped him gain a measure of revenge against the people who put him in a wheelchair, he still insisted that I pay for his and Herzog's dinner. Oh, well.

Still, you had to give Finnegan his props. Everyone went to

prison on a potpourri of criminal charges including drug trafficking and distribution, conspiracy, extortion, first degree and second degree murder, attempted murder, kidnapping, assault and battery, even assaulting federal officers. Carson Brazill took the hardest fall, life without parole, mostly because he refused to identify the serious businessmen based in Chicago that he mentioned in the videotape that served as a virtual confession at his trial. The softest tumble went to Randy Bignell-Sax, who drew only twenty-seven months—paroled in eighteen—at the Level 1 minimum-security prison in Lino Lakes, about a forty-minute drive from Cambridge. His family's exceedingly high-priced attorneys had a lot to do with it by convincing the court that Randy was merely a foolish and hopeless pawn of the drug lords—not a particularly hard stretch when you think of it. But I believe it was Erin Peterson's impassioned plea for leniency that made the difference.

Salsa Girl was portrayed by Finnegan as a heroic victim who was betrayed by her partner, who nevertheless persisted against terrifying odds to defeat the bad guys, an assertion readily adopted not only by the juries she testified before but also by the media that adored her good looks and humble, innocent, little-girl persona—yes, she had that tool in her Swiss Army knife, too.

Christine Olson was never mentioned, not even by Brazill or Levi Chandler, who more or less adhered to omertà, organized crime's code of silence.

Which isn't to say that everything was sunshine and lollipops. Apparently Erin's business deal with Central Valley International fell through. I say "apparently" because neither John Ripley nor anyone else at CVI would return her calls to make it official. Still, whatever disappointment she felt was short-lived at best, because a few days later, Marilyn Bignell, newly installed chairperson of the board of directors of Minnesota Foods and Bignell Bakeries, announced that the company had successfully concluded negotiations to purchase sixty-five percent of Salsa Girl Salsa with an option to buy the remaining thirty-five percent in three years. Bobby suggested that the deal was sealed when Erin petitioned the court on behalf of Marilyn's son—and refused to speculate about who might have blown up one of her trucks—but he's always been cynical like that.

After that, though, Salsa Girl disappeared. I thought she had taken the money and run until she reappeared at a gathering held at Dave Deese's house holding Ian Gotz's hand. They had spent about ten days together—they didn't say where—during which she told Ian exactly who she was and what she had done. Ian's response was to ask her to marry him.

Alice Pfeifer was to be her maid of honor. She was hoping that Nina and Shelby would agree to be her bridesmaids, a request that was met with much loud squealing—this after the somewhat less than generous things Nina had said about Erin when she saw what Brazill and his minions had done to my face and ribs.

Afterward, Erin spoke to me.

"I don't have family," she said. "I'm like you, McKenzie. My friends are my family. I was hoping, if it wasn't too much of an imposition—would you give me away?"

I was shocked into silence. It was a condition that didn't go unnoticed.

"Oh my God," Shelby said. "You've left him speechless. I've never seen that."

"McKenzie," Nina said. "No quips? No witticisms?"

Bobby snapped his fingers at me.

"McKenzie, say something?"

I don't know how, but I managed to choke out the words. "What are friends for?"